Mayhem on Mackinac Island

By Bill Blewett

To: Amber

Bill Blewett

11-20-21

Mayhem on Mackinac Island

Bill Blewett

Editor: Karl Lehmann
Assistant Editor: Barb Blewett
Associate Editors: Sophie Blewett, Jack Blewett
Medical Advisor: Charlene Blewett R.N.
Photos: Bill Blewett, Tom Poiggione
Photo Assistance: Kelsey Bolt

ISBN: 978-0-578435381

Printed in the United States of America
First Printing, 2019

Layout: Stacey Willey, Globe Printing
www.globeprinting.net

Other books by Bill Blewett
Mayhem on the Dead River
Mayhem on the Michigamme
Mayhem in the Superior Peninsula
Coming in 2020: Mayhem on Manasota Key
Coming in 2021: Mayhem in the Mitten

I dedicate this book to my mother. She always gave more than she received and never asked for anything.

Acknowledgment

I would like to take this opportunity to thank everyone who helped write these stories. Many thanks to my family, friends, editors, and publisher, for without all of you, this endeavor would not have been possible.

Table of Contents

Characters That Appear in All of the Stories

- John Baldwin, Retired Military Soldier
- Tyler Baldwin, Needleton Police Sergeant
- Bill Bennett, Retired Sheriff of Mesabi County
- Barb Bennett, Wife of Bill Bennett
- Mark Kestila, Retired Military Police Officer
- Ben Meyers, Retired Police Officer

Characters That Occur in Murder on Mackinac Island
- Ned Beals, Richard Randall's Hired Henchman
- Shawn Beals, Ned Beals' Son
- Paul Brown, Bridgewatar Corp. PR Rep.
- John Crane, Detective and Friend of Bill Bennett
- State Trooper Jenni Durant, friend of the Pseudo-Detectives
- Peggy Holmes, Citizens for Pure Water Receptionist
- Lieutenant Menendez, Commander of the local State Police Post
- City Marshal Karl Ramsey, Mackinac Island Police City Marshal
- Julie Randall, Richard Randall's Spouse
- Richard Randall, Julie Randall's Spouse
- State Trooper Kelly Sanderson, Friend of the Pseudo-Detectives
- David Wells, Eco-terrorist Leader

Characters Appearing in Contrition on Mackinac Island
- Bishop Grant
- Father Al Clevins
- Sheila Tarnisky

Characters Appearing in the Visa Scandal
- Rick Bonetelli, Poker Player Extraordinaire
- Dan Martin, Immigration and Naturalization Employee
- Shontal McKenzie, Immigration Attorney
- Tanesa Simpson, Jamaican Immigrant

Characters Appearing in the Governor's Assassination
- Asher Clarke, New York Governor
- Ben Conrad, Michigan Lieutenant Governor
- Michael Davis, Illinois Governor
- Theodore Harris, Pennsylvania Governor
- Fred Gainer, Bridge Painters' Union President
- Evelyn Harrison, Ontario Premier
- Dorothy Hutchinson, Michigan Governor's Wife
- Jim Hutchinson, Michigan Governor
- Ed McCallister, Governor Hutchinson's Aid
- Olivia Moore, Ohio Governor
- Howard Pearce, Governor Davis' Staffer
- George Thompson, Indiana Governor
- Lee Trembly, Quebec Premier
- Mitsy Webster, Bridge Painters' Union Steward
- Charlotte White, Minnesota Governor
- Ethan Wilson, Wisconsin Governor

Characters Appearing in the Odorous Murders:
- Mary Archer, Mackinac Island Chamber of Commerce Director
- Elliot Brown, Sewage Scow Deck-Hand
- Sandy Evans, Mackinac Island Mayoral Administrative Assistant
- Brick Griffin, Sewage Scow Deck-Hand
- Axel Hale, Sewage Scow Deck-Handy
- Jeff Mitchell, Mackinac Island City Marshal
- Abby Rodman, Mackinac Island Mayor
- Rock Winston, Sewage Scow Skipper
- Characters Appearing in A Robbery Gone Awry
- Mrs. Anderson, Kaiser Middle School Principal
- Eddie Sawyer, Robber
- Gunner Slade, Robber
- Mick Thorne, Robber

Introduction

In the early 17th century, the predominant Native Americans in this area were three Algonquin tribes; the Ojibwa, Ottawa, and Potawatomi. These people had long ventured through the area to fish, hunt, and trade.

Because Mackinac Island has the shape of a turtle, the Indians had a creation myth based on it. The Straits of Mackinac was the center of two routes vital to the fur trade: one to Montreal in the east and the other to Detroit in the south via Lake Huron.

The first European to pass through the site of Mackinaw City was Jean Nicolet in 1633 who was sent to explore and map the western Great Lakes. His exploration resulted in the French government providing funds to send settlers, missionaries, traders and soldiers to the Great Lakes region. Father Jean Jacque Marquette had established a mission on Mackinac Island in 1671.

Mackinaw City's first European settlement came in 1715 when the French built Fort Mackinaw. They lost it to the British during the Seven Years' War in 1763.

As a part of Pontiac's Rebellion, Chippewa and Fox warriors captured the fort on June 2, 1763. In a surprise attack during a game of lacrosse; the British were taken prisoner that resulted in most of them being executed. After reoccupying the fort, the British troops moved it to Mackinac Island. What the British did not take with them, they burned.

The British scored an important early success when a detachment, learned of the declaration of war before the nearby American garrison at the important trading post on Mackinac Island. A force landed on the island on July 17, 1812, and mounted a gun overlooking the fort. After the British fired one shot from their cannon, the Americans surrendered. This early victory encouraged the natives to help the British. Because of the victory, it gave the British total control over the access to the Ohio Valley.

Despite this outcome, the Treaty of Ghent of 1815 forced the British to return the island and it remained under the control of the United States government until 1895.

During the Civil War, the fort was used as a prison for three years to hold Confederate sympathizers.

In 1875, Mackinac National Park became the second National Park in the United States after Yellowstone.

Auto ferries began running in the early 1900s until they were replaced by the Mackinac Bridge in 1957 connecting Upper and Lower Michigan.

Train ferries crossed the Straits until 1984. Today, Mackinaw City remains an important port city for tourists traveling by passenger ferry boats to Mackinac Island.

Through the course of time, the main industry of Mackinaw City became almost strictly tourist-oriented, with other sources of employment supplementing it.

Part I

Murder on Mackinac Island

Chapter One

The hum of the ferry engine drowned out the sound of the waves splashing against the boat hull as it neared its destination. The seagulls arrived as usual hoping for a tidbit cast overboard by a disinterested tourist. As they approached the island, the famous hotel became even larger than they imagined.

Richard spoke first, "That's where we're staying," pointing to the majestic hotel high above everything.

Julie responded, "You shouldn't have. It looks so expensive."

Richard retorted, "It's well worth it. It has a lot of amenities and in the evening, formal dining."

"I remember. That's why I packed my chiffon dress as well my diamonds."

Julie and Richard Randall prepared to disembark on the island of magical dreams. They hoped to rekindle their dying marriage amid years of disgruntlement. Richard had booked the excursion leaving their problems behind in Montreal and hoping to persuade his wife to forgive his infidelities. He had heard Mackinac Island was such a place.

They stepped off the ferry and after exiting the port tunnel, they were awed by the activities. Hundreds of tourists were squirming through gift shops. Many of them carrying bags while enjoying the island's famous fudge.

Julie displayed a perplexed look and asked, "Where are all of the vehicles?" Richard chuckled and replied, "That's the beauty of this island. They only have emergency vehicles. Most transportation is by bicycle or horse-carriage."

Richard and Julie meandered through Main Street taking in the sights. They held hands as the clip-clop of horses was heard as carriages passed. When crossing the street, they were careful to miss the droppings of the horses.

For a brief moment both Julie and Richard forgot their

differences and were enjoying the festivities.

Julie believed it was just like old times. They had met in college years ago and knew they were meant for each other. Julie was majoring in art history and Richard in business. She was awed by his personal charm and sweetness, he by her beauty and grace. Their senior year was nirvana. They enjoyed going to many social events together.

Within a year they were married. Neither came from money, and the first few years were hard. They decided children were not in the picture; both being devoted to each other.

However, the reality of life set in and both went their separate ways over the years. Richard rose up the corporate ladder and Julie threw herself into various charities. Eventually, Richard's eyes wandered and one affair followed another as it was easy to take advantage of the secretarial pool.

Julie found tell-tale signs of other women. His shirts smelled like perfume and there were phone numbers in his jacket pockets. Did she want to divorce him and start all over again or ignore his infidelities and make her own life? She chose the latter.

It had now reached a crescendo and she felt she couldn't take any more embarrassment. She knew he was currently seeing another young woman, but this time his romantic interest must have been outside of the corporate office. He would disconnect his phone conversation when she entered the room. She knew he was setting up a rendezvous later that night and when he said he was called back to work, she never made a fuss.

As payback, she decided to test the waters herself, and sure enough there were other fish in the sea. All she had to do was be home before him when he worked late. What he didn't know didn't hurt him. None of the relationships meant anything. Actually, they were exciting. She would meet her romantic interest in a hotel in downtown Montreal. She gave herself to her suitor as quickly as possible in order to be home before her wandering spouse returned.

Julie had endured countless Christmas parties, pretending she didn't see Richard whispering in some young girl's ear; both giggling. She never asked why he was late every night from work. She just quit caring.

Now years later, they were going to make one last try to reconcile. It had started out great, but could it continue?

It was easy to get caught up in the buying frenzy as shoppers were only too happy to pay exorbitant prices as long as they depicted the Mackinac Island logo.

After a few purchases, Julie uttered, "Let's check into our hotel. I don't want to take a chance and lose our reservation."

Richard agreed, saying, "Good idea. Once we're settled, we can come back and see more of the sights."

Hailing a carriage, they were soon whisked up the daunting hill to the large hotel overlooking the Straights of Mackinac.

Stepping onto the porch that sported Adirondack chairs, Julie gasped, "I can't wait to sit in one of them and relax."

Richard responded, "All in good time, my dear."

Julie eyed Richard and stated, "It's almost as if we're transported back in time."

Richard nodded affirmatively and said, "I agree it's almost magical. Maybe, we can go back in time ourselves. Believe it not, they made a movie regarding that very topic back in 1980."

They entered the extravagant lobby and proceeded to the check-in desk. While Richard filled out the forms, Julie enjoyed browsing through the brochures that promised fun-filled events.

Once the check-in was completed, Richard returned to Julie and she said, "Promise me we can go for a moonlight carriage ride."

Again, Richard smiled and said, "I promise we'll do everything you want."

Checking in to their room, Julie approached their window and enjoyed the view of the clear blue water below. Ships could be seen in the distance as they maneuvered their cargos to faraway destinations.

Julie teared up and said, "I don't want this to ever end. Promise me we'll never leave this island."

Richard, trying to placate his wife, replied, "Even after we leave this island, we can always keep the memories in our hearts."

Julie threw her arms around her new-found love and embraced him. Richard returned her embrace and gazed over the water.

After unpacking and strolling through the hotel grounds, they smiled as they walked through the tea room. Richard murmured, "We can have our tea later this afternoon and tonight they show a movie."

Julie replied, "I think I can get used to being pampered like this."

Strolling past the pool, they were almost drenched by youths who were enjoying an afternoon swim. The two love-birds had to avoid being splashed and laughed at the possibility of being soaked. Walking past the pickle-ball courts, Julie stated, "I think I'd like to give that a try."

Richard replied, "It's a date. We'll play tomorrow. They have a pro that gives lessons. We'll have to take advantage of that. Later in the week, we can play some golf. They have a nice 18-hole course that's supposed to be challenging. I haven't played in a while, but I'd like to. Will you join me?"

Julie answered, "Maybe, if I can get the rust off, I'll see if I can beat you."

They left the hotel and proceeded back to the Main Street. As they gazed in a fudge shop window, Richard saw a familiar face in the reflection.

Chapter Two

"Listen dear, is it okay if I look for a newspaper. I'm dying to find out how the Blue Jays did yesterday?" Richards asked.

Julie looked at Richard and replied, "Sure, but don't be late or there won't be any fudge left."

Richard gave Julie a peck on the cheek and watched as she entered the fudge emporium.

After being sure she was inside the store, he turned and walked past his acquaintance without acknowledging him. Once he was sure they were out of view of his wife, Richard turned on his heels and stared his associate in the face and snorted, "Are you crazy? What do you mean following us? I told you I would text you when I was ready."

His co-conspirator replied, "I'm the one that's going to have to kill her. I want to make sure we have a plan that'll work."

"Listen, Beals, I make the decision when and how she's going to be killed. I'm not ready yet; I want to establish a visible alibi that I'm a loving husband and that I'm trying to reconcile with her. Tomorrow, we're playing pickle ball in the morning and later we're playing golf. I'll let you know when it's time, now lay low until I text you."

"Okay, but don't wait too long. If I don't like the plan, I'm out of here and you can get somebody else to do your dirty work."

"My wife should be tired by tomorrow night and she'll go to bed early. There's a place on the island called Skull Cave. I saw it in the brochure. Meet me there tomorrow night at sundown."

They mutually departed and Richard returned to the fudge shop.

As he entered, Julie held up a plastic spoon with a fudge sample and said, "Honey, taste this. It's delicious. It has peanut butter in it."

Tasting it, Richard agreed saying, "Mmmmm, that is good fudge."

"By the way, how did the Blue Jays do yesterday?" asked Julie.

"They got beat again," answered Richard.

"I hope they have better luck tonight," stated Julie.

After leaving the fudge shop, they sauntered toward the end of town.

"Look, the lilacs are in full bloom," stated Julie.

"Yes, I wish we had flowering trees like that," answered Richard.

Meanwhile, Ned Beals boarded a ferry and returned to the Lower Peninsula. As the boat sped through the water, he hated the prospect of killing someone, but he was desperate. His whole life was dedicated to protecting people. Sure, he had a pension from the state, but it wouldn't be enough to take care of his grandchildren. If he could get a small fortune from Randall, he would feel better when he went to the great beyond which wasn't too far in the future.

Strolling past St. Anne's Church, Julie stated, "Let's go inside and say a prayer. I heard it's good luck to make a wish each time you enter a church for the first time."

Together, they entered and enjoyed its antique beauty. Kneeling at the altar, Julie whispered to Richard, "Make a wish and it'll come true."

Complying, Richard knelt and closed his eyes. Shortly, Julie and Richard stood and exited the church. Julie looked at Richard and said, "Okay, out with it."

Richard responded, "What do you mean?"

Julie replied, "What was your wish?"

Before he could answer, he looked at his watch and shouted, "Look at the time. We'll be late for afternoon tea."

Julie answered, "I declare, you are becoming a gentleman. What's a girl to do?"

Richard took Julie's arm and they motioned to the closest horse carriage and returned to the hotel.

After entering the tea room, the new love birds sought out a table near the window to enjoy the beauty. The flowers were in full bloom and provided a spectacular backdrop as they consumed their tea and treats.

Julie reiterated, "I'm having a wonderful time. How about you?"

Richard gazed into Julie's eyes and said, "Me too. Tomorrow we can play pickle ball in the morning and golf later in the day. I want to pack as much excitement into every day."

"By the way, I had my company fly our jet here for the week. What do you say we take it for a little spin and we can see the island?" asked Richard.

"That would be great. Let's do it," replied Julie. With that they took a carriage ride to the top of the island and saw the Bridgewatar Corp. plane sitting on the runway.

Chapter Three

Richard entered the small tower and after obtaining permission and a flight plan, he emerged and motioned for Julie to join him.

Taxying to the runway, he waited for clearance from the tower. Soon they were gathering speed and the lift off was smooth as silk. As they were gaining altitude, Richard said, "I read the brochures and I've learned a lot about the island. It's approximately 8 miles in circumference and about 4 square miles in total area. The highest point of the island is the historic Fort Holmes which is 320 feet above lake level and 890 feet above sea level. That's the fort over there."

"I can see why the British built it. The fort looks impregnable," she answered.

"As you can imagine, the population is pretty small. According to the latest census, the island has a year-round population of about 500. The population grows considerably during the summer as hotels, restaurants, bars and retail shops, open during the summer season, and hire short-term employees to accommodate as many as 15,000 visitors per day."

"That's impressive. The stores must make a killing on the tourists," Julie responded. She continued, "What about the geology of the island?" Julie asked.

Richard replied, "I was getting to that. The island was formed as the glaciers of the last ice age began to melt around 15,000 years ago and the bedrock under the island is much older. During one period of low water, the Straits of Mackinac shrank to a narrow gorge which discharged its water over Mackinac Falls, located just beyond Arch Rock."

"I'll take us down to Arch Rock," stated Richard as they descended.

"Wow, what a magnificent display of nature. I can't believe that rock formed that way," Julie replied.

"We'll bike to it while we're here. It's a very easy ride. As you can see, the terrain around the perimeter is perfectly flat, but it rises in the interior. Look, there's the Gem Golf Course. That's the course we're going to play," Richard added.

Julie replied, "I can't wait."

"Look over there. That's Round Island. It's uninhabited, but I think people sneak on the island by boat. The island has an area of about 400 acres. Almost the entire island comprises the Round Island Wilderness Area. It's part of the Hiawatha National Forest and is protected by the U.S. Forest Service. The sole building on the island is the lighthouse. According to the brochure, it's being restored. The channel between Mackinac Island and Round Island is lit by the Round Island Lighthouse. Now as we fly southeast, you can see a much larger island, Bois Blanc. It's actually located in Lake Huron. The island covers about 34 square miles and is about 12 miles long and 6 miles wide. Believe it or not it has 6 lakes."

Richard added, "The local Chippewa tribe gave the island to the United States government as a gift in the Treaty of Greenville in 1795. The treaty ceded most of Ohio and a slice of Indiana to the government, as well as sixteen strategic sites well within the Indian Territory."

"I have some more history for you," Richard continued, "During the War of 1812; U.S. Navy Captain Arthur Sinclair's fleet took shelter at the island while waiting to attack the British at Fort Mackinac."

Displaying his knowledge of the island's local history, he stated, "In addition, I have a human-interest story for you. In 1880 the island provided a refuge to accused murderer Henry English who escaped from Pennsylvania authorities before his trial. He was arrested on Bois Blanc by Pinkerton agents, returned to Pennsylvania and acquitted.

I'm pretty sure, Pointe Aux Pins was the first resort community on the island. Much of Bois Blanc Island is state-owned forest land containing White and Norway Pines. As recently as the 1950s, the island provided lumber to Mackinac Island where woodcutting was prohibited.

Richard said, "If I remember right, "Bois Blanc Island was without electric service until 1964. At that time, there were approximately 200 structures on the island. Later, an electric service upgrade replaced the original cable with two cables spanning the Straits of Mackinac. As I've told you, no private automobiles are located on Mackinaw Island, but that's not true for Bois Blanc. Commercial motor vehicles are transported to Bois Blanc Island by ferry. Even though, there are no paved roads, a county road extends from the island's northeast corner to the far western tip. A fire access road bisects the island and is also the route used for public access to two interior lakes. There are many walking trails. The island has a paved landing strip on the island. We could land there and walk around if you want," asked Richard.

No, that's okay. I only go where they take credit cards," replied Julie smiling.

Reinvigorated, Richard finished his diatribe regarding the islands saying, "During some winters, an ice road is marked by cut evergreen trees, allowing travel over the ice between the island and the mainland. The route generally runs from Pries Landing on the mainland, to Sand Bay on Bois Blanc."

"Thanks a lot, honey, I really appreciated the aerial guided tour of the area, but I'm tired, let's return to our hotel."

"I'm way ahead of you as the plane veered northward to their landing strip. Replicating his take-off, the landing was also tranquil.

They emerged from the plane and Julie and Richard embraced and kissed.

Chapter Four

The next day was filled with action. The lovebirds learned to play pickle ball and after lunch, played the island's Gem Golf Course.

As they were playing, Richard stated, "If people want, they can play like they did a hundred years ago with old wooden clubs and a leather golf ball."

Julie responded, "No thanks. This game is challenging enough without adding that to the mix."

The view from the top of the island was gorgeous. Julie commented, "I can actually see both peninsulas from here. I feel so close to God and you right now."

Richard answered, "Yes, it's a beautiful sight and we have the rest of the week to enjoy it." After finishing their round and satisfied they had wrung as much out of the day as possible, they returned to the hotel to soak in an old-fashioned tub.

Julie finished her bath first and said, "If you don't mind, I think I'll go to bed. I want to get an early start tomorrow when we bike around the island."

Richard nodded his head and said, "Sure, I'll let you sleep in and we can always bike later in the day." It wasn't long before he could hear her enjoying a deep sleep. It was now time to rendezvous and put his plan into action.

Borrowing a bicycle left unattended in the front of the hotel, he traversed the distance to the other side of the island to meet his co-conspirator, Ned Beals.

Upon arriving, he stepped over the low barricade and approached the entrance to the shallow cave.

"Beals," Richard whispered. "Are you here?"

He continued to whisper his accomplice's name as he foraged through the thickets. Removing his cell phone to provide some light he continued on the trail. He tripped over an obstacle that must have been a log. Kneeling down, he realized not only wasn't it a log, but it was his co-conspirator, Ned Beals. Shinning the light on his face, he felt for a pulse, but the man was stone dead. As he removed his hand, he felt something wet. Holding his hand up to the light, it was blood. The only thought that crossed his mind now was he had to get out of there and quick. He couldn't risk being seen.

He returned to the hotel and placed the bicycle back on the rack. He waited for the desk clerk to become preoccupied before he entered the lobby. Arriving in his room, he quietly undressed and slipped under the covers of the bed. Julie opened her eyes and smiled. She whispered to herself *the Blue Jays didn't play yesterday.*

The next morning, the hotel restaurant was alive with conversation. Most of it relating to the body discovered near Skull Cave. Listening intently, the couple ascertained a body was found on the trail but the police weren't releasing any other information.

Julie started by saying, "I feel so sorry for the person's family. I wonder if they are a tourist or a local."

Richard retorted, "I'm sure we'll find out who the person was in time. What do you want to do today?"

Julie didn't answer, but only continued to sip her coffee and gaze out the window at the magnificent flower gardens.

With Richard's prompting, they returned to Main Street and continued to browse through the shops. The feeling was quite different this time. Richard had a faraway look and Julie appeared to be disinterested.

Chapter Five

Meanwhile, in Mesabi County, with our adult children having plans of their own, we were gifted with caring for six grandchildren. We could either entertain them in our house or find someplace else to destroy. We chose the latter.

My wife, Barb, started the conversation, "Why not go someplace where we can all have fun?"

I didn't think the little ones would like sitting in a bar for a week so I countered with a possible trip to Mackinac Island.

After mulling it over, my wife and grandchildren agreed it would be fun to visit the quaint island and enjoy some quality time together.

Reservations were made in Mackinaw City at an affordable hotel with the only requirement that it possess a swimming pool. From Victorious to Mackinaw City was a three-hour drive that was made doable only with the young ones playing games on electronic tablets, nooks, and as a last resort an old-fashioned laptop computer. It could be said, collectively, they saved my sanity. Upon arriving at the hotel, it wasn't long before our little lovelies were screeching and hollering as they bailed in and out of the pool. My patience was tempered by a cold refreshing beverage that I kept replenishing.

In reading the local paper, Barb pointed out an oddity that a body was found on Mackinac Island. I was relieved for once, that I was not part of the scenario. The grandchildren screamed, "Watch me, grandpa." I acknowledged each one as they plunged into the water squealing upon resurfacing. It was a perfect day as grandma and grandpa relaxed by the pool and the grandkids wore themselves out taking time to devour pizza and sodas. I should have known it was too good to be true.

As the last of the pizza disappeared, I saw a uniformed officer enter through the glass door. As he approached, he said, "I assume you are Bill Bennett. The clerk at the front desk told me you and your family were in here. I'm City Marshal Ramsey from Mackinac Island."

I replied, "Nice to meet you. This is my wife, Barb, and the six hellions are our grandchildren. Their parents all booked convenient trips and we were asked to pinch hit. Rather than try to preserve our house, I thought it would be better to wreak havoc on this hotel. How can I help you?"

City Marshal Ramsey responded, "As you may know, we have a body that was discovered on our island yesterday. The state police have already interceded and they have taken jurisdiction over the case. I would like another pair of eyes and I heard you were vacationing here so I thought I might ask for your input."

I answered, "I'm flattered, but if the state police are involved, they are far better equipped than I am to solve the mystery"

"That's where it gets complicated," City Marshal Ramsey replied. "You see, the body was Ned Beals. He was a retired Michigan State Trooper. If I rely simply on the state police to look into the case, there might be claims of impropriety."

I answered, "I don't want to step on anybody's toes, especially the state police."

City Marshal Ramsey retorted, "I'm under a lot of pressure to solve this case. As you can probably imagine we have a small police force and a very limited budget. I've heard you and your crew have done great things in Mesabi County solving a lot of horrible crimes. I need your help. Won't you consider giving me a hand?"

I looked at Barb and I've seen that look many times. She nodded her head and said, "Take a few days and see what you uncover. I can hold the fort down here."

After saying my good-byes and watching my grandchildren canon ball a few more times, I left the light-hearted atmosphere for a gruesome experience.

Accompanied by City Marshal Ramsey, I took the ferry to Mackinac Island and walked the short distance to the police headquarters.

Once in his office, he pulled out a folder that I assumed had the pertinent information and photos. Perusing the contents, it was clear Beals had a stellar career as a trooper recently retiring as a sergeant.

The photos were gory to examine with his death probably being caused by a garrote. It would take a person with sizeable strength to hold Beals while the murderer turned the wire tight.

I said, "I doubt if a woman could have done this considering the size of Beals, it would take a pretty big man to control Beals while he was being strangled."

"That's what I thought," replied the City Marshal, and he continued, "Do you want to visit the murder scene?"

I agreed knowing full well by now there probably wasn't any evidence left since the tourists and ghoul mongers would have trampled it. I complied and soon we were looking at the entrance to Skull Cave pretending we knew what we were doing. Nosy onlookers photographed us as we tried to imitate investigators. As I suspected, there wasn't much left in the form of evidence, but I was curious as to how Beals arrived at the scene.

I asked the City Marshal, "Have you checked the horse carriage companies to see if any of them dropped a fare off in this vicinity?"

"Yes, I did and they promised to get back to me as soon as all of the drivers can be interviewed," responded City Marshal Ramsey.

"Who's doing the autopsy?" I asked.

"Old Doc Dunstan is supposed to do it, but he's getting up in years and his health isn't very good," replied the City Marshal.

"Well, if you don't mind, I have a highly skilled pathologist that works in Mesabi County and she wouldn't miss anything?" I replied.

"Is she certified by the state?" asked the City Marshal.

"Not only that, but she is one of the best. She's probably the reason we have solved so many crimes in the county. I can give her a call and I could even get the rest of my crew here. They are all crack detectives and we work well as a team."

"I'll run it by the village council, but I don't think it'll be a problem. Go ahead and give your crew a call and I'll get back to you," answered City Marshal Ramsey.

I phoned Carolyn Baldwin and upon her answering, I said, "Don't hang up. This is your favorite retired sheriff. I'm on Mackinac Island and we have a body that needs an autopsy. Are you interested?"

There was a moment of silence. "Don't you think I have enough work without you digging up extra bodies?" Carolyn Baldwin replied.

I could tell I still had her eating out of the palm of my hand. I continued, "They found a murdered man on the island and because he was a former state police trooper, the local City Marshal wants an outside investigation. Are you interested?" I knew she couldn't resist a good challenge.

She replied, "Clear it with the local authorities and I'll check my schedule."

"I'm going to ask the entire crew to come including your husband if he can get the time off from his police duties in Needleton," I added.

Carolyn retorted, "Call me back and let me know if the local hospital and police are on board with me doing the autopsy."

I answered, "Sounds good."

Later in the day, my phone chimed. "It's City Marshal Ramsey. I've cleared it with the powers that be so your M.E. can perform the autopsy and the state police have assured me they will work with you as long as you don't interfere with their case."

"That's great. I'll make a few calls and get my team here by sundown," I answered.

I tapped a familiar number on my cell phone and waited for an answer. It wasn't long before my old friend, John Baldwin, answered and I started, "How's everything in Mesabi County?"

John replied, "It's pretty quiet right now. What's up?"

I answered, "I'm on Mackinac Island and the local City Marshal has asked me to help check into the murder of a man that was found on a remote part of the island. Because the local pathologist isn't up to the task, I've cleared it for Carolyn to step in and perform the autopsy. Because the victim is a retired state trooper, the City Marshal has asked me to help avoid any improprieties that might arise. Are you up for it?"

John replied, "That sounds interesting."

"Do you want to see if the rest of the guys want to help?" I asked.

After disconnecting I thought to myself, I have been fortunate to remain friends with some great senior gentlemen who were once unequaled in their respective detective fields. My best friend, as I mentioned, is John Baldwin, having twenty years military detective experience, now retired. His son, Tyler, is a police sergeant in a nearby community, Needleton. Tyler's wife, Carolyn, had also become a regular. As I already mentioned, she is a great medical examiner and had helped solve numerous crimes. My old duck hunting partner, Mark Kestila, had earned his detective stripes while serving in the Army in Europe during his younger years. Ben Myers was a retired police officer from my hometown, Victorious. Ben had almost single handedly closed many meth labs. We had helped solve a lot of crimes in Mesabi County the last few years and were somewhat of celebrities. I was hoping we could help solve this one also.

Chapter Six

It was no coincidence why Randall chose Mackinac Island as his choice for a romantic get-away. In addition to his marital problems, Randall was also the Vice-President of MichCan Corp. Midwest Division. It's an international oil transport company that is responsible for the pipeline that carries nearly 20 million gallons of crude oil every day. It passes between the state's Upper and Lower Peninsulas.

His main adversaries are a coalition of local businesses, municipalities, Native American tribes and environmental and conservation forces. They are concerned that the straits' strong currents and corrosion-causing forces could cause the pipeline to rupture, creating a catastrophic oil spill that would spread through the Great Lakes.

Those who want MichCan Corp. to repair, could replace or remove the pipeline have a powerful example of what could go wrong: A newer pipeline ruptured in 2010, spilling 1 million gallons of heavy crude oil into the Kalamazoo River — the largest and most expensive onshore oil spill in U.S. history. MichCan Corp. had to restore or create damaged wetlands on top of the $1 billion the company spent to clean up the oil.

However, conservationists argued MichCan Corp. pipelines experienced more than 1,000 leaks in the U.S. and Canada from 1999 to 2013. Freshwater mollusks could harm the protective coating on the pipelines, according to university researchers and government agencies. The NTSB said that the 2010 spill was the result of multiple small corrosion-fatigue cracks that gradually grew together. Many scientific experts said they believe the mollusks could exacerbate that process.

It wasn't good enough that the state had passed a proposal to authorize a tunnel to be constructed 100 feet below the Straights 4-miles long and would connect the two peninsulas. MichCan would underwrite the $500 million price tag. The finished petroleum pipeline would be encased in concrete.

To the environmentalists, that wasn't enough. They wanted the pipeline shut down until the underwater tunnel was completed in 2024. They pointed out that 23 million gallons of petroleum poured through the pipeline daily and was an eco-disaster waiting to happen.

A state university worst-case scenario of a spill was done to demonstrate how quickly currents could spread throughout the Straights. It took just 12 hours, to reach the island, and about a day to reach both lakes. The study concluded that the Straits are "the worst possible place" for an oil spill in the Great Lakes region.

Richard was hoping to quell the groundswell against his company while simultaneously win his wife back if possible. If she wasn't receptive to a harmonious re-union she would have to die.

To the media, he emphasized the economic benefits of the pipeline. Last year he told the state government task force that 15 percent of total U.S. oil imports arrive through the MichCan Corp. system and that the company pays millions in state taxes each year.

In addition, earlier this year, he told the state investigative committee, any leak on the pipeline could be isolated in a few minutes.

Fearing retribution, Randall hired Beals. At first, Richard just wanted the former state trooper to act as a semi-bodyguard fearing for his own safety. There were many threats on the internet and letters promising retribution if MichCan Corp. didn't revamp their pipeline. As time progressed, Beals took on a more important role even going so far as to carry out clandestine attacks against MichCan Corp.'s eco-terrorists. The oil transportation corporation's enemies started having problems of their own. In addition to the eco-terrorist's offices being fire-bombed, some of the protestors were beaten.

As the opposition to MichCan Corp. increased, so did Beal's

role in the organization. He became Randall's right-hand man, always able to deal with protests.

Richard was now willing to bring Beals into his inner circle of trust hoping he could not only down play the role of the environmental opposition, but also help come up with a plan to eliminate his wife. It was a gamble, but he felt he could rely on the former trooper.

When first broached on the subject of murdering Randall's wife, Beals hesitated. After a six-figure payment was promised, the former trooper agreed.

That's when the two of them hatched the plan for Richard and his wife to bike around the island and at the right time near Arch Rock, Beals would wait in anticipation. Richard would lure his wife to the top of the arch and at the right moment, when nobody was in sight, Beals would throw her over the ledge. It would be a perfect crime. Richard would act the part of the grieving husband and Beals would disappear. Case closed.

But now with Beals dead, Richard would have to cook up a new scheme that he would have to carry out himself. *Could he lure his wife to the top of Arch Rock and carry out his plan? Was it possible one of the eco-terrorists murdered his henchman? Was he next on the list?*

Randall's public relations advisor, Paul Brown, encouraged him to get out in front of the opposition and participate in public charities such as relief for the homeless and aid to veterans. Many photos of Richard made their way into the media showing a smiling MichCan Corp. vice-president handing out blankets to the downtrodden as well as giving checks to needy charities. The ruse seemed to be working. If the media would only get off the company's back the opposition would melt away.

Unbeknownst to Randall and his cohorts, the eco-terrorists weren't without resources. One of which was Randall's own wife. After his infidelities, she was not going to take his deceitfulness lying down. It could be said, she was not an environmentalist. Far from it, but she would use the opposition to MichCan Corp. as a tool to undermine her husband.

After making inroads to the Citizens for Pure Water conservation group, she gained their trust by divulging correspondence between her husband and the state. In the infamous communication, MichCan Corp. admitted that it had not complied with the state's original easement requirement that allowed the pipeline to be built. In that agreement, the company said the pipeline should have anchor structures installed every 75 feet along its length at the bottom of the Straits to prevent sections from dislodging. The agreement would have required MichCan Corp. to hold $1 billion in liability insurance for their pipeline.

The correspondence Julie Randall turned over to the eco-terrorists was invaluable. They now had the upper hand. No matter how much positive publicity MichCan Corp. did could not overcome its deceitfulness.

On the flip side, upon learning of the published letter, Richard could not figure out how Citizens for Pure Water could have gotten their hands on it.

Chapter Seven

The next day the pseudo-detectives arrived at our hotel with great fan-fare. After hugs and many hand- shakes, we got down to brass tacks. We discussed our strategy over a cold beverage while my grandchildren continued to plunge into the hotel pool.

Carolyn Baldwin started, "I can perform the autopsy on the body at the local hospital."

John said, "Tyler and I can visit the state police and see what they have."

Ben interjected, "Mark and I can check with the horse carriage companies to see if they've located a driver who dropped off the victim."

I summarized, "I'll look into Beals' background to see what he was doing on the island."

After adjourning, Carolyn made her way to the local hospital and was impressed with its facilities. It didn't take long before she was standing over the murdered victim and preparing to conduct the autopsy.

John and Tyler found the state police headquarters and upon entering, smiled as they gazed on two old acquaintances, Troopers Jenni Durant and Kelly Sanderson. A few years prior, the two troopers were saved from a life of prostitution in Mexico by the pseudo-detectives and me. Jenni and Kelly overcame the horrible nightmare and had become successful law enforcement officers.

John started, "I can't believe my eyes. What are you two doing here?"

Jenni responded, "We've been reassigned to this post. It's nice to see you. What's up?"

Tyler answered, "The whole crew has been asked to try to find out how Beals was murdered. We know it's your jurisdiction, but because he was a former state trooper, the City Marshal has asked us to help avoid any question of impropriety."

Kelly Sanderson interjected, "You know that wouldn't happen. Our department would conduct a thorough investigation."

John answered, "We know, but nevertheless, we have been asked to follow the leads."

"Where can we find the lieutenant in charge of the investigation?"

Jenni nodded to the back room and said, "You'll find Lieutenant Menendez in her office. It's nice to see both of you and say "hey" to Bill and the rest of the gang."

John and Tyler approached the back office and knocked on the door.

The lieutenant motioned for them to enter and upon doing so, John stated, "Good morning, my name is John Baldwin and this is my son, Tyler. We've been asked to coincide the investigation into the death of the victim, Beals, found yesterday on Mackinac Island."

The lieutenant responded, "I'm Lieutenant Menendez and yes, that's what I understand. You're free to investigate and we'd appreciate it if you show us anything you come across, but we can't divulge anything we find."

Tyler replied, "I see, then we'll both investigate the murder simultaneously without sharing any information. Good bye."

The two pseudo-detectives left the state police post without bidding farewell to their former colleagues, Jenni and Kelly.

Ben and Mark had much better luck after interviewing several horse-carriage rentals.

"This is the last one on the list," stated Mark as they entered the stable.

"Watch your step or you'll sleep in your own room tonight," added Ben Meyers.

They walked past several young employees shoveling hay into the stalls and approached an older person in the barn. "Hello," Mark started, "I'm Mark Kestila and this is Ben Meyers. We're helping solve the murder on the other side of the island."

The man turned and replied, "I'm Dag Taggert. What do you

want to know?"

"Do you know if any of your drivers dropped a fare near Skull Cave that night?" Ben asked.

The stable boss walked into his office and tapped a few keys on his computer. He said, "The last one to come in that night was Fred Michaels. You can find him on Main Street."

Ben and Mark scurried away hoping to catch the driver before he picked up another fare.

Once on Main Street, the two senior sleuths saw a line of horse-carriages waiting at the port entrance. They worked their way down the line of carriages asking the drivers if they were the elusive Fred Michaels. Some tourists were boarding the first carriage in line, when Ben shouted, "Are you Fred Michaels?"

The driver turned and said, "That's me, but as you can see, I'm busy right now."

Mark quipped, "It'll only take a minute. The other night, did you drop a fare off on the other side of the island near Skull Cave?"

Michaels thought for a moment and responded, "Yes, as a matter of fact I did. Why is that important?"

"We're trying to discover if he met anybody." Ben answered. After you dropped him at the cave, was anybody waiting?"

The driver responded, "No, I didn't see anybody and mine was the last carriage ride for the night."

Mark produced a photo he had been sent by Carolyn and showed it to the driver. "Is this the man?"

The driver nodded his head and said, "I think it is. Do you mean that I dropped a guy off and he was murdered?"

Ignoring the question, Ben asked, "Do you remember anything about him?"

The driver contemplated a minute and then replied, "He asked when the last ferry left?"

"Anything else?" asked Mark.

"No, but he kept looking at his watch as if he was waiting for someone. I don't know who it could have been. There's no more carriage rides after mine and the bike shops were closed," he answered.

Ben concluded, "Well, thanks for the information."

With that the driver shook his reigns and the horse obediently started.

Meanwhile, I had given myself a challenge trying to ascertain the background of the victim without any help.

Typing in the victim's name into my smart phone, I uncovered some interesting information. Naturally, his police career was sealed, but I did learn that he had a former wife. That would be worth investigating as well as his two adult children. Apparently, after retiring from the state police, he started his own security business. That definitely would have to be scrutinized. His hometown and the residences of his ex-wife and children were in the Midland area. I would have to explore those possibilities post haste.

After returning to my hotel, I explained to my wife that I would be out of town for a few days. After all these years, she had come to expect the unexpected and just wished me luck.

I texted the other senior sleuths and told them I would be incommunicado for a few days as I was on my way to Midland to see what I could uncover about our victim.

Chapter Eight

After arriving in Midland, Beals' ex-wife's residence was a well-kept modest home. Knocking on the door, I was surprised to see a young child. I knelt down and asked "Does Mrs. Beals live here?"

Without saying anything, the young child closed the door. I hesitated to leave believing I had the right address. Shortly, the door opened and a middle-aged woman opened it a crack and whispered, "Yes." I answered, "My name is Bill Bennett and I'm looking for Ned Beals' ex-wife."

The lady responded, "That's me. I haven't seen him in days." As we were conversing, the same child slid her head between the woman's legs and looked at me.

Trying to win the woman's approval I stated, "My, but you're beautiful."

Mrs. Beals responded, "This is one of my granddaughters, Lizzy. I babysit her and her sister, Carrie, while their father works."

Not wanting to leave empty handed, I asked, "May I come in?"

"I suppose, but I don't know anything about Ned."

"Then you haven't heard?" I asked.

"What do you mean?" she asked.

"I'm sorry to have to be the one to tell you, but he was found murdered on Mackinac Island a few nights ago."

"No, that can't be. Nobody would want to hurt Ned. Sure, he could be short tempered at times, but he would never cause trouble."

"What sort of business was he doing?" I asked.

"I guess he was conducting surveillance for people. Sometimes, he even got big jobs from companies to spy on their competitors," she answered.

"Do you know who he was working for recently?" I asked.

"I don't know for sure, but he said he was going to be busy for months. He phoned me a few days ago and wanted me tell the grandchildren he wouldn't be around for a while. Lord, what am I going to tell the little ones now?"

"You mentioned these are his grandchildren. They must live in Midland also."

"One of them does. Our oldest, Shawn, lives across town. He's divorced and has custody of these two. Their mother left long ago," she answered.

"Are there any other children?"

"Yes, but Don lives in Los Angeles. I'll have to call him and tell him the bad news," she replied.

"Could you tell me where your ex's office is?" I asked.

She gave me the details of his location and I thanked her for the information and smiled at Lizzy as I left.

I checked in at the local Holiday Inn and waited for darkness. I knew I had to uncover more information regarding Beals and the only place was his office.

Once nightfall made its presence known, it was easy to slip the office door lock and enter the retired trooper's lair. Turning on his computer, it was password protected. Remembering the two little girl's first names, I typed them into the computer and it opened. Sometimes I even impress myself.

Starting with the most recent accounts, I saw MichCan Corp. apparently had him on retainer for the year. Paul Brown signed the checks and that would be worth exploring at a future date. Continuing browsing through the clients' transactions, he probably made a lot of enemies. Many husbands were identified in immoral trysts with their secretaries. One account stood out regarding the illegal dumping sewage into the Great Lakes. Being horrified of that possibility, I was reading with great interest when a wire was strung around my neck and I felt the pressure instantly chock off my airway. Within seconds I would be unconscious and that would be the end.

I managed to slip some fingers between my throat and the garrote. The pressure was intense and I could feel the wire cutting through my fingers. I stomped on the attacker's toes as hard as I could and grabbed the assailant from behind and tossed him over my shoulder resulting in a summersault.

Normally, I would have manhandled the would-be murderer, but I was too weak to do anything. The attacker raced out of the office into the darkness.

I knew if I texted any of my comrades, they would only chide me for not taking them along. Instead, I composed myself and thought to myself *I must be getting close.*

Returning everything to its rightful place, I locked the door as I exited Beals' office. I just had to figure out which client would want him dead.

I remembered the name, Paul Brown, as the contact person for MichCan Corp. I decided to locate him and see if I could divulge any information.

After returning to Mackinaw City, I called a meeting of the pseudo-detectives. We shared our information with each other. Ben and Mark collaborated that a horse-carriage had dropped off our victim near Skull Cave. John and Tyler confirmed that we would get no help from the state police due to their policy of nondisclosure. Carolyn had completed her autopsy and validated the obvious that he was indeed murdered by a garrote. I shared that I was attacked in Beals' office and almost killed. I told them, "I think it might have been an amateur because if it was a trained killer, I'd have been unconscious in seconds. I doubt if I could have been able to slip my fingers under the wire."

I asked, "Ben, could you and Mark nose around the island and see if there are any reasons why Beals would be killed. Maybe, it might have been a local problem like an angry husband."

Ben responded, "We can do that."

"John, could you and your son try to get something out of Jenni and Kelly. I know they can't reveal much, but maybe, they'll agree to work with us."

"We can do that," replied John.

Mark asked, "What about you."

I replied, "I think I'm going to have to visit our friendly neighbor to the north, Canada. MichCan Corp.'s main office is in Montreal."

"Be careful, you know how something just seems to happen to you" warned John.

Chapter Nine

The wheels touched down at the Montreal-Pierre Elliot Trudeau International Airport. After clearing security, I boarded a bus for the city. Arriving at my destination, 1000 de La Gauchetiere, I exited and was immediately impressed by its architecture. It was built in the early 1990s and reached 47 floors which are the most allowed in the city. It had a distinctive triangular red roof as well as four copper-capped entrances at the tower base corners.

Upon entering the monstrosity, I perused the lobby directory until I saw my mark, MichCan Corp. Contemplating how I was going to conduct my ruse, I was still weighing my options when I entered their office on the fifteenth floor.

Standing at the front reception desk was a beautiful brunette who could have been a model. She asked, "May I help you sir?"

I replied, "I'm looking for someone who would be involved in security. A man was murdered in Michigan and he was employed most recently by your firm."

"One minute please?" she responded. Soon, a burly man appeared displaying a square jaw and an athletic build. He extended his hand and said, "My name Avellino Dubois. I am in charge of security for our corporation. How may I assist you?"

I responded, "There was a murder in Michigan a few days ago and he was in your employment. I wonder if you could provide me some insight into what he might have been doing."

Dubois responded, "What was his name?"

I answered, "Ned Beals."

Dubois thought for a moment and then replied, "I'm sorry to hear of his death. I remember he was brought on board to run interference for our pipeline in the Straights of Mackinac. As you probably know we have received some bad publicity and some eco-terrorist threats and he was hired to keep track of them. Let me introduce you to our public relations person. He also worked with Mr. Beals."

It wasn't long before we were entering another beautiful suite of offices. Dubois spoke in French to the receptionist and we were escorted into the inner office.

Approaching the man behind the desk, Dubois spoke in French again and the man seated appeared to comprehend. After a few minutes of dialogue, Dubois speaking in English said, "This is Mr. Paul Brown. He is our public relations advisor. He worked more with Mr. Beals than I did. He's at your service." With that, Dubois departed leaving us to continue. After appropriate greetings were exchanged, I asked, "What exactly was his role in protecting MichCan's interests?"

Brown retorted, "As I understand, he was supposed to keep an eye on the eco-terrorist groups like Citizens for Pure Water. He did a good job. Occasionally, he had to get rough with them, but these people aren't choirboys."

"Do you know why Beals would be at a remote part of the island?"

Brown responded, "I can't think of any reason. We have no interests in the back of the island. Our pipelines run through the Straights. Maybe, he was conducting surveillance on some nut job and they ambushed him."

I continued to press but was unable to divulge anything of importance. Just then, the land line beeped and Brown said, "Excuse me. I have to take this. It's my boss calling by coincidence from Mackinac Island."

"Yes, Mr. Randall. I'll look into it. By the way did you know the man that was found murdered on Mackinac Island was an employee of ours?"

After listening, he replied, "Yes, in fact I have an investigator in my office now asking why Beals was on the island."

Listening again very intently, his face suddenly lost its color and after disconnecting, he said, "I'm sorry I can't divulge any more information. MichCan Corp. has an official "No comment" on anything relating to Mr. Beals demise. Now if you'll excuse me, I have work to do."

Brown's receptionist quickly showed me to the door and within minutes I was standing on the street corner wondering *what the hell just happened?*

I wondered if Brown was up to the task of garroting someone, but the security chief certainly could. I entered his name into my smart phone and before long; I was looking at a litany of Avellino Dubois' accomplishments. Last but not least was a hitch in the Canadian Special Operations Regiment (CSOR). It was Canada's answer to our Special Forces. With my curiosity piqued, I pursued the training the OSOR received. Reding further in the report, I learned the unit depends on its ability to conduct and support a broad range of operations.

Wanting to know more about the CSOR, I contacted my source, John Crane, who was deeply involved in black ops. We had worked together over the last few years and although he could be crusty at times, he was a good friend.

After researching Dubois and his training in the Canadian Special Forces, John informed me CSOR is a Special Forces unit with the capabilities and responsiveness to operate throughout any conflict. The regiment provides extra support to The Canadian Special Operations Forces Command (CANSOFCOM).

After studying the training Dubois received, it convinced me that he could certainly use a garrote, but in my case, he would have succeeded in killing me instantly. I felt I could rule him out for now. However, Brown was a different story. He knew Beals and I felt he was hiding something.

As I was being escorted from the reception area, I picked up a brochure on MichCan Corp. Once outside, I examined the pecking order in the corporation. Working up the ladder I came across the name Richard Randall-VP for the Midwest Operations. If anybody would be concerned about the pipeline in the Straits, it would certainly be this prodigal son.

Chapter Ten

Watching her eyes flutter as she was enjoying some much-needed REM sleep, Richard contemplated who could have given that incriminating letter to the Citizens for Pure Water. Perhaps an employee of the company developed a conscience and felt compelled to safe-guard the Great Lakes water supply.

Richard really wanted to believe that, but truth-be-told it just didn't seem plausible. He only had the letter at home and then destroyed it. There was no way an employee, no matter how well intentioned they may have been, could have gotten their hands on it.

It had to be someone in his own home and the maid wouldn't have known what it was even if she saw it on his desk. Besides, he always kept his desk locked when he wasn't present. Only his wife knew where he kept the key. Thinking it through carefully, it had to be her. Could this whole week-end just be a cover to lead him on as she gathered evidence to destroy him? Julie could retain a good divorce attorney and literally clean him out financially.

His first plan to have Beals throw her from the cliff near Skull Cave was no longer a possibility. A new plan that still had the appearance of an accident would have to be developed.

He continued to watch his wife deep in slumber bliss. Any attempt at reconciliation was now out the window. *She had to die, but how?*

Julie opened her eyes and saw Richard staring into hers.

"Good morning, my love," he quipped.

Julie feigned a smile knowing there was no feeling left for this two-timing Casanova.

"Would you like some coffee? I can have it delivered," Richard continued.

"That would be wonderful," Julie answered.

"After breakfast, let's go scuba diving. I saw there was a rental place on Main Street. I can call and book us for this afternoon," he added.

"Wow, I haven't dived in a few years. I would need a refresher course before I do," she said agreeably"

"It's set then. I'll call the scuba office while you shower," Richard stated.

Julie slowly rose from her bed and gazed out the window at the azure water that looked so peaceful.

Richard had his plan and all he had to do was make her death look like an accident. He could jury rig the equipment so she ran out of air and then he would make sure he was far enough away when she started to struggle.

As he heard the shower water running, he made the arrangements with the scuba shop and they promised both of them a refresher course before they entered the water.

After Julie had showered and dressed, she re-entered the bedroom.

Richard grinning from ear to ear stated, "Great news. They had a cancellation this afternoon and we can meet them at the dock at 1:00. They'll even give us a crash course to refresh our diving skills. The other couple cancelled because the water is supposed to be a little choppy but we'll manage."

Julie knew she had to keep her guard up. Richard was being way too accommodating. *He wouldn't dare do something on the dive* she thought.

Arriving on time, they graciously shook hands with the captain and the first mate.

The captain said, "I'm Captain Glen and this is my first mate, Ron. When we're on the water, remember I am in command." Both Julie and Richard nodded their heads and then sat quietly as the captain reviewed all of the scuba diving procedures.

Captain Glen was emphatic that they know the 20 basic hand signals and insisted on reviewing them. The skipper said, "Scuba diving is great, but you have to know the hand signals, especially decompression and low-on-air hand signals. After Richard and

Julie demonstrated their command of the signals, the captain repeated, "Are you sure you know them?" Both Richard and Julie nodded their heads in affirmation. The captain continued, "This could be fun but you have to be careful and obey the rules, especially the buddy system."

Once completed, they left for a reef that was ten miles from shore. There were some old sunken schooners that were popular dive areas and the captain had taken countless diving groups there.

The boat bobbed like a cork cutting through the waves. While they were in transit, both Richard and Julie checked their gear carefully. Finally completing a check of her equipment, she excused herself to use the head. Now was Richard's opportunity to seal his double-crossing wife's fate.

First, he reversed the valve that controls the back-up tank and he would wait under water for her oxygen to expire knowing that increased pressure underwater causes a diver's body tissues to absorb more nitrogen gas than they would normally contain at the surface.

If a diver ascends slowly, this nitrogen gas expands very slowly and the excess nitrogen is safely eliminated, but if the diver tries to surface, too rapidly, the body can only eliminate nitrogen so quickly. The faster a diver ascends; the faster nitrogen expands and the diver endures too great of pressure change too quickly. Their body can't eliminate all of the expanding nitrogen and the excess nitrogen forms bubbles in their tissues and blood.

Nitrogen bubbles would cause Julie to suffer from decompression sickness. Once, the blood was blocked to her organs, she would become unconscious. He had seen first-hand rapid pressure changes years ago while he was still a novice diver and knew well the dangers of decompression, also called "the bends." He adjusted her equipment and was finishing his own check-list when she re-appeared.

"Five minutes to dive," shouted Captain Glenn.

Both Julie and Richard strapped their equipment on and made sure their computers were working. The boat slowed to a crawl and the captain said, "You'll find the wreck of an old schooner about 70 feet down. You should get some great pictures even though the water isn't very clear. Remember to descend and ascend slowly. I'll expect you back in one hour. Good luck and have fun."

Both Julie and Richard flipped themselves backwards into the water and they slowly descended stopping at fifteen feet to give their body time to acclimate. After five minutes of enjoying the beautiful aquatic life they continued downward.

Before long, they could see the old schooner and they swam toward it. To put Julie at ease, Richard stayed right by her side as she pointed out the gorgeous nuances of the lake. As the captain had told them the visibility was murky.

Giant Sturgeon, Lake Trout, Carp, and Muskellunge swam by them and didn't even act nervous. Richard and Julie tried several times to get close to the gargantuan fish, but they slowly maneuvered away at the last minute.

Richard kept an eye on his watch as Julie enjoyed peeking inside the sunken schooner. The would-be murderer now put his plan into action. He swam to the other side of the sunken ship knowing Julie was not paying attention to the time. After the hour had expired, Julie looked around and panicked. Richard was nowhere to be seen. Julie switched to her back up tank, but no oxygen came through. She knew she had to surface quickly and risk decompression. As rapidly as she could, she tried to swim to the surface, but something was holding her down. It was Richard. He had grabbed her legs and was hanging on with all his strength. Julie tried to kick free, but it was no use. The struggle continued for minutes until she lapsed into unconsciousness. By now, Richard had switched to his back up tank and before allowing her to float away he reached for his wife, but the current pulled her away. *Good-bye my love,* he thought as she disappeared.

He now had to surface slowly and play the role of the hysterical husband. After waiting at the appropriate depths for his lungs to acclimate, he emerged shouting, "Is Julie on board?"

"No," came the reply. "We haven't seen her."

He re-submerged and again after waiting at the fifteen-foot depth, he continued downward. He assumed he would find her floating somewhere near the schooner. That didn't happen. Swimming toward the surface, the captain and one of his deck hands had donned scuba gear and were swimming toward him. He motioned he had to resurface and they nodded as they swam to the bottom. Richard waited on deck expecting his wife's body to surface. The captain and his deck-hand both bobbed up after an hour and after stepping on the boat, the captain said, "We have to contact the Coast Guard. Hopefully, she floated away and some fisherman rescued her."

Richard now had to act the role of the concerned spouse. He reiterated over and over again, "It's my entire fault. I went around to the other side of the schooner and when I returned, she was gone."

It seemed an eternity before the Coast Guard appeared. A helicopter flew over and contacted through the radio they would fly in a grid pattern while several Coast Guard boats maneuvered back and forth.

Nightfall set in, and the Coast Guard told the captain over the radio, they were suspending rescue operations.

Upon arriving at the pier, there were several media personnel waiting along with the Coast Guard and City Marshal Ramsey. Richard was taken into a small room and grilled for hours. The Coast Guard and the City Marshal asked a thousand questions.

Naturally, Julie's health and ability as a swimmer were raised. Richard was able to fend them off easily saying she was a strong swimmer and in perfect health. They both qualified as divers several years ago and both had over fifty dives. He admitted they were a little rusty, but the refresher workshop was adequate.

Chapter Eleven

We were enjoying a cold beverage on our hotel's front porch when I heard some weeping coming from below the veranda. Naturally, an investigation was in order Looking over the flowers, I saw a young woman crying into another lady's arms. I asked them, "Is everything okay?"

The consoling lady responded "Go away."

I persisted, "Maybe, I can help. My friends and I are pretty resourceful."

"We have government problems," the weeping lady whispered.

Stepping into the garden, I approached them and tried to console her saying, "Sometimes, if you tell someone it helps."

The whimpering lady nodded her head and reiterated, "Nobody can help us. My husband is in Jamaica and I'm here."

I pursued saying, "I assume you have immigration problems. Is that right?"

The other lady said, "I'm an immigration attorney from Detroit. She's just been told her husband has been denied his visa."

I replied, "I heard they're cutting back. Maybe, if we phone our congressman, he might be able to do something."

The attorney bristled and responded, "Are you kidding. He's from the same party as the President. He's not going to rock the boat. Congress just rolls over and plays dead."

I asked, "What exactly is the problem?"

The attorney said, "My name is Shontal McKenzie and this is Tanesa Simpson. I'm on the island to arrange visas for the employees. Unfortunately, our government has drastically reduced the number. Our government maintains that the immigrants are taking away jobs from Americans, but the truth is these jobs are so low paying; Americans won't work for these wages. Immigrants are happy to come here on a work visa and return to their home in the fall. The program has been working for decades, now all of a sudden, the immigrants are considered dangerous."

"How many people are we talking roughly?" I asked.

Shontal McKenzie responded, "The federal government sets a limit of 66,000. Today, some hotel and restaurant owners in the tourist industry of Mackinaw City and Mackinac Island say they are suffering from a severe shortage of foreign workers because of a drop in federal visas. Foreign workers annually receive visas from the H-2B program, but it didn't used to count returning foreign workers against the cap. In late September 2016, Congress refused to renew the exemption for returning workers as Donald Trump campaigned for the White House decrying foreign workers took jobs from Americans.

But the reduction has hurt Mackinac Island, which depends on foreign workers to fill summer jobs. Businesses need more workers. I think the island has less than 500 people living on the island and there are only about 11,000 residents in the whole county," she concluded.

"Can't the government see how bad this idea is?" I asked.

"It's been a nightmare," said the attorney. "Whole families have been separated. Some workers got visas and some didn't and had to remain in Jamaica. It's a travesty."

"We were lucky to get what we have," Ms. McKenzie continued, "adding that many employees haven't received a day off in six weeks." I could only listen dumbfounded.

While holding the young Jamaican lady close, she continued, "Some restaurants can only open certain times of the day and even had to raise prices to pay the few employees they have.

By contrast, this hotel is not having problems because, as the island's largest hotel, it starts the tourist season earlier and can request H-2B workers sooner. Some businesses will get relief before the tourism season ends in October because the U.S. Department of Homeland Security last month approved a one-time influx of more foreign workers. Businesses across the state are struggling to fill openings with an unemployment rate below the national average and are actually at a 17-year low. As bad as this year is, next year may be even worse. H-2B visas for next year may be impossible to obtain."

"The President's hardline position on immigration doesn't help."

I said, "My name is Bill Bennett and those ugly old codgers sitting on the veranda are my friends. We're here to help solve a murder, but I think we can take some time to look into this."

Shontal McKenzie said, "What do you think? You make it sound so easy. that you and your friends can accomplish more than we can! You're dreaming!"

I responded, "Ms. McKenzie, you might be right, but it won't hurt to look into it. Besides, my friends and I like to cause trouble." Departing with a wave, I returned to my senior sleuths.

Chapter Twelve

In between dealing with Beals' murder and the disappearance of Julie Randall, I squeezed some time aside to pursue looking into the government denying Tanesa Simpson's husband a visa.

Searching the internet, I found as a whole, immigrants contribute greatly to our state. While less than 7 percent of the state's residents were born in another country, they make up a vital, educated share of Michigan's labor force. Nearly 40 percent of immigrants in the state possess a college or higher degree, and more than four in five report speaking English fluently. Our state benefits from the various way's immigrants participate in the economy. They are employed in many professions. In addition, they comprise nearly 11 percent of the state's healthcare practitioners. As workers, business owners, taxpayers, and neighbors, immigrants are an important part of Michigan's successful communities and make great contributions that benefit all.

More than half of all immigrants in Michigan are naturalized citizens.

I now wanted to find out more about the Jamaican contribution on the island and in the United States.

It was impressive to learn almost 15,000 Jamaicans work in the United States on H-2B visas. After Mexico, Jamaica sends more guest workers to the U.S. than any other foreign country.

They earn the same wages and benefits that locals would get. A season's worth of earnings in the states can exceed what a Jamaican might make at home in a full year. These visas are good for up to six months.

Back in their homeland, The Jamaica Central Labor Organization, for its part, actively encourages its citizens to seek job opportunities in the United States through its Overseas Employment Program.

On the down side, it disturbed me to learn that more than 70,000 U.S. citizens in Michigan live with at least one family member who is undocumented. There are over 130,000 undocumented immigrants living in Michigan.

I learned that more than 10,000 Deferred Action for Childhood Arrivals or DACA recipients live in Michigan.

I also discovered over 400,000 immigrants make up our state's labor force. It was plain to me, our state needed immigrant workers and I had to help Tanesa Simpson get her husband a work visa.

It usually took a lot to upset me, but this bureaucratic hog wash was over the top. I contacted my elected representative, but just as Ms. McKenzie had predicted I ran into the usual red-tape. It was to their credit, they connected me to the Immigration office in Detroit.

After I explained the entire dilemma, the Immigration employee summarized his side of the problem. Listening to his diatribe on the hold-up on immigration work visas, he did mention perspective employers only had to fill out Form I-129 H-2A and that immigrant would be eligible for a visa.

I asked the Immigrant agent, "So, if I guarantee his employment, this non-immigrant can come to this country." I queried.

"Certainly," the government pencil pusher confirmed.

"How long will the paper work take?" I asked.

The government employee replied, "Maybe, a year?"

I almost went ballistic as I screamed, "Are you nuts? Let's get real!" I shouted.

"I'm sorry, but that's how long the process will take. I thought you knew the quota has been met for this year," answered the government agent.

Controlling my temper, I replied, "Well, send me all of the paperwork. Maybe, I can speed it up on my end." After giving him my hotel address, we disconnected and I had to admit I wasn't too optimistic. I had one more ace up my sleeve. I again phoned my old friend, John Crane, who seemed to be able to make things happen.

Listening to the dial tone, I cringed at what he would say. I wasn't disappointed. "Hello, John. How are you?" I asked.

"What do you want? Do I have to come there and bail you idiots out again?"

"No, nothing like that. I'm trying to help a non-visa person get a visa so he can work on Mackinac Island. Do you think you could help?" I asked.

"I already gave you information on Dubois. Why should I help you again?" was his reply,

"How about a case of suds? Your favorite. Come on John. The immigrant's wife's already here and he can't get a visa to come."

"That's just what I need, another charity case dropped on me. Let me work on it and see what I can come up with. What's his name?" asked Crane.

"His name is Herne Simpson. Thanks, John. I appreciate it."

"You better. I'm keeping track and your debt is getting pretty high," he said as he disconnected.

Chapter Thirteen

Returning to our current problem, the local news was all over the missing female diver. The pseudo-detectives and I, along with our spouses, had gathered in the hotel lobby to watch the events unfold.

We only saw a glimpse of the bereaved husband on television as he was led into the City Marshal's vehicle and slowly disappeared through the crowd.

The announcer stated that the boat had left to examine a schooner wreck in the middle of Lake Michigan. The captain was an experienced old salt and had conducted hundreds of such trips without any mishaps. Search and Rescue boats were scouring the region and hopefully would find the missing diver.

Once I heard the name, Richard Randall, my police instincts clicked in. *Was it possible that it could be the same Richard Randall I was going to interview?* I would have to find out.

Meanwhile, during the television commercials, we exchanged updates on our investigations. Ben and Mark had no luck on the island and John and Tyler also struck out. I had to admit I hadn't made much headway either, but I had returned with the very same name that was now the husband of the missing diver. *Was that a coincidence?*

The next day I decided to pay a visit to the eco-terrorist organization, Citizens for Pure Water.

It's not like you can find them in the yellow pages or even on my smart phone. Through diligence I was able to locate their headquarters on a back street. The windows were covered with environmentally friendly posters encouraging everyone to become more politically active. Walking through the front door I wasn't sure what to expect. Instead of seeing a messy room with long haired youths, it looked like a well-organized group of eager staffers. Everyone was busy working on a computer or photocopying.

I approached the first young lady at a desk and asked, "May I speak with the person in charge?"

She retorted, "Are you with the police?"

I had hoped it wasn't that obvious after all these years. I responded, "No, not exactly. I am investigating the death of a man a few days ago on Mackinac Island."

She responded, "What does that have to do with our organization?"

"Well, the victim worked for MichCan Corp. and I thought someone here might have an insight into his death," I answered.

"Are you implying we're murderers?" asked the young lady.

"No, as a matter of fact, I was hoping your organization could shine some light on why he was killed," I replied.

"I'll see if David's available. Wait here," she retorted.

Before long a middle-aged man emerged from a back room and extended his hand. After introducing myself, he responded, "My name is David Wells. I'm in charge of this kangaroo court. We're trying to save our water supply before big businesses like MichCan Corp. and the government destroy it. You know once it's gone it's gone."

I said, "I agree with you. I don't want to see our water supply destroyed any more than you do."

"What's this about the murder of that man on Mackinac Island being tied to us?" he asked.

"My friends and I have been asked to look into Beals' death to avoid any improprieties by the state police. So far, we haven't gotten very far. We know Beals was probably working for MichCan Corp. when he was murdered. We don't know what he was doing on the island since he had no reason to be there especially that late," I answered.

"A month ago, someone threw a Molotov cocktail through our front window. The fire destroyed our computer system and, in fact, we just got it up and running yesterday. One of our young interns got the crap beat out of him last week. Kenny was in the hospital for several days, but he never saw who hit him. We can't even press charges in either situation," he answered with a scowl.

"In talking with City Marshal Ramsey, I understand you have collided your boats with MichCan's repair vessels. Some divers have even destroyed some of the closed-circuit cameras attached to the pipeline. In addition, the local politicians have gotten death threats. Don't you think that's going a little too far?" I asked.

"Do you want to drink contaminated water? We have some in the back room from the Kalamazoo River as well as some from Flint. Would you like to have a taste?" he asked.

"Okay, you made your point. But someone is going to get hurt if you continue down this road," I replied.

"We'll do everything we can to stop MichCan Corp. They say if there's a leak, they can have it repaired in minutes. We don't believe that. It's time big business and the government is made accountable," he replied sternly.

I wanted to go down a new road so I asked, "Why in heaven's name don't you just wait for MichCan to finish the tunnel?"

The editor replied, "We can't wait that long."

"So, if I understand correctly, you're going to keep pressure on MichCan but you're denying any involvement in Beals' death?" I retorted.

"We do not condone violence, but we will take whatever measures short of that to save our water. Now if there's nothing else, I have to get back to work," he said as he turned and walked back into his office.

I left the office and decided to wait for it to close. Maybe, one of the young idealistic interns would be more forthcoming.

As I was waiting, a van arrived and a group exited. I couldn't see who they were as the building blocked my vantage point.

I felt something was amiss. I texted John Baldwin and told him to bring everyone. I gave him the street address, and meanwhile I checked my Glock to make sure it was loaded. Within minutes, the pseudo-detectives arrived dressed in tee shirts, cut-offs and even swim wear.

I told them something suspicious was going down. A van

arrived and a group entered the back door, but I couldn't make out what they were up to. John asked, "What if they're just carrying in posters?"

Tyler added, "We could get in big trouble if we charge in with guns and they're just having a party."

Ben and Mark concurred. It was just too risky to barge into a business brandishing firearms.

We decided to wait and see what happened. As the sun was setting, the employees left the office and I noticed the young receptionist who greeted me when I entered the office, was making her way to her vehicle.

So as not to frighten her, I exited my vehicle and shouted, "Miss, can I have minute of your time?"

She seemed nervous and increased her pace to her automobile. I added, "I just want to talk to you about the murder on Mackinac Island. I've been asked to help find out who may be responsible?"

She seemed to calm down and turned and waited for me. As I approached, I said, "My name is Bill Bennett and my friends and I have been asked to help the state police get to the truth. We know Beals was working for MichCan Corp. Do you know anybody who would want him dead?"

She shook her head and noticing the others sitting in their vehicle next to mine and became agitated. "I don't know anything. I just answer phones and sort the mail," she responded.

She kept looking back at the office so I asked, "Is there something in there that's dangerous. You know if you know a felony is going to be committed it's called aiding and abetting, and you can go to prison for that."

She started to cry and mumble under her breath. I could see she was cracking. I continued, "You're too young to go to prison. What's happening?"

She murmured, "They have her."

"What do you mean? Who do they have?" I asked.

"Julie Randall!" she blurted.

I said, "Get in your car and get down." I immediately waved to my compadres and I ran to the front door of the eco-terrorist's office.

The door was locked but my Glock made quick work of it. I swung the door open and aimed my pistol at the crowd. I shouted, "Hands, I want to see your hands!"

My compatriots were right behind me, albeit they didn't look too menacing in their tank tops and swim suits.

All of the office personnel raised their hands as ordered and David Wells stepped forward very carefully.

"It's not what you think. We didn't kidnap her. We're protecting her," he said.

I shouted, "Who the hell are you talking about?"

From behind the group stepped an attractive woman and she said, "I'm Julie Randall. They rescued me from Lake Michigan."

Needless to say, the pseudo-detectives and I were thunder struck.

"We'll have to call City Marshal Ramsey and the state police."

"No, you don't understand. My husband tried to drown me today. I was pretty sure he would try something so I contacted my friends and they followed us out and stayed out of sight from our dive boat. Before we entered the water, I checked my gear one more time and noticed the back-up tank wasn't operational. I opened the valve and after my husband tried to drown me, I feigned unconsciousness and floated away from him. I was able to swim to their boat and now I'm hiding. If I accuse my husband of trying to murder me, he'll simply deny it. Will you help us?"

"I guess we owe you an opportunity to explain everything." Julie reviewed the entire ruse and after she was finished, I stated, "We'll help you on one condition."

Julie asked, "What's that?"

"While we're helping shield you from the law, these goofs don't do anything stupid like sabotage the pipeline or blow up something."

She looked at Wells and he nodded in agreement.

Chapter Fourteen

Now that we were getting involved with an eco-terrorist group, I wanted to know just exactly who these people were. In my investigation, I discovered the government defines eco-terrorism as the use or threatened use of violence of a criminal nature against innocent victims or property by an environmentally-oriented, subnational group for environmental-political reasons, or aimed at an audience beyond the target, often of a symbolic nature. The FBI credited eco-terrorists in our country with over $200 million in property damage between 2003 and 2008. A majority of states in the US have introduced laws aimed at fighting eco-terrorism.

Eco-terrorism is closely related to civil disobedience and destruction of the environment. Some of those labeled as eco-terrorists do not commit violence against humans, but only against property. This has led to a debate that touches on whether or not to classify these actions as terrorist. In the United States, the FBI's definition includes acts of violence against property, which makes most acts of sabotage fall in the realm of domestic terrorism.

Some "eco-terrorists" are people fighting to preserve their environment with the belief that they are preserving their existence.

My study led me to uncover that the reason behind eco-terrorism rose from the radical environmentalist movement that gained momentum during the 1960s. Ideas that arose from liberal environmentalism are founded on the belief that capitalism, patriarchal society, and the Judeo-Christian tradition were responsible for the destruction of nature. It's also characterized by the belief that human society is responsible for the depletion of the environment and, if current society is left unchecked, it will lead to the complete destruction of our world.

I found that eco-terrorists believe that human beings are just an ordinary member of the biological community and that all living things should have rights and deserve protection under the law. Some eco-terrorists are motivated by other aspects of deep ecology, like the goal to return the environment to its pre-industrial state.

There are a wide variety of tactics used by eco-terrorists and groups associated with eco-terrorism. For example, one popular method is known as tree spiking. This is a common tactic that was first used by members of one group that involved hammering a spike into the trunk of a tree. Their goal was damaging chainsaws and/or seriously injuring a logger. Spiking trees became a federal offense in the United States when it was added to the Drug Act in 1988.

A more common type of eco-terrorism is arson; which is a tactic most associated with recent activity by one eco-terrorist organization. This organization has been blamed for arson at sites such as housing developments, and other urban sprawl locations.

The FBI has stated that "since 2005, investigations have resulted in indictments against 30 individuals." In 2006, the FBI brought charges of domestic terrorism against eleven people associated with two eco-terrorist groups. The indictment included charges related to arson, conspiracy, use of destructive devices, and destruction of an energy facility.

A third technique used by radical eco-terrorists is bombings. While this tactic is rare, on some occasions, explosives have been used.

In 2008, one eco-terrorist was convicted of plotting to attack targets including a fish hatchery, a dam, power stations, and cell phone towers. An undercover FBI agent exposed the plan. In addition to the leader, two others were also convicted. In 2008, the eco-terrorist leader was sentenced to 20 years in prison for conspiracy to damage or destroy property by fire and explosive.

Organizations accused of eco-terrorism generally come from grassroots and do not have a hierarchal structure. They usually only want to solve their immediate goal and are not linked to a national organization.

There was another side to the coin. The government was not always in the right. I scrutinized one report that cited what it called other FBI acceptable practices in its monitoring of domestic groups in the years between the September 11, 2001 terrorist attacks and 2006.

In some cases, agents began investigations of people affiliated with activist groups for unsubstantiated reasons and without adequate proof they improperly kept information about activist groups. Activists affiliated with one eco-terrorist group were improperly put on a terrorist watch list, the report said.

I found out that sabotage and eco-terrorism are two different crimes. Sabotage is the destruction, or threatening to destroy, property while eco-terrorism refers to acts of violence committed in support of ecological or environmental causes, against persons or their property.

In 1990, two organizers of one group were injured when a motion-detecting pipe bomb detonated beneath the driver seat. Authorities alleged that the bomb was being transported and accidentally detonated. The pair sued investigators, alleging false arrest, illegal search, slanderous statements and conspiracy. In 2002, a jury found that FBI agents and Oakland police officers violated their constitutional rights to free speech and protection from unlawful searches of the organization!

A recent example of one eco-terrorist group claimed responsibility for arson was the March 2008 burning of luxury homes in an expensive Seattle suburb. In 2009, this organization claimed responsibility for the destruction of two radio towers in Seattle. In 2001, the FBI called this group "one of the most active extremist elements in the United States". One eco-terrorist group was mentioned in an FBI testimony as a group that was responsible for a series of arsons in Arizona. Using similar tactics, they have caused more than $5 million in damages.

I found the most infamous eco-terrorist, Ted Kaczynski, also known as the Unabomber, injured as many as 23 and was

74 Mayhem on Mackinac Island

responsible for three deaths through letter-bombs.

A number of "local" organizations have also been indicted under federal laws related to eco-terrorism.

In 2008 the Federal Bureau of Investigation said eco-terrorists represented one of the most serious domestic terrorism threats in the U.S. today citing the sheer volume of their crimes (over 2,000 since 1979); the huge economic impact are losses of more than $110 million since 1979; the wide range of victims from international corporations to lumber companies to animal testing facilities to genetic research firms; and their increasingly violent rhetoric and tactics.

I also learned that under the Animal Protection Act of 1992, it became a federal crime to cause more than $10,000 in damage while engaged in physical disruption to the functioning of an animal enterprise by intentionally stealing, damaging, or causing the loss of any property used by the animal enterprise.

In 2006, this was updated and renamed the Animal Enterprise Terrorism Act. The updated act included causing personal harm and the losses incurred on "secondary targets" as well as adding to the penalties for these crimes.

By the time I finished my study of the eco-terrorists, I felt I had a good understanding of these diverse organizations. They may not be organized nationally, but with dedicated local individuals willing to go to the wall for their cause, they were certainly a force.

Chapter Fifteen

The next day, the ferry docked and scores of enthusiastic tourists disembarked looking forward to a fun-filled day. They were oblivious to the ongoing tragedy that was unfolding on the island. Among the tourists were two professionals that had a job to do. Paul Brown, MichCan's public relations executive, and Avellino Dubois, the corporation's head of security, strode through the port tunnel and emerged onto the island's main street. They hailed a horse-carriage and grunted the name of their destination to the driver. Within minutes, they were knocking on Richard Randall's door.

Upon opening it, they saw a very distraught and downtrodden mid-west corporate vice president.

Paul Brown started the conversation, "Have you heard anything from the Coast Guard?"

Randall replied, "No, not a word."

Dubois added, "Hopefully, she got picked up by a yacht and they haven't been able to call in yet."

Randall retorted, "If someone had rescued her, we would've heard." Randall knew he had to act the part of a worried spouse in case these two were called to testify someday as to his mental state. He continued, "I don't know what I'll do if she doesn't make it." He buried his head in his hands for effect.

Paul Brown said, "You know MichCan's entire apparatus is at your disposal. I've talked to the CEO and he has told me; the corporation will spend any amount of money to help locate your wife."

Avellino Dubois added, "Absolutely, I will have the entire corporation security team here tomorrow if they're needed."

"We're here at your complete disposal," stated the public relations executive.

Randall replied, "I really appreciate it. We had such a great time diving near the sunken ship this afternoon and then she wasn't there. I can't believe it."

Both Brown and Dubois put an arm around him to console him.

Randall finally asked, "Do you mind if I'm alone for a while? I have to think about everything."

Both Brown and Dubois shook their heads in agreement and left Randall's hotel room.

Brown said, "I'll try to get us a room."

Dubois replied, "That sounds good. I think we're going to be here for a while."

Paul Brown was just getting settled in his bed when his cell phone rang. Tapping his phone, he heard a familiar voice. "This is the voice from beyond the grave. Did you miss me?"

Paul Brown sat up and couldn't believe his ears. "I've been worried sick about you. Where are you, Julie?"

"I can't tell you that but I'm safe and I'm with friends," she muttered. "The idiot tried to drown me, but I was too smart for him. I got away and my friends saved me. I'm in hiding and I have to stay out of sight until my beloved husband is caught."

Brown responded, "I couldn't think straight all day. Is there anything I can do to help?"

"Not right now. You took care of Beals and you almost took care of that old detective. I appreciate everything you've done for me," answered Julie.

"I have to see you," gasped Brown.

"Not right now. The timing isn't right. Stay near Richard and I'll phone you in a few days. I'll need you then," replied Julie.

Brown responded, "Dubois is here and he's told Richard he could bring his whole security team to the island."

"Get rid of him. Then try to dispose of those pesky old detectives," Julie ordered.

"I can probably get rid of Dubois, but I don't know how to get rid of those old guys," Brown said.

Julie responded, "Think of something. I want to deal with my husband on my own terms and I don't want any outside interference."

With that encouragement, the next morning Brown was only too happy to tell Dubois he was needed back in Montreal.

Brown started the conversation over coffee, "I've just been notified that there's been a cyber-attack on our computers at corporate."

Dubois responded, "Why wasn't I informed of this?"

Brown said, "Can I be candid?"

Dubois answered, "Of course."

Brown said, "I understand your second-in-command, Chuck Sutton, has made it known that he wants your job. He specifically told me not to tell you and that he can handle the attack. He assured me it's probably just an eco-terrorist organization trying to short circuit our system."

Dubois responded, "Is that so? I'll be on the next plane to Montreal. Tell Richard I was called back on an emergency. When we get the cyber- attack controlled, I'll return."

Brown replied, "I'll pass it on to him. Good luck."

Without even finishing his coffee, Dubois left the dining room and prepared to return to Montreal.

Brown smiled as Dubois left the restaurant saying to himself *one down and one to go.*

Chapter Sixteen

Hearing a knock on his hotel door, Richard opened it and Trooper Durant was standing in the hallway.

"May I come in?" asked Jenni Durant.

"Have you heard anything?" asked Richard.

"There's no easy way to tell you, so I'll get right to it," said Jenni.

"They've found a scuba fin a few miles away. They're going to start dragging the area."

Richard acting the part of a distraught husband responded, "Oh, my God. Is it possible the current could have blown her that far?"

"We don't know, but right now it doesn't look good. Nobody has seen anything and the Coast Guard and Search and Rescue have been over the area thoroughly. We have to tell you, they're switching to a recovery mode," answered Jenni Durant.

"What does that mean?" asked Richard.

"It means they're not optimistic she's still alive and they're looking for her body," replied Jenni. "I'm sorry to have to tell you this, but we think you should be ready for the worst. Is there anybody I can call?" asked Trooper Durant

"I appreciate your candor. It's hard to believe she could have drowned. Two of my associates arrived yesterday so I'm in good hands," quipped Richard.

"If there is anything we can do, let us know," added Jenni as she left the room.

As Paul Brown entered the elevator, he passed Jenni Durant and politely nodded.

After knocking on Richard's door, the distraught VP opened the door and said, "Come in." Paul Brown started, "I just passed a state trooper in the elevator. Is there any news?"

"I guess you could say that. They said, they found a diver's fin several miles away and they're switching to a recovery mode. They're assuming she's dead."

"I'm sorry to hear that. By the way, Dubois was called back to Montreal to deal with a problem. But if there is anything I can do, let me know."

"Thanks. You're a good friend," answered Richard.

Richard was savoring a glass of wine when his phone chimed. Tapping his cell phone, he said, "Hello."

"Mr. Randall, my name is Shawn Beals, my father was Ned Beals. Do you have a minute?"

Richard responded, "This isn't a good time right now. My wife is missing on Lake Michigan and I'm hoping the Coast Guard can find her."

"I understand this is a terrible time, but I have to tell you something important about my father's murder. Could you meet me tomorrow at Protestant Point about noon?"

Richard responded, "I can't promise anything. If something comes up, I'll have to take care of that first."

After disconnecting, Richard mused *what could Beals' son have discovered that would shed light on his father's death?*

As Jenni exited the elevator, Kelly Sanderson was sitting in the hotel lobby.

"How did it go?" asked Kelly.

"About as expected. He seemed upset that the Coast Guard is switching to a recovery mode, but then we have a good idea he's probably faking his remorse."

Coincidentally, the pseudo-detectives and I were entering the hotel lobby when we bumped into Jenni and Kelly. I asked, "We're on our way to talk to Randall, but that can wait. Do you have time for a cup of coffee?"

After making ourselves comfortable, Jenni started, "It's been a long time since we saw you. You know it goes without saying you guys literally saved our lives several times. We've been assigned to investigate Beals' homicide and work with you up to a point."

I retorted, "You mean you'll help us as long as you don't

divulge anything critical."

Kelly replied, "We want to work with you, but we have to do it within parameters. Lieutenant Menendez would have our badges if we divulged anything. However, there's nothing that says we can't exchange information. For example, we know Randall's PR man has a record. He has served time for aiding and abetting. We're actually looking at him as a suspect in Beals' homicide."

"Why would Randall want to murder Beals?" John asked.

"That we haven't figured out yet. We're going to get a copy of his lugs and see who he has been communicating with," replied Jenni.

Kelly added, "We're pretty sure Dubois is clean although he has the training to kill anyone."

"What about Randall himself?" I asked.

"He's in the middle of a messy separation. He and his wife's trip to Mackinac Island was a last-ditch attempt to save their marriage. He has a million-dollar life insurance policy on her. Now with her missing, he's our prime suspect," said Kelly.

"What have you fellows uncovered?" asked Jenni.

Tyler stated, "Carolyn has completed her autopsy and as you know, Beals was garroted. The irony is he had pancreatic cancer and probably only had a few months to live."

"Anything else?" asked Kelly.

The pseudo-detectives and I looked at each other and I blurted out, "Okay, I have to tell you. We found Julie Randall with the Citizens for Pure Water eco-terrorists. When they were scuba diving, she claims her husband turned off her back-up air valve before they dived. She said she turned it on before the dive, and he later tried to drown her. She wants to prove he tried to kill her so she went down a rabbit hole."

Jenni replied, "We have to tell our commander, but we won't release that to the media. If we can keep the husband into thinking his wife is dead, he might make a mistake."

Kelly said, "I have an idea, "He likes his liquor and his women. What if we wait for Randall to come into the lounge for a drink? I can pose as an easy mark."

I replied, "It sounds like our scheme in Michigamme a few years ago. It might work. We can mic you up and since he doesn't know most of the guys, we can have the lounge covered."

Once in their cruiser, Kelly started, "As Bill said, we did it once, maybe, we can do it again."

Jenni replied, "I think we better not tell our CO about our little charade. I doubt if she would buy into it."

Kelly added, "It's always better to ask forgiveness than permission."

Chapter Seventeen

I just couldn't get Tanesa Simpson's plight off my mind. I asked Siri for the immigration attorney that was trying to help.

After dialing her number, I heard, "Hello."

I started, "Hello, Ms. McKenzie, this is the fellow that spoke to you at Mackinac Island near the hotel. You were consoling Tanesa Simpson and I tried to help."

She responded, "Oh, yes, now I remember. What can I do for you?" she asked.

"I just can't forget her. I researched the problem and I understand there's a quota that has been reached. Is there any way we can get around it? I even phoned my congressman and just like you said, I got his voice mail and I'm not holding my breath for him to return my call."

"I appreciate your concern, but there's nothing legally we can do," she responded.

"What about illegally? I'm not one to brag, but my friends and I have bent the law a few times to achieve the result," I replied.

"I can't condone breaking the law," Ms. McKenzie quipped.

"Nobody's asking you to break the law, but do you know something that could be done to undo this injustice. We're talking about one non-immigrant who has a great work record and is needed at the hotel. I understand he can make as much in the summer as he could an entire year in Jamaica," I added.

"Well, I can't tell you over the phone for obvious reasons, but if you were to talk to me off the record, I might be able to help you."

"I'll see you in the morning. Where do you want to meet?" I asked.

She answered, "I live in Detroit and I have breakfast at the corner of Marshall and 8th Street every morning. When do you think you can make it?"

I replied, "I'll be there in the morning."

"It's a long drive on I-75," she replied.

"Order a cup of coffee, black." as I disconnected.

The next morning, Ms. McKenzie smiled as I approached her in her restaurant. She began, "My, that's impressive. I didn't think you'd make it."

"I'm pretty resourceful when I put my mind to it. What do you have for me?"

She responded, "First of all, call me Shontal."

"Shontal, it is. And just in case you forgot, I'm Bill, Bill Bennett."

"Now that we got our introductions out of the way, I will deny any knowledge of our conversation. Let me have your cell phone, just in case," she stated.

I handed her my phone and I replied, "One can't be too careful."

Shontal began, "I'm not sure, but there's an Immigration agent that has a gambling problem. People have told me he spends just about every night at the casino. I don't know if that helps, but that's all I have."

"What's his name?" I asked.

Shontal replied, "Charles Martin."

We continued to talk into the early afternoon as I was getting an in depth look into our immigration policy. I developed a tremendous respect for Shontal and the other immigration attorneys.

Finally, I thanked her for the information, finished my coffee and left the diner. I knew only one great poker player so I decided to place a call.

After the phone rang several times, I heard a low moan that passed for an "hello." "Hey, Rick, how's it going?" I asked.

"Do you know what time it is?" asked the voice.

"A better question is do you even know what day it is?" I asked.

"Leave me alone. I was in the middle of a beautiful sleep," replied the voice.

"Aw, c'mon on. You can sleep anytime. I have a proposition for you."

"I'm not interested. Good-bye," he replied.

Before he disconnected, I shouted into my phone, "It involves a lot of money."

There was silence on the other end and then, "What do you mean a lot of money?" he asked.

"The truth is, I need your help. There's somebody in Detroit that has a gambling problem and I want to take advantage of it. You're the best poker player I know and I want you to come here and clean him out of every cent. I need him to do a favor for me. I want him to pull strings to get a non-immigrant worker from Jamaica into the country."

Rick Bonetelli replied, "Is that all? I must be dreaming. Not even you are that stupid. Good-bye!"

"Listen, I'm desperate. I want to help the wife who is on Mackinac Island and she wants her husband to join her. There is a quota of 66,000 allowed in annually, and they've reached that quota already. Have a heart and so something nice," I begged.

"I help little old ladies across streets. I think that's enough," he said smugly.

"You can make a difference and have fun doing it." I retorted.

Finally, he said, "Where and when?"

"Be on the next flight to the Detroit airport and I'll fill you in as we drive to the casino. Hopefully, I will have everything in place by then. Adios."

We disconnected and I had a few things to do before Rick's plane landed. I decided to rent a limousine for the night. I stopped at a decal store and purchased two large stick-on prints of the local casino. By this time, Rick was emerging from the airport terminal. I motioned to him and he was impressed with my vehicle.

Rick started, "You didn't have to rent a limo just for me."

I replied, "Don't let it go to your head. It's all part of the ruse. I'll take you to the casino and later, I'll deliver our fall guy."

After dropping Rick at the casino, I drove to the federal building and hoped my plan would work.

Parking in front of the Federal Immigration and Naturalization Building, I held up a sign displaying "MARTIN". Fortunately, an older portly gentleman approached the vehicle and I asked, "Are you Mr. Martin?"

He responded, "Yes, but what's with the limo?"

I responded, "The casino wants to show their appreciation for your patronage. Please get in."

He smiled and complied. Once inside, he helped himself to the champagne and caviar much to my dismay.

Driving to the casino, I asked, "I have to have your name for my log book."

He answered, "Martin, Dan Martin."

I asked, "What's your favorite game at the casino?"

Martin replied, "I only play five card poker in the back room."

"Are you pretty lucky?" I continued to ask?

"Luck's got nothing to do with it. I count cards and I know when to ante and when to fold," Martin responded.

I continued to press, "You must be pretty good to go as often as you do?"

"I make my own luck. Now if you don't mind, I'd like to get there sooner than later," he retorted.

"Yes, sir." I answered and drove the rest of the way in silence.

Dropping him in front of the casino, the doorman had a quizzical look as Martin exited the limo. I'm sure he was wondering how did this fellow rate getting a ride in a casino limousine. Before the doorman could say anything, I quickly drove the limo into the rear parking lot.

Rick's phone chimed and he answered, "Hey, Rick. Your mark is coming through the front door. He's wearing a blue suit with a striped tie. Do you see him?" I asked.

Rick responded, "I see him now and he's moving to the back of the casino."

I replied, "He said he only likes to play five card stud. That's your specialty. Good luck."

I changed into some casual clothes and made my way into

the casino. After playing a few slots, I found myself in the back room watching intently as the main table became the center of attention.

Hours passed and most of the players disappeared. Only Martin and Rick were left along with the dealer. By now, Rick had accumulated a tidy sum and Martin was sweating profusely.

Martin murmured, "I can write a check for the balance. I'm good for it."

Rick Bonetelli retorted, "Keep your checks in the bank."

Martin now completely despondent begged, "Is it okay if I take a minute and visit the washroom?"

Rick replied, "You got one minute."

Martin left the table and walked toward the restroom with yours truly following close behind. After Martin had taken care of his needs, he rinsed his face in cold water. He straightened his tie as I handed him a paper towel.

I started, "It looks like you're having a run of bad luck."

Martin replied, "Luck's got nothing to do with it."

He walked toward the door and I again followed him.

Martin laid a blank check on the pile of chips and said, "I'm good for it. Any bank in town will cash it."

Rick now believing he had his mark, replied, "I guess I can take the check. But it better be good."

Rick laid down his cards. A full house. Kings over Queens. Martin put his cards by his belly and looked completely despondent and said, "Well, all I have are five little ones. Rick started to pull the pile toward him when Martin interrupted him and said, "But they're all the same suit and all in a row."

Rick released the pile and his mouth dropped open. Martin started to pull the pile in his direction when I reached down and flipped his tie over. There sitting snugly on the bottom of the tie was a small clip. Immediately, two security guards dragged Martin toward a back room. I followed close behind hoping to make a deal.

One of the security guards swiped his card through the reader and the door opened. The guards with Martin in tow slid through the doorway. I dived through knowing I was probably going to be in trouble myself. A behemoth pulled me off my feet and was preparing to hurl me back through the doorway when I shouted, "I have a deal for the idiot? If you agree to release him into my custody, my friend will return all his winnings?"

The manager sneered and said, "What's in it for you?" "This fool and I have some business to discuss. Could we have a minute?"

The casino manager motioned for one of the security guards to release Martin. I maneuvered the confused Martin to a corner. He started, "I don't know you. I'm not making a deal with you or anybody else."

I said, "Look around stupid. Your ass is in a jam. Either you listen to me and cooperate or they're going to pound you to a pulp before they throw you in jail. On top of that, stupid, you're going to be banned for life from every casino in the state. Do you want to hear my offer?"

Martin shrugged his shoulders which I took as a yes. I started, "There's a certain Jamaican fellow, Herne Simpson that wants to come to America. He needs a non-agricultural visa. I know they have all been dispersed, but I bet you know how to get one more non-immigrant into the country. Don't you?"

He   responded, "I can't do that. How dare you even propose such a thing? I could go to prison."

"Listen buddy, right now, you don't have a whole lot of choices, do you? Either you walk out with me and find one little non-agricultural visa or they're going to beat the piss out of you. What's it going to be?"

We returned to the casino crew and I looked at Martin and I asked again, "What's it going to be? I walk out of here with you or without you? Frankly I don't care."

Martin, with his head hanging, nodded affirmative.

The manager said, "One more thing, Martin. If I catch you in here again, you'll disappear. Ya got it?"

I dragged Martin toward the door and after being allowed to

exit, I breathed a sigh of relief. There was only one more little problem. I had to tell Rick he wasn't going to be able to keep his fortune.

Rick had already cashed his winnings and was preparing to exit the casino. The manager along with a small security force followed us to the front. Rick smiled while he examined his check. I grinned at Rick and asked, "Could I see it?" Rich looked like he was on top of world said, "As long as you give it back."

Taking the check, I passed it to the manager who promptly departed. The security guards remained ensuring we found the exit. After stepping through the doors, Rick looked at me and screamed, "Are you nuts? I'm assuming you made some kind of half-ass deal to trade my money for this idiot."

I responded, "You got it. Now this fool's going to figure out a way to get our friend into the country. Aren't you Martin?"

"What's to keep me from reneging on my deal? After all, the casino has the check and there's no proof I cheated the casino," he reported smugly.

"You forget the casino has everything on video. I'm sure your higher-ups would like to see you getting caught cheating at cards," I answered, "I want that visa by the end of the week. Here's my address you can mail it to me," I ordered.

A disheartened Rick Bonetelli boarded his flight back to the Superior Peninsula. As he departed, I consoled him saying, "You can feel better knowing you did a good deed."

By the end of the week a plain manila package arrived with Herne Simpson's papers inside. When Tanesa Simpson was given the package, she hugged me and I was happy to have solved the *visa problem*.

Chapter Eighteen

The next morning Richard Randall was up early and phoned the younger Beals. Shawn Beals answered, "Yeah."

Randall said, "I have some time this morning what is it you want to tell me?"

Shawn Beals answered, "I want to meet in a place where nobody will recognize either of us. Besides, after what happened to my dad, I can't be too careful."

"Okay, how about Protestant Point in one hour?" replied Randall.

"That's fine. I'll see you there," answered the younger Beals.

Richard Randall arrived at the destination and sat on a park bench. He didn't realize he had a host of people watching. Besides the media, me, and the state police, he had become a minor celebrity.

As Shawn Beals approached, he could see the entire area was under surveillance. He quickly phoned Randall and said, "Look around you. You have more people watching you than a Hollywood celebrity. We'll have to meet another time. I'm not walking into that trap."

Randall thinking quickly, asked, "What do you have on me?"

Shawn Beals answered, "Okay, here goes. I hacked into my father's computer and I examined your file closely. According to his file, you were going to have my dad do something illegal. Since your wife is missing, is it possible you wanted to have him murder her?"

Randall replied, "How much is it going to cost?"

Shawn thought for a minute and said, "How about a half-million dollars?"

Randall replied, "Are you nuts, I'll give you two-hundred and fifty thousand dollars. Take it or leave it."

Shawn Beals replied, "No problem. I can just walk into your

surveillance party and hand the thumb drive over to the cops."

Rethinking, Randall agreed saying, "Okay, a half-million it is, but it will take me time and obviously the police and the media are watching my every move. I'll call you when I have the money."

Shawn Beals replied, "Okay, let me know when you have transferred the money. Have your banker wire it to this number." He proceeded to give Randall an off-shore bank account number and disconnected.

Richard Randall thought to himself, *I'll take care of that amateur Sherlock Holmes.*

Returning to his hotel, he felt he deserved a reward for planning his next strategy. He entered the hotel lounge and seeing only one person at the bar decided he could use some company.

"Is this seat taken?" asked Randall.

"No, as a matter of fact, my date stood me up. I need a shoulder to cry on," said the gorgeous blond.

"I have very strong shoulders. You can borrow them if you like," disclosed Randall.

The gorgeous blond feigned feeling his shoulders and replied, "You're right. You do have big ones."

Randall leaned in and said, "My name is Richard Randall."

The gorgeous blond replied, "I'm Kelly."

More drinks were ordered as the day progressed. Randall showed his charm much to Kelly's delight. The hours whiled away as more drinks were consumed. The pseudo-detectives were now taking turns keeping the new friends under surveillance.

I was sitting in the hotel lobby when John sat next to me. He stated, "Kelly hasn't lost her touch. She can sure play up to that joker."

I agreed saying, "She's almost wasting her talents in the state police." Our plan was working splendidly until Paul Brown entered through the front door.

I nudged John and said, "I don't like the looks of this. We better get our girl out of there or risk her cover being blown. Brown doesn't know Kelly, but we have to keep our ruse as simple as possible."

John replied, "Let me handle this."

John approached Brown and did a double-take. Looking at Brown, John shouted, "Hey, I know you. You're Mark Meacham from Kalamazoo. It's nice to see you again." Brown retorted, "I'm sorry you must have me confused with someone else. Excuse me."

John continued, "You're not getting away that easy, Mark. Remember when we had those two hookers in our hotel room when your wife knocked on the door?"

While John kept Paul Brown busy, I was able to enter the lounge and signaled Kelly to make her departure.

After seeing my motion, Kelly looked at her watch, she said, "Oh, look at the time. I have to meet someone."

Richard Randall replied, "Can I see you again? What about tomorrow, same time, same place?"

Kelly nodded and slid out the front door as Brown was entering after eluding the public relations executive.

Brown continued into the hotel lounge and sat next to his boss. "Any word from the Coast Guard?" he asked.

Randall replied, "Still nothing. I'm starting to think she might have drowned and I may never see her again. I had hoped this trip to the island would help us reconnect. I guess that's not going to happen."

"I've put together a news release and I'd like you to check it," replied the public relations employee.

Randall said, "Sure," and after skimming through it he handed it back to Brown and said "That's fine. I guess it doesn't matter anymore."

Brown gave him a pat on the back and departed.

With his wife out of the way the next problem was silencing Shawn Beals.

He tapped his phone and soon a voice was heard on the other end. "I'd thought you'd be calling. Have you transferred the money to my account?"

"Yes, they were able to expedite the transaction. Let's meet at

Arch Rock. I'll expect you to have the flash drive."

"I'll have it. Just make sure you have proof of your transaction. Bring your smart phone and I'll double-check it," growled the younger Beals.

They both mutually disconnected and Randall smiled at the possibility of tidying up that loose end.

He returned to his hotel room and was surprised to see a scuba fin leaning against his door. Looking both ways in the hallway hoping to see someone, he picked up the fin and entered his room. Upon closer scrutiny, he realized it might be his wife's. *Could someone be playing a sick joke?* It could be some nut case, maybe, even a media person. They would like nothing better than to throw a scare into him and print a wild accusation. First things first. *Shawn Beal had to disappear.*

Chapter Nineteen

(Contrition on Mackinac Island)

"Hey, Grandpa, watch this," shouted one of my grandkids as they performed a backflip into the pool.

"That's great," I responded.

My wife and I were enjoying an afternoon relaxing while our six little ones continued to terrorize the hotel pool and its guests. Fortunately, there weren't many guests present and the few lounging told us they had grandchildren also, and it didn't bother them.

Knowing I would have to return to the island to help solve some horrible crimes, I was enjoying my reprieve.

My wife and I were soon joined by my comrades and their wives. Good times were rolling and I felt it was too good to be true. I was right.

The boys even persuaded me to take a dip and the immature behavior started. As bad as my grandchildren were, my friends and I were even worse. Whole rows of loungers were dripping when we finished. I didn't realize most of the guests were willing to tolerate children splashing, but couldn't stand old men making fools of themselves. I guess it just came naturally.

As I was drying myself, a clerk from the front desk approached and said, "Mr. Bennett, there's a phone call for you."

I acknowledged the clerk and proceeded to the front desk expecting to hear some bad news regarding one of the cases. I would be so lucky.

I answered saying, "Hello."

The voice on the other end responded by saying, "Is this Mr. Bennett?"

"Yes, it is. To whom am I speaking?" I asked.

"This is Bishop Grant. We have a problem and I would like to speak to you about it."

"Go ahead. I'm listening," I replied.

"I think it would be better if we met face to face," replied the Bishop.

"Suit yourself. But I'm pretty tied up at the moment," I replied.

"Could you spare me some time tomorrow and come to the cathedral?"

I responded, "Sure, How's about 1:00?"

"Very good. God be with you," as Bishop Grant disconnected.

I returned to my family and friends and said, "I just had an interesting phone call. Bishop Grant wants to meet with me tomorrow afternoon."

Naturally, the boys had to supply some good-natured ribbing.

"I hope the walls don't fall down."

"Maybe, he's going to perform an exorcism."

"They must have found that dollar you put in the collection plate and discovered it was counterfeit."

I was sorry I had mentioned it, but my interest was piqued. The next day I entered the cathedral and was impressed with its beauty. A priest approached me and I said, "I have an appointment with Bishop Grant."

He nodded his head and said softly, "Follow me."

Before long I was in the Bishop's residence. I could see the vow of poverty was not something they took seriously.

A great door opened and I stood to greet Bishop Grant. Not sure what to do, I extended my hand and said, "Your Excellency."

The bishop extended his hand and displayed a powerful grip.

Bewildered, I decided the best thing to do was keep quiet and let him do the talking.

He motioned for me to be seated and said, "Thank you for taking time to see me. I know you're very busy. I have checked and it appears you're the best qualified for what I'm going to ask."

"The Catholic Church has been more concerned about protecting its reputation than it was in removing pedophile priests and helping the victims," argued Bishop Grant.

He was now getting emotional as he stated, "My son, we have

a great scourge on our church. We have spent almost $3 billion settling lawsuits related to this crisis and there may have been as many as 100,000 victims of sexual abuse."

Somehow, I got the nerve to ask, "It is a great tragedy, but how does that affect me?"

He replied, "I have a great favor to ask you."

I nodded my head and waited for him to proceed. I could only imagine.

"My son, we are trying to save some of our priests and we have arranged a retreat on Mackinac Island. We want them to have intensive counseling and time for reflection."

I said, "I still don't see what that has to do with me."

He paused and said, "There have been many death threats against our defrocked priests. Many parents have vowed to take measures into their own hands."

"Okay, I think I know where you're going with this," I quipped.

"Mr. Bennett, I am asking you to provide security for these confused souls. I'm hoping we can save them."

My first thought was to say, Hell, no. I don't have any compassion for these perverts, but I bit my tongue and replied, "Do you honestly think they can be saved?"

Bishop Grant answered, "I have to."

I continued, "Don't they have legal problems. There must be dozens of criminal charges pending against these perverts."

He replied, "I know the whole world is against them, but our universal church isn't just for the saints, but also the sinners."

He answered, "I'm asking you not to judge these misguided individuals. Yes, they are probably going to prison, but before they do, I want them to have a chance to self-reflect and maybe, through prayer, they can be saved before they begin their incarceration. Will you help me?"

I answered, "I'll have to talk to my friends. There are a number of them that would have to become involved."

"Certainly. I understand. Could you get back to me as soon as you can? The priests arrive tonight and they begin their seclusion tomorrow. I pray you and your friends help. We will pay whatever you ask!"

I said, "I will talk to my partners tonight and I will let you know."

Bishop made the sign of the cross as I shook his hand and left.

How do I sell the boys on this cockamamie plan? I arrived at the hotel and I could tell by their expressions they were eager to hear why the bishop wanted to see me. I took a deep breath and laid it out for them. There was total silence, then Mark shouted, "Is he crazy. If I had my way, I'd hang every last one of them."

Ben agreed saying, "Of all the disgusting things to ask us to do, that has to be the lowest."

Tyler said, "Give me a gun and five minutes and I'll cure their disease."

John sat quietly and I waited for his opinion. Finally, after a long lapse of time, he spoke saying, "What's the upside of guarding them?"

I said, "We get paid a lot of money and fulfill our sacred duty. In addition," as I produced my favorite book, I said, "I think I have an appropriate quote from John 1: 8-10

If we say that we have no sin, we are only fooling ourselves, and refusing to accept the truth. But if we confess our sins to him, he can be depended on to forgive us and to cleanse us from every wrong. And it is perfectly proper for God to do this for us because Christ died to wash away our sins. If we claim we have not sinned, we are lying and calling God a liar, for he says we have sinned.

I heard a universal growl from my compatriots. John retorted, "You don't play fair."

Mark asked, "How close do I have to get to them?"

I answered, "I know you'll be professional."

Ben smiled and said, "Now, I guess I've done everything."

Tyler said, "I hope God is watching. I deserve some brownie points for this."

I patted him on the back and replied, "He is."

Chapter Twenty

In the morning, we were at the dock waiting for the church entourage to arrive. It wasn't long before a black van approached and I said, "Get ready."

The van drove as far as possible onto the dock before stopping. There were already dozens of tourists waiting to embark on the ferry.

Leading the group, Bishop Grant stated, "Thank you my son. I am forever indebted to you and your friends." We knew we had to protect them, but it made our skin crawl to think what they had done. The bishop introduced each of them; I barely heard their names. After the introductions were over, I said, "Let's get on the boat now. I don't want them in the open." We boarded the ferry and I motioned for the defrocked priests to sit in the rear. I wanted to be as inconspicuous as possible.

The former priests obediently obeyed and I could tell they were nervous. I heard Mark grumbling and I motioned for him to stop. As the tourists filed in, some of the youngsters began to investigate their surroundings. One youngster turned around in his seat and smiled at the row of former priests. I made a gesture for the youngster to desist and he had the audacity to stick his tongue out. I heard one of the defrocked priests whisper, "My God, I am sorry for my sins with all my heart. In choosing to do wrong and failing to do good, I have sinned against you whom I should love above all things. I firmly intend, with your help, to do penance, to sin no more, and to avoid whatever leads me to sin. Our Savior Jesus Christ suffered and died for us."

I knew they were human beings, but it was hard for me to see them as such.

After arriving, the ferry docked and everyone stepped out into the beautiful sunshine. An obscure individual followed us to the horse carriages and watched as we departed to our retreat.

After our clients entered the sequestered home, the boys and I walked around the perimeter. It was a very plain older house that I assumed was especially selected just for that reason.

Mark said, "Ben and I can take the first watch. You boys can relieve us later."

The three of us returned to Main Street to enjoy some of the island's famous food.

The rest of the day was uneventful and I replaced Mark and Ben in the early evening. I felt it would be too conspicuous if I sat on the front porch. Finding some Lilac bushes along the side of the house, they would provide ample cover. The only sounds were those of the horses pulling their clientele through the streets. By sundown, the streets were empty and it would make it harder if a perp tried to enter the premises.

The hours ticked away as I felt my watch would soon be over and I could get some sleep.

Suddenly, there was movement in the bushes and my first thought was *Great. Now I'm going to get sprayed by a skunk. John and Tyler would never let me live it down.*

Straining to see, it wasn't an animal, but a person.

They were trying to enter the back door. I removed my Glock and stepped toward the individual and asked, "How do you want to do this?" The individual froze and placed their hands in the air. I kept my weapon trained on the back of their head as I applied wrist ties.

Demonstrating almost perfect timing, John and Tyler appeared out of nowhere and I heard John say, "What do we have here?"

I exclaimed, "I just caught this jaybird trying to sneak through the back door!"

Tyler stated, "Well, let's get this person to some light and see what we have."

Dragging our captive to the street we were surprised to see our would-be assassin was a young lady.

I asked, "What's your name?"

She answered, "Sheila Tarnisky!"

I stated, "I assume you wanted revenge against one of the

former priests."

She answered, "You got that right. I want to kill Clevens for what he did to my little brother."

I replied, "I can sympathize with you but we can't allow you to take the law into your own hands. I'll have to phone the City Marshall and turn you over to him."

Meanwhile, the commotion created a disturbance and the front porch was soon filled with the former priests.

One of them stepped forward and said, "Sheila, please forgive me."

Our young captive replied, "Go to Hell. That's where you belong!"

The defrocked priest stated, "I'm trying to obtain forgiveness. I don't know if I'll ever get absolution."

She replied, "I hope there's a special place in Hell for you."

After one of the deputies removed the young Tarnisky, I felt compelled to enter the house and reassure the men they were safe.

Sitting at the kitchen table, Clevins asked, "Would you like some coffee?"

I replied, "That would be fine."

Most of the priests returned to their bedrooms, but Clevins remained which I assumed meant he wanted to talk.

He introduced himself and I reciprocated.

After pouring a cup of coffee for me, he joined me at the table and he started, "She's right to hate me. I loathe myself. I didn't think I was doing anything wrong. I told myself I was helping the young boys. They needed a father figure and I was there for them. You have to understand the parishioners come to depend on their priest. He has to be there for everyone. Sometimes it was simple like helping them find money to pay a utility bill, clothing or food. After a while, the whole congregation came to trust me implicitly."

He continued, "My parish was very poor and most of the children came from broken homes. I organized a lot of camping trips in the summer."

After taking a sip of coffee, Clevins stated, "It all started one night when I was wrestling with a young man and I reached over and touched his genitals. He didn't resist. He just laid there. I told myself I was helping him. It continued until he became too old and was able to fend off my advances. But by then, I had found a new teenage boy to replace him. Sheila's brother, Tim. Our relationship lasted for over a year and then he too, became old enough to say no."

I didn't know what to say. I was no therapist and at that time I wished my wife was here. She was a trained counselor and would know the right words to say. I began with hesitation, "Have you had any contact with your victims since?"

Clevins said, "Yes, I have been allowed to write a letter to each of my victims asking forgiveness."

He continued, "I know when I go back, I'll be facing several trials and imprisonment. Our purpose this weekend is to talk among ourselves and help us come to grips with our sickness."

I could only think of a few things to tell this former priest. I stated, "Maybe, you can do some good in prison. I'm sure they need faith. You could organize Bible study groups. Possibly, you could help others to look inside themselves and see what goodness they can do."

He seemed to appreciate my amateur advice.

Clevins responded, "Thanks for listening." He stood and retired to his room. I was left wondering if somehow, he could find absolution.

Chapter Twenty-One

The next day, we knew it would be a very intense therapy session for the defrocked priests. We set up camp on the front porch and enjoyed the sunshine.

I thought it might be worth my while to pay a visit to the local jail to see how Ms. Tarnisky was doing. Entering the City Marshall's Office, I saw it was empty except for one deputy. I approached him and introduced myself. He responded, "I'm deputy Rogers. Can I help you?"

I began, "Do you think I could see the prisoner?"

He reflected for a moment and then stated, "I guess it couldn't do any harm. Ten minutes."

I replied, "Thanks," as I followed him to the cell.

I had to break the ice. "Ms. Tarnisky, may I call you Sheila?"

She answered, "You can call me what you want. Just go away."

I said, "Last night after you left, Mr. Clevins poured his heart out to me. He's sick about what he did. He knows he's going to prison. I can't imagine the hatred you have for him. I would feel the same way."

"You have no idea how I hate that man. If I could have gotten inside, I would have killed him," she spewed.

"I'm glad I stopped you. You would have achieved your revenge, but you would have ruined your life. Besides, how would you be able to help your brother if you're incarcerated?"

"My brother doesn't have a future nor do I," she grunted.

Your brother has been dealt a terrible blow. He's going to need help. Is he getting counseling?" I asked.

"What good does counseling do? The damage is done. That pervert took my brother's innocence from him," she snorted.

"Maybe, you and he could organize a group therapy session. I'm sure there are many victims of the church's abuse that need to discuss their attack among other victims. You and I know they need to deal with this abyss if they're going to lead productive lives. Killing Clevins would make you feel better, but the problem would still be there."

I could see she was half-listening and I wondered if I was doing any good. I finished saying, "Why don't you think about what we've discussed?"

She turned her back to me and didn't respond when I said, "Good-bye."

On my way out of the office, the deputy said, "Nice try. Maybe, you did some good."

I answered, "I hope I did."

When I returned to the defrocked priests' house there was a small crowd gathering in front. I could see this had the possibility of getting out of hand. Once inside, I whispered, "Do the former priests know it's getting a little ugly outside?"

John nodded his head and said, "I think we're going to earn our pay today."

In the living room, the former priests were having a therapy session and I could see they were opening their hearts to one another. The noise outside was getting louder, and I said to my compadres, "We need a back-up plan in case things go south."

We discussed several options, but since there were no vehicles available, we were limited how we could respond if the crowd charged the house.

Mark stated, "Maybe, deterrence might work. I'll sit on the front porch with my shotgun."

I replied, "That's a start. Make sure the doors are locked and pull the shades. If the crowd rush the front door, we force our way out the back and try to get to the police station. We'll have to fight a rear-guard action."

Ben said, "That's not much of a plan."

I smiled and asked, "Do you have a better one?"

The front door opened and Mark stepped in covered in egg yolk and tomatoes. The rest of us couldn't help but snicker. He mused, "What's Plan B."

The crowd was getting restless and suddenly a brick crashed

through a window. Shouts of "Freaks" and "Cowards" could be heard from the crowd. I looked at John and stated, "With all the modern communication available word can travel quickly."

He agreed saying, "Maybe, we should escape out the back and Tyler and I can try to buy you time to get to the City Marshal's Office."

I responded, "I think it's too late. There must be over a hundred people out there. Every hour the ferries bring more reinforcements. I dialed 911 and said, "We are being bombarded with rocks and bricks. I'm afraid the mob is going to rush us. Can you send help?" After giving them our address, we hoped we could keep them at bay until help arrived.

With a thud, the back door fell in and dozens of angry men rushed inside. The boys and I tried to push them back, but there were too many of them.

Some of them grabbed Clevins and dragged him outside. We tried to fight through the crowd but couldn't. As much as I wanted to use my pistol, I was hoping it wouldn't come to that.

Unexpectedly, a shot was heard and we rushed outside with our Glocks drawn. Clevins was clinging to a tree with a man pointing a gun at him. I could see Clevins was wounded but I couldn't tell how seriously.

The man was preparing to shoot again, when we heard. "**Stop**!" Time stood still for a minute while we looked to see who shouted. Standing in front of the crowd was Sheila Tarnisky. Deputy Rogers had brought her there hoping she could defuse the crisis. Sheila shouted, "I want him dead more than anybody, but I realize it won't undo what's happened. He molested my younger brother and we're going to have to cope with it. If you shoot him, you won't be any better than him."

The man holding the gun dropped it and Ben quickly put it in his pocket. Sheila walked over to me and said, "I thought about what you said. I have to try to help my brother and let God deal with Clevins."

I said, "I'm very proud of you. I know it took a great deal of compassion to overcome your anger. You might still hate

Clevins, but right now your priority is to help your brother."

She responded, "I like the idea of Tim and me setting up therapy sessions for abused sexual victims."

I replied, "Who knows? You might benefit also."

We escorted Clevins to the hospital and hearing the bullet didn't hit any vital organs, he received stiches and was in the recovery room when we entered. I said, "I hope you find your penance."

Clevins replied, "The Sacrament of Reconciliation is one of the most unique aspects of Catholicism. Christ established it so we can obtain forgiveness for our sins and reconcile with God. I have to forgive myself and ask God's forgiveness."

I shook his hand and left feeling better towards him and more importantly about myself. I felt better we had achieved a *priest's contrition.*

Chapter Twenty-Two

Stepping out of the hotel into the cool crisp air, Paul Brown felt things were going his way. He had his boss buffaloed and his sweetheart was just a phone call away. He had done Julie's dirty work by helping her in her battle with her husband. Now she might show her appreciation. Together, they could destroy Richard. Julie could have her divorce and her husband's money and he could make a bid for Richard's job. As he walked to Main Street to catch the next ferry, he wondered who actually murdered Beals.

Julie had asked him to get rid of those pesky senior detectives. *Why not start with their leader?*

He boarded the next ferry back to the island and prepared to cut the head off the snake.

Meanwhile, I decided it was time to pay a visit to the City Marshal to ascertain if anything new had occurred.

I entered the City Marshal's office and it was pretty much what I expected. It was cramped with a half dozen wanted posters on a bulletin board. There were stacks of papers on counters and file cabinets, with a holding cell along the back wall. I wasn't sure if he was messy or they just didn't care.

I began, "Hello, how's it going?"

He retorted, "Okay, but I wish they'd find that lady diver's body."

I knew I couldn't disclose Julie was still alive. I trusted the state police to keep it quiet, but small-town police departments have a way of letting the cat out of the bag. If I told the City Marshal about Julie's escaping and hiding under the Citizen's for Pure Water auspices, it would be the gossip at the local lunch counter tomorrow.

I felt bad for all of the people involved in the search and rescue operation, but I had to keep a tight lip. I related, "They'll probably find her somewhere on shore where the current has taken her. I assume they'll call off the search in a few days."

"Yes, the Coast Guard will continue and then hope to retrieve what's left of the body on shore."

I waved to the City Marshal as I walked into the beautiful star-filled night. Looking up enjoying the brilliant vista of twinkling lights, my star-gazing was cut short by a wire strung around my neck. This time I tried to do a body roll, but without success. The attacker stayed behind me and rode me to the ground. I waved frantically trying to hit the mugger in the face or stomach. I could feel myself slipping into unconsciousness when I reached for my pocket knife and stabbed the assassin in the leg. Instantly, the pressure on my neck was relieved. I now went into action. After getting some oxygen into my lungs, I turned and went commando. I pummeled the attacker with everything I had. I didn't let up until the assailant was unconscious. I immediately phoned John and told him where I was and what had happened. Grabbing the mangled body, I dragged him to the nearest light. I was surprised to see it was Paul Brown.

Within minutes, John and the crew were there. I was still trying to catch my breath when I repeated the events that transpired.

Mark said, "Let's take this piece of garbage out of sight and make him talk."

I said, "As much as I like the idea, I don't think he's able to tell us much right now."

Tyler added, "Let's put him on ice for the night and question him in the morning."

We agreed that was probably the thing to do, but where could we find a place to hide this sorry excuse for a human being.

Ben interjected. "Let's take him to one of our rooms."

John shook his head, "Look at the condition he's in."

Mark removed a fifth of brandy and doused the sad looking sap and said, "Now, he just smells like he had too much to drink."

I added, "The problem with that is when we question him, we'll have to keep him gagged and we can't get any blood on the floor."

Mark replied, "You take all the fun out of everything. Give me some time and let me see if I can get something out of him."

We threw our interrogation subject into Ben's vehicle's trunk. A few hours later, Mark returned brimming from ear to ear as he disclosed, "I've found the perfect place. It's about an hour west of the bridge." Stepping into Ben's vehicle, we knew we had to get information from Brown without getting ourselves in trouble.

We crossed the bridge and drove along US 2 for miles. Mark said, "Slow down. It's up here on the right." We saw a zoo sign, but it was obvious it was closed. Everyone smiled as we fist-bumped Mark. We exited our vehicle and dragged the soon-to-be animal's midnight snack toward the cages.

Ben opened his trunk and I shook Brown saying, "It's time to meet your new friends." Being gagged Brown was only able to mumble loudly and Ben cracked him on the back of the head. "Keep it down or you'll wake the owners."

I started, "I know you don't want to reveal any details of why you tried to kill me. That's okay. I understand that, but you see if you don't tell us everything. We're going to let one of the critters make a meal out of you."

Mark removed Brown's gag and Brown exclaimed, "You're crazy. I know you're only pretending." I replied, "Do you want to make friends with Mr. Alligator or Mr. Tiger. You decide. But please hurry."

Brown whispered, "You can go to hell. I know you're bluffing."

I motioned for Tyler to open the 'gator pen. The 'gators were in the bottom of their pool but I could see some eyes surface. "Last chance buddy. Bon Appetite!"

The boys dragged the attempted assassin into the 'gator pit and tied his arms to two sturdy trees. The boys closed the gate and we sat down. Brown was struggling furiously as one by one the gators emerged and maneuvered toward their meal. Brown now turned and through his gag was able to mumble he was willing to talk. The boys and I re-entered the pen and herded the 'gators back to their pit. I approached Brown and said, "If you're just stalling, we won't come back for you next time. Do you understand?" He nodded his head and after we removed his gag, he said, "Get me out of this hell-hole and I'll tell you everything."

The boys dragged him out of the pit and Tyler slammed Brown against a tree and whispered, "Now tell us what you know or so help me I'll personally feed you to the 'gators."

Shaken and trembling, Brown muttered, "Julie and I were working as partners. If we could get rid of her husband, she could divorce him and I might have a chance at his job."

"Okay, that explains some of it, but why did you try to kill me?" I asked.

"It was Julie's idea. She wanted you and your crew out of the way. You were snooping around and might stumble on to something," Brown murmured.

"Did you kill Ned Beals?" I asked.

"No, as God is my witness, I don't know who killed him," Brown responded.

"Do you know who attacked me in Beals' office a few days ago?" I asked.

"No, I don't know anything about that." Brown continued to disavow any knowledge of either attack.

Meanwhile, back on the island, Richard Randall had just finished renting a bicycle with a ride-along cart. He stopped at the hardware store to pick up a few items. Once the items were secure in his bicycle cart, he pedaled toward Arch Rock. The sun was setting as the last of the tourists were descending the hill.

On top of the rock, he could see a man who he assumed was Shawn Beals. Randall removed a few items from the cart and ascended the hill. Shawn Beals asked, "Are you Randall?"

Randall responded, "That'd be me. Let's wait until the last of the tourists are gone." Once nobody was in view, Randall said, "Okay, let's do this."

Shawn Beals asked, "Do you have your Smartphone to confirm the financial transaction?" Randall stated, "This hurts me more than you can imagine. Yes,

I have my phone in the bag. Let me retrieve it and you can see for yourself. I assume you have the flash drive."

Shawn Beals expressed concern, "First, I want to see that the transaction's complete."

Randall removed his laptop and turned it on. He said, "I had to liquidate most of my assets, but you have your money in your account. Here, see for yourself."

Shawn Beals leaned into the computer to get a clear look. Once he did, Randall pulled out a rag doused with chloroform, grabbed the young black-mailer and held the rag over Beals' mouth until he was unresponsive. Confident, that Beals was fully unconscious; Randall shoved the burly would-be black-mailer down the hill. After checking to make sure there were no late midnight bikers approaching, he laid out a large tarp on the ground and then dragged the moaning Beals on top of the tarp. To guarantee silence, Randall held the chloroform over Beals' mouth again until Beals was totally unconscious. Donning a plastic suit, he removed a portable circular saw from his cart and proceeded to dismember the would-be black-mailer. Once the messy job was completed, he wrapped the pieces and placed them in the cart. Picking up the saw and tarp, he checked to make sure there was no tell-tale evidence. He smiled at how he had metamorphosed into a cold-blooded murderer.

Pedaling toward town, he realized he had to discard the body without it ever being discovered. He remembered a house was being remodeled on the north side of the island. Stopping in front of the house, an idea popped into his head. The contractor had placed pylons in the front of the structure that would eventually be filled with cement. Taking advantage of this opportunity, he removed the body parts and dropped them in the pylons. It took longer than he anticipated, but soon the job was done.

He returned to his hotel and locating a hose alongside of the building, he used it to sanitize the cart using bleach courtesy of the custodian's closet. Mission accomplished. He retired to his room believing he was in the clear. The one-million-dollar insurance check was as good as his.

Once in his hotel room, he felt for the flash drive in his pocket, but it wasn't there. Frantic, he returned to the site of the remodeled house and searched. No luck. He thought about returning tomorrow, but the area would be filled with construction workers. His only hope was that it would be stepped on carelessly.

Chapter Twenty-Three

Paul Brown, or at least what was left of him, was returned to Mackinaw City.

Before we dropped him at his hotel, Mark pinched his nose and said, "Mister you better take a shower."

I added, "I assume you'll cooperate with the authorities when the time comes. Until then, you're to keep quiet or we'll come back. Understand?"

Brown shook his head as he trudged into his hotel, hearing his cell phone chime as he entered.

"Paul, darling, I'm glad I caught you. I have been trying all day. Where have you been?"

"You'll never guess. Those old farts you wanted me to get rid of kidnapped me and took me to a zoo. They threatened to turn me into 'gator bait if I didn't tell them everything."

"Did you?" Julie asked.

"Of course, I did. These guys weren't kidding. Now what do we do?" Brown asked.

"Let's meet and we can come up with a plan. The Citizens for Pure Water have a boat and they'll let me use it. I'll come by shore near Fort Michilimackinac and get you. I'll see you soon honey."

"I'll have to shower and change, but I can meet you there," he relayed. The chance to see his beloved girlfriend was too hard to resist.

It wasn't long before he was sitting on the beach overlooking the Straights with the old fort behind him. A small boat approached and knowing she couldn't be seen in public, he was willing to carry out this clandestine meeting. Once Brown was aboard, they were soon speeding into the twilight with the lights of the bridge illuminating the horizon. As they were motoring through the Straights, Brown asked, "What's under the tarp?"

Julie replied, "I packed some wine and cheese as we enjoy the moonlight."

Once out of sight of land, Julie turned the engine off and turned to face her new love.

She snuggled into his arms feeling the bruises on his face. "My God, it must have been terrifying. I'm glad you're alright. You could have been killed by those animals," Julie expressed.

"You're telling me. I didn't think they would let the 'gators devour me, but until I pleaded with them, they weren't going to help," Brown disclosed.

"I have to deal with my husband, but I can't have any outside distractions. You understand," whispered Julie. "Close your eyes and let me kiss your cuts. Maybe, it will make you feel better."

With that encouragement, Brown closed his eyes and waited for Julie's sweet kisses. Instead, he felt something tighten around his ankle. He opened his eyes and saw there was a shackle attached to a cinder block.

He screamed, "Julie, what are you doing?"

Julie said, "Remember, I told you, I can't have outside distractions and you're one of them. Adios." With that she threw the cinder block over the side of the boat with a screaming Brown following close behind.

The next morning, the pseudo-detectives and I gathered for breakfast. I was the last one to arrive and as I took my seat, John asked, "Did you hear?"

"Hear what?" I asked.

"Paul Brown has disappeared and nobody has seen him since we dropped him off at his hotel last night."

"That can't be good," I stated.

"Maybe, he took a flight back to Canada," added Mark.

"I hope so, but we have our own work to concern us. We have to keep an eye on lover boy when he's with Kelly. Remember what Jenni and Kelly told us, Randall could receive a cool one-million-dollars."

John added, "I've been thinking. I don't believe Julie is as innocent as we think."

Ben interjected, "I agree with John. If she's in cahoots with that eco-terrorist group she's not squeaky clean. I've heard about wives that would undermine their husband to get more money in a divorce? Besides, if Randall is convicted of attempted murder, she gets everything he owns without a divorce."

Tyler stated, "It's possible both the Randall's have dirty laundry. Naturally, we'll keep an eye on Randall when he's with Kelly. As for Julie, she has gone underground and I doubt if we can find her."

"I have another idea. You fellows keep an eye on Kelly when she's with Randall and I'm going to check out the Citizens for Pure Water receptionist. Maybe, I can glean something out of her," I said.

We finished our breakfast and went our separate ways. The four comrades-in-arms agreed to watch Randall in shifts while I bee-lined to the eco-terrorist office.

In an attempt to keep track of Kelly, John phoned her and said, "Hello, Kelly, this is John. What's your schedule for today? Are you going to see Randall?"

Kelly replied, "I'm scheduled to meet him for lunch at the hotel."

"Great, we'll be there," replied John.

Meanwhile, I was babysitting the eco-terrorist's office as the workers filed into the small shabby building. I finally saw my gal exit her automobile and I decided to renew my acquaintance.

As I was walking across the parking lot toward the young receptionist, a tremendous explosion erupted inside the building. I tackled the young girl and used my body as a shield to protect her. With debris raining down everywhere. I laid there allowing the fragments to land. By the time the young gal and I sat up, there was nothing but a fiery inferno where the office used to exist. Fire erupted from the gas line and I grabbed the young girl and together we raced across the parking lot as fast as possible.

Finding some grass, I could feel my heart pounding. I managed to ask, "Are you okay?" She shook her head while still shaking.

City Marshal Ramsey arrived and he surveyed the firestorm.

He looked at us and asked, "Are either of you hurt?"

I replied, "I think we're okay. If this young lady had been a minute earlier, she would have been blown to bits."

City Marshal Ramsey asked, "Can I ask your name?"

The young gal replied, "Peggy. Peggy Holmes. I am. I mean I was the receptionist for Citizens for Pure Water."

The City Marshal said, "You two stay right here. Someone will take your statements."

I nodded in agreement as I removed my coat and placed it around the shaking receptionist.

I continued, "I know you're naturally upset, but you have to look at the bright side. You're alive and if you had been any earlier, you'd be dead. Just relax now and we'll talk to the officers later."

I phoned John to tell him about the disaster. After answering, he stated, "I can see the smoke from here. Ruling out a gas leak, there could only be a few possible reasons why they blew up the eco-terrorist headquarters."

I stated, "I agree, maybe, MichCan Corp. had someone do it or possibly Julie Randall could be tying up loose ends. After all, if everybody in the building was killed, the only people that know she's alive are us and the receptionist."

After we disconnected, I had time, so I researched Avellino Dubois' background a little more thoroughly. A call was put into my slightly unusual friend, John Crane. He was an expert in every conceivable military scenario. There was nothing he couldn't accomplish. I asked him to forward me a dossier on Dubois, and after the usual complaining, I waited for the fax to come through.

Finally, from Crane, I learned Dubois was educated in advanced munitions skills for an additional 24 months in Improvised Explosive Devices (IEDs).

By the time he left the Canadian military he had obtained the level of a Grade 10. There was no doubt Dubois could be our boy.

The next order of business was to check with John Baldwin

and discuss the same question. After he answered his phone, I started, "How are things going on your end?"

John answered, "Pretty dull. Kelly's going to meet with Casanova later for lunch. Hopefully, she can get the bum to reveal something about the attempt on his wife."

"I was just wondering, Dubois had special explosive training in the Canadian military. We'll have to wait until we get the state explosive report back," I stated, "but do you think he could be the bomber?"

John pondered and then responded, "You're probably right. He certainly has the training. I'm just not sure about his motive."

We mutually disconnected and I returned to comfort Peggy Holmes. I realized her life may be in danger now that she was the only person left alive from the Citizens for Pure Water organization.

As I was consoling Ms. Holmes, I texted "C-4" into my cellphone. I discovered to make C-4 blocks, explosive manufacturers take RDX in powder form and mix it with water to form slurry. Next, they add the binder material, dissolved in a solvent, and mix the materials with an agitator. When the chemical reaction begins, the C-4 decomposes to release two gases; nitrogen and carbon oxides. The reaction destroys everything in the surrounding area. To the observer, the explosion is nearly instantaneous; one second, everything's normal, and the next it's totally destroyed. I learned the explosion actually has two phases. The initial expansion inflicts most of the damage. It also creates a very low-pressure area around the explosion's origin because the gases are moving outward so rapidly that they suck most of the gas out from the center of the explosion. After the outward blast, gases rush back in to the partial vacuum, creating a second, less-destructive inward energy wave.

After reading this information, I wondered how difficult was it to obtain C-4.

After texting, I ascertained that only the United States government has it, but somehow it has turned up on the black market, especially in Iran.

I could see MichCan Corp. spending a fortune to eliminate a pesky eco-terrorist group.

Chapter Twenty-Four

City Marshal Ramsey returned and I asked, "If you don't mind, I think it would be a good idea if my comrades and I put Ms. Holmes in protective custody."

The City Marshal replied, "That's probably a good idea since we don't know who's responsible for the explosion. The state fire marshal found the incendiary device and it's pretty sophisticated. I doubt if just anyone could rig the bomb. With the bomb detonating a few minutes after nine o'clock, the bomber wanted to kill everyone inside."

"I have a hunch it's probably someone that wanted to make sure the Citizens for Pure Water were eliminated completely. It's the reason that it was blown up that bothers me."

We watched as Carolyn Baldwin was busy placing the body parts in bags.

The City Marshal replied, "We'll have to wait until the state lab examines the device closer. It's going to be a hard job identifying the bodies. Is that your Medical Examiner over there?"

"Yes, but I'm sure she's not going to be thrilled dealing with such a mess. I've learned not to bother her when she is on the scene. I'll have to pay her a visit later."

Approaching the young receptionist, I knew she wouldn't be happy to think she might be the next victim.

I began, "Peggy, we're going to have to put you in protective custody. I have some friends that are experts at guarding people whose lives are in danger."

She shook her head, "No way. I'm out of here."

I replied, "I don't think you realize the gravity of the situation. Somebody wanted the entire eco-terrorist organization eliminated. Whoever did this will track you down and kill you."

"I'm not without resources. I have a brother in Peoria, Illinois. I can hide there until this is solved," she answered.

I continued, "If they have the ability to plant a sophisticated bomb and blow up an entire building, they can track your credit cards. You'll only be endangering the people you love."

She gazed at Lake Michigan and reminisced when she and her family came to Mackinaw City years ago. She loved walking down Main Street looking in the windows. At night it was so exciting. Those days were gone now. Her parents were killed in an automobile accident when she was only fifteen. Coming back to reality, she looked at me and reluctantly agreed. "Okay, what do I have to do?"

I answered, "For starters, let's get out of here. The sooner we can get you undercover the better."

Meanwhile, my compatriots had placed the hotel bar under scrutiny as Tyler took the first shift.

Just before noon, Richard Randall entered and ordered a drink before sitting at the bar. Tyler texted the others, *the fox is in the hen house.*

The others gathered outside to await their turn baby-sitting the corporate VP.

Kelly approached the senior sleuths and continued through the entryway without acknowledging them. One couldn't be too careful.

After settling in next to Randall she sipped her cocktail.

"It's nice to see you again, Kelly. You look more ravaging every time I lay eyes on you," Randall started.

"Boy, you sure know how to sweet-talk a girl," replied Kelly.

"What would you like to do this afternoon? Let's get out of this stuffy bar and go someplace quiet," Randall asked.

"What do you have in mind, as if I didn't know," replied Kelly.

"Nothing risqué, I would like to go for a carriage ride around the island," quipped Randall.

"That sounds pretty innocent," retorted Kelly. "Can I trust you to be a gentleman?"

Randall retorted, "That depends. Do you want me to?"

Before she could answer Randall's cat-and-mouse game, a fire erupted in the main foyer of the hotel. Instantly, the room was filled with thick black smoke. Confusion and chaos reigned. The employees professionally ushered everyone to the exits. Minutes passed until the smoke started to clear. When Tyler returned to the bar, Randall and Kelly weren't there.

Tyler instantly tapped his phone and shouted, "Randall and Kelly are gone."

Ben, Mark, and John were inside the bar in seconds. Looking around they saw what was probably Kelly's cell phone on the floor.

John kicked open the Men's bathroom door and Mark did the same with the Women's, but to no avail.

Ben shouted, "How could they escape?"

John replied, "Did they escape or were they kidnapped?"

The four sleuths scoured the hotel from top to bottom. No one saw them.

Ben began, "They couldn't have just vanished."

"I agree. There are no vehicles available to steal," answered John.

As we were trying to survey the crowd of onlookers, the fire department arrived. Within minutes, the fire was extinguished. Someone had planted a combination of antifreeze which contains glysterone and potassium permanganate. Did Randall set the delayed fire to kidnap Kelly?

Jenni caught up with them with a terrified look on her face. "How could this happen? You were supposed to have Kelly covered."

The four senior sleuths and Jenni continued to scour the island asking everyone if they saw a couple fitting their description. It was as if they had vanished into thin air.

After being contacted, I took the next ferry to the island and met them on the Great Porch of the hotel. Just looking at their faces, I could tell they were downtrodden and berating them would accomplish nothing. I suggested, "Let's see if anyone left by boat."

We returned to the marina and asked every boat owner if they saw anyone fitting Randall's and Kelly's description. Again, no luck.

Let's take the trail around the island and see if anyone saw the two.

We had no luck searching the perimeter of the island and as we rendezvoused, I suggested, "There's only one place he could possibly have taken her." With that we looked at the hill and knew we had to take the trail leading to the airplane runway.

Renting some bicycles, we pedaled uphill, but as determined as we were to arrive at the top of the hill, our bodies told us it wasn't going to be easy. Through diligence, we finally reached the apex of the island and the runway was in sight.

"Let's go," I shouted.

Tyler was able to lead the way as he zoomed downhill with us following close behind. I could hear Mark complaining that he was exhausted, but we persevered. Kelly's life was at stake. Pedaling onto the runway, there was a small plane taxying to the runway. We had to get to the runway and stop that plane.

We could see the *MichCan Corp.* logo on the side of a small twin-engine Cessna. The pilot had lowered the plane's flaps and was increasing its speed. It was now or never. Tyler was able to reach the runway and tried to block the plane's escape. Randall simply swerved around him and continued gaining speed.

I now had to get to the plane before it lifted off even if it cost me my life.

As I approached the plane, I could see Randall was at the controls and I lunged toward the wheels. Tackling the left wheel, I hoped my weight would keep it from lifting off the ground. I guess I didn't know much about airplanes. The plane lifted off and flew at tree top level. If it was able to gain altitude, I knew I was a goner. I continued to hang on praying for a miracle. Apparently, my weight was able to keep the plane from climbing. Some miracle.

Randall now started to flutter the plane's wings in hopes of knocking me loose. By now I had wrapped one leg around the wheel and was holding on for my life. He opened his pilot's door and prepared to shoot. At this time, Kelly, even though her hands were tied, lunged at her kidnapper, causing the plane to nose dive. Watching the two of them struggle, I lifted myself up the undercarriage and grabbed the cockpit door handle. Meanwhile, the plane was flying in every direction but straight. Lunging at the door handle, I reached it and pulled with all my strength. I grabbed Randall as he was pointing his pistol at Kelly. With the wind whipping across my body, I grabbed Randall's neck and wrapped my arm around him and held tight. Kelly was able to wrestle the pistol away from him and pulled him toward her.

Once, inside the plane, I slammed the door shut and I watched as Kelly pulled Randall into the back of the plane. Making use of my ample weight, I threw myself on top of Randle while Kelly jumped into the pilot's seat. Using my belt, I tied Randall's hands behind his back rendering him harmless.

Kelly had grabbed the controls and was attempting to right the plane. With one slash of my pocket knife I cut her writs free and she shouted, "I got this!"

Kelly leveled the plane and circled back to the island's runway. As we neared the landing strip, I was finally able to regain control of my emotions. I whispered over the hum of the engine. "I've never been so happy to see those ugly comrades of mine." They were now waving and cheering as the plane set down gently and slowly rolled to a stop. I hugged Kelly and said, "I owe you one."

She replied, "No, you don't. I owe you. If you hadn't risked your life to hang onto the plane's wheel, Randall would have gotten away and who knows what he would have done."

The senior sleuths threw open the side door and dragged the would-be kidnapper out of the plane. Kelly and I emerged and after lots of hugs and high fives, we settled down as the City Marshal and his deputies drove onto the runway.

The million-dollar question was why did Randall try to kidnap Kelly.

Reconvening at the Marshall's office, we had an unlimited number of questions for the assailant. However, giving Ramsey credit, he ushered him into a cell and said, "He has to be arraigned first and we have to follow the law."

With that being said, we left the City Marshal's office just thankful that Kelly and I were alive.

We had a lot of unsolved questions to be answered. For example, *who murdered Ned Beals? Where was Julie Randall? Who was responsible for blowing up the eco-terrorist building? Did Paul Brown return to Canada or was he murdered? Why did Randall try to kidnap Kelly?*

Relocating to our hotel bar, we enjoyed a few cold toddies. John started, "I think we have to find Julie Randall. She's the key to everything. She fooled us into thinking she was the poor victim of spousal abuse."

John stated, "Who would have the know-how to blow up the eco-terrorist building and why was it blown up?"

Tyler chimed in, "I think the answer is sitting in the Mackinac Island jail. We need to talk with Randall before he lawyers up."

I agreed, "Let's check with Randall in the morning. Right now, I think we could all use some sleep. We adjourned until the next morning hoping we could have some answers to our questions when we confronted Randall.

We didn't know we were being watched.

Chapter Twenty-Five

After enjoying a well-earned breakfast, we took the ferry to the island hoping to persuade the VP to come clean with some answers.

We were about to enter the City Marshal's office when there was an internal explosion. We were blown to the ground by its force and smoke billowed out of the office. Waiting for the fumes to diminish, we inched inside. The entire back wall of the City Marshal's office had been blown away. The deputy on duty lay on the floor and after checking for a pulse, there was none.

The City Marshal arrived shortly after and knelt over his friend. We tried to console him, but at times like this, words are meaningless. Some of the senior sleuths ran into the alley behind the office hoping to see the escapee, but that was a lost cause.

"Who could have done this?" asked City Marshal Rawley.

"Someone that knew explosives and had no regard for human life," I answered.

"Look at this," Ben shouted.

He was holding up the remnants of a bomb and after smelling it, said, "C-4."

We all knew what that meant. Whoever detonated the bomb was skilled and it was no amateur job.

"It's probably the work of the same person that blew up the eco-terrorist building," I said.

John asked, "Why wasn't Randall killed?"

I responded, "He probably knew it was coming and hid behind his bed."

City Marshal Rawley looked at me and said, "This is personal now. I want whoever killed my deputy to face justice."

I replied, "We'll do our best."

While we were investigating the ruins of the jail, Kelly Sanderson appeared and shook her head as she stepped into the office. She stated, "My God, what happened?"

I said, "Somebody blew the back wall of the City Marshal's office out, killing the deputy on duty. Randall escaped and I can only guess he's trying to commandeer a boat."

Kelly retorted, "That bum told me he was going to have his way with me once we landed in Pellston. Somebody tipped him off I was a state trooper. He kept muttering he had to kill his wife. He had completely lost his mind."

I replied, "According to his wife, he did try to drown her the other day. We talked to her the night before the eco-terrorist building was blown up."

"Why didn't you tell us that? You were supposed to share information with us," she responded."

I answered, "I know, but she took us into her confidence and begged us not to tell anyone. She wanted to set a trap for her husband to prove he did want her dead."

"Well, look at the mess you caused now. I hope you're satisfied," Kelly snorted as she strode out of the smoldering office.

"I probably had that coming," I said under my breath. "Well, let's get to it. We have a lot of work to do. Ben, how about you and Mark check the marina to see if any boats have left?"

"John, would you and Tyler check ferry boats to see if Randall would be dumb enough to try to blend in with the tourists?"

There was something bothering me, but I couldn't quite put my finger on it. I thought to myself *how come the good City Marshal always shows up immediately after the explosions?*

This was not a good time to search the office for the City Marshal's background folder. I would have to return that evening when nobody was around. The other deputies spent the day removing critical files and weapons. Carpenters arrived and boarded up the back of the office waiting for the state fire marshal to begin the investigation.

The search for Randall proved fruitless as I suspected. He probably had a pre-planned get-away and would not be foolish enough to use public escape routes. I told the boys I was going to check out a hunch that had been nagging me.

That evening with only the clip-clop of horses being heard on the streets, I returned and pried the boarded-up plywood loose and entered the City Marshal's office.

After stepping past the yellow tape, I scoured the burned ruins for the records cabinets. The vault was damaged from the explosion, and I could peer inside. I thumbed through the folders until I spied Ramsey's personal file. I examined it and after perusing it carefully, I realized everything was coming together. His file showed he had spent a hitch in the army and was trained in explosives.

Could the City Marshal be the bomber of both the eco-terrorist building and his own office? Why would a man knowingly help a vicious individual escape and murder his own deputy? Sliding the file back into the cabinet, I slithered away into the darkness.

I caught the last ferry to the mainland and returned to my hotel where I shared my information with my compadres.

John stated, "As crazy as it sounds, it probably makes sense. But why would the City Marshal get involved with Randall?"

I answered, "Money."

Chapter Twenty-Six

Back in the Lower Peninsula, Julie Randall was trying to initiate her next move. She had eliminated brash Paul Brown who could have ruined everything. How could she get even with her husband who she heard was temporarily in custody but escaped from the cracker-box jail on the island?

As Julie was deep in thought, her door opened to her hotel room and Avellino Dubois entered.

"How do you feel today, my love?" asked Dubois.

"Lousy, it's driving me nuts that my ne'er-do-well husband has escaped from jail on Mackinac Island. I can't believe they had him in custody and let him get away. I want you to help me finish him once and for all. If it was up to my nefarious husband I would have been drowned and he'd have the one-million-dollar life insurance policy."

"I'll do anything you want. Haven't I proved myself to you by blowing up the eco-terrorist headquarters? Didn't I tip you off that your hubby was going to try to kill you?" replied Dubois.

"Yes, I know. You've been great. I owe you a debt of gratitude," answered Julie as she continued, "if we could only get rid of that receptionist that survived the blast it would help."

Dubois stated, "I'll take care of Holmes. Those old farts are probably hiding her. All I have to do is find where they're keeping her and put a bullet in her brain. I'll check their hotel and if they try to move that secretary, she'll be dead meat."

"If you could do that, we could plan how to trap my soon-to-be late husband and get rid of him as well. Once those two are out of the picture, I'm all yours," continued Julie.

With that encouragement, Dubois said, "You stay here and I'll track that bimbo down and erase her. I'll call you when I'm finished. Later, when the receptionist is dead, we'll plan our revenge on your husband. See ya later."

Dubois closed the door and after she watched him leave the parking lot, she tapped a number into her phone.

The party on the other end responded, "I see you're still kicking. You're like a cat with nine lives. I wish I was as lucky as you. I appreciate the tip you gave me about Dubois planting the bomb at our headquarters. I doubt if they'll ever be able to put all the bodies back together. What's up?" asked David Wells.

Julie responded, "Dubois is on his way to kill the receptionist, Peggy Holms. He thinks the old detectives are hiding her and once he locates her, he'll kill her. He doesn't know I tipped you off and that you're alive."

"I want our plot to finally finish MichCan Corp. If we play our cards right, MichCan will be blamed for blowing up our headquarters, your husband accused of murder, and their P.R. and security head accused of collusion would just about put an end to the pipeline."

"That would be great. I'll be able to ride off into the sunset with my husband's money and live in luxury. I'll talk to you later after Dubois kills the receptionist. Then we'll need a plan to get rid of him."

Wells answered, "I really liked Peggy, but she is collateral damage. By the way, I have some Strychnine left over from one of our protests. When the time comes, you can simply slip some into your husband's drink."

Julie Randall replied, "I like how you think. We make a good team."

Wells responded, "If it wasn't for you giving us that letter showing collusion between MichCan Corp. and the Michigan legislature, we'd still be at square one. That letter really got things moving. I'll talk to you later after you hear from Dubois."

They mutually disconnected and planned their next moves.

Chapter Twenty-Seven

Accompanied by the pseudo-detectives, Kelly, Jenni, and I had gathered in Peggy Holmes' hotel room to discuss our plan. Looking at Peggy, I asked, "Who do you think blew up your headquarters?"

Peggy Holmes thought for a moment and replied, "It could only be someone that wanted all of us dead. The likely suspect would be MichCan Corp., but that would be too obvious. I've been giving it a lot of thought and I've concluded it must have been that woman that we were hiding."

I replied, "You'd make a great detective. That's exactly what we were thinking."

She continued, "I don't know who would have the ability to devise a bomb that sophisticated."

I answered, "I have a suspect in mind and I think he's the one that's going to pay us a visit. It's safe to say, the would-be assailant will probably locate us so we're going to need a ruse to entice him to try to kill you. We'll have one of our state trooper friends, Jenni, disguise herself as you and then we're going to give our assassin a glimpse of them in the open, but before he can do anything one of us will nail him. We're all crack shots. Jenni will be wearing a Kevlar vest, but we know nothing is fool proof."

"Are you kidding? That sounds much too dangerous," replied the receptionist.

"We've done this before. You're right. It's very risky, but that's what we do. We'll need your cooperation to stay out of sight while we conduct this sting. Will you stay low until it's over?"

Peggy Holmes replied, "Certainly, that's the least I can do, but I do feel guilty all of you risking your lives to save me."

It was still dark the next morning when our crew took their

positions. Assuming our would-be assassin was nearby, the boys and I established 360-degree surveillance around our hotel. The ruse called for Kelli to shepherd Jenni to the cruiser. From a distance Jenni looked quite like Peggy. They were both the same height and with wig and Peggy's clothes, Jenni could pass for the receptionist as long as the would-be murderer didn't get too close.

Dawn was just breaking, when Kelly opened her hotel door and proceeded to escort Jenni toward their vehicle.

"Movement at 10 o'clock," John whispered over our walkie-talkies.

"Got it," I responded. The others reciprocated.

We watched as the assailant crawled ever closer among the vehicles in the parking lot to his intended victim. The would-be murderer raised his rifle and waited for the perfect shot.

I whispered into my radio, "I want him alive if possible."

"Roger that," came several responses.

It was now or never as the assassin was poised to pull his trigger when a thought crossed my mind. I leaned out of my tree and from my vantage point; I had the perfect angle from behind. Rather than take a head shot, I lowered my scope and fired one shot into his buttock.

The assailant screamed in pain. All of us held our position while Kelly and Jenni dived into their cruiser. Nobody moved. We now trained our weapons on the hit-man as he groaned in pain. I saw the would-be shooter start to crawl toward the trees from where he had emerged. He wasn't going to get away. We deployed quickly and keeping our weapons trained on him moved toward him. I repeated my request, "I want him alive, guys!"

Mark mused, "How about one little shot in the groin?"

By now we had gathered his rifle and rolled him facing us. He was in deep anguish, but mercy was not on our minds.

John and Tyler pulled the thug to his feet and he winced in pain. The murderer was thrown against a vehicle as he was searched from head to toe.

Tyler pulled out an address book that would prove useful.

I asked, "Okay, I recognize you. Aren't you the security chief for the MichCan Corp.?"

The would-be murderer replied, "Yes, I'm Avellino Dubois."

Many questions regaled him at once, but he just shrugged and shouted, "I don't have to tell you anything! Call your police and let's get on with it."

John sneered, "In your dreams. Who's paying you? Out with it."

Dubois responded, "I've been trained by the best. I am immune to torture. Do what you want."

"Mark responded, "I was hoping you'd say that. Come on boys. It's time to start carving."

With that, Dubois started to struggle saying, "I have rights in your country. You must turn me over to the police and I have the right to see an attorney. That's the law."

Ben replied, "The only law that exists is the law of the jungle. We've carved prisoners up before. We usually start with their manhood."

Dubois had been trained for every special type of interrogation, but he hadn't been questioned by us. The girls, Kelly and Jenni emerged with Peggy in tow and approached us. Peggy looked at the man wincing in pain and stated, "I don't even know this man and he was going to shoot me."

Dubois looked away and spat. John turned him to face Peggy and grunted, "Well, big man, you're not so tough now, are you?"

Seeing the innocent receptionist weeping caused him to relent. Dubois spoke, "The girl was supposed to be killed in the blast. I was just doing my job."

"Killing innocent people isn't part of any job," I replied as I continued, "Who put you up to this?"

Dubois realizing it was over spilled his guts, saying, "Julie Randall and I are lovers. I blew up the environmental headquarters to hide the fact that Julie was still alive. She promised me she would go away with me if I did."

"How did you meet her?" asked Tyler.

"She approached me while I was working for her husband. As you know, I'm in charge of security for MichCan Corp. I was able to pass information to her, and she likewise gave it to the Citizens for Pure Water."

With his usefulness now fulfilled, we debated what to do with him.

Mark suggested, "If we turn him in, his mistress will find out and she'll disappear. In addition, we want to find the center of everything, her husband. Let's hide Dubois until we can catch both of the Randalls."

Sometimes, Mark makes sense, but I related, "No, we have to let Kelly and Jenni bring him in, but maybe, we can put a twist on it. Troopers, would you be willing to keep him and tell the media Dubois is unconscious?"

Kelly replied, "I think we can fly that past our post commander.

I added, "It's important that you don't even tell the local authorities."

"Why not?" asked Jenni.

I replied, "I don't know if we can trust the local police. Someone blew that wall out of the jail and I think it was an inside job."

"Okay, we'll admit him and keep him isolated."

"Thanks, now let's come up with a plan to trap the mice with our cheese," I stated.

As our plan unfolded, we followed Dubois to the hospital and, sure enough, he underwent surgery to remove the bullet and later was isolated at the end of the recovery hall.

A state trooper was posted in the hallway and I was pretty sure someone would be sent by one of the Randall's to finish Dubois.

Hiding behind a curtain in Dubois' room, we took turns being careful not to be seen. When we were not protecting the recovering assassin, the rest of us occupied a room across the hall.

Sure enough, that evening an apparent surgeon approached the state trooper and using a chloroformed rag subdued the trooper. The surgeon prepared to enter Dubois' room when we burst out of our room and John shouted, "Go ahead, and do something stupid!"

Mark joined in, "Make a sudden move and you'll be dead before you hit the floor!"

The surgeon turned and raised his arms saying, "Don't shoot. I'm unarmed."

"We'll see," shouted Tyler as he pulled the surgical mask from the would-be murderer. Standing in the hallway was David Wells. He was white as a ghost. I ordered, "You're supposed to be dead. Where's your partner-in-crime, Julie Randall?"

He whispered, "I don't know."

We applied wrist ties to Wells and watched as the local police escorted him out the door. I thought to myself *now the cat's out of the bag. Whoever blew out the back of the jail will certainly know Wells is in custody.*

As Wells was being escorted down the steps of the hospital, a shot rang out and Wells collapsed into a heap. The local police scanned the perimeter, but the assassin departed. There were so many houses, it was impossible to tell where the shot originated.

We raced to the scene and scoured the area, but no perp was located.

The only leads we had was a wounded cohort of the wife and we knew her husband was probably still in the area trying to eliminate her.

After meeting the next day, the pseudo-detectives and I decided to gamble. We would bring Peggy Holmes into the Mackinac Island jail (or what was left of it) and try to lure the two felons out of hiding. It was a long shot, but we were desperate.

Peggy Holmes agreed to the ruse providing we didn't leave her side. We took the first ferry to the island and walked toward the rubble that now passed for the City Marshal's office.

As we walked through the street, my eyes fell on an open window above one of the fudge shops. I motioned to the others to keep an eye on it. A rifle barrel soon appeared through the window's opening and I shouted, "Gun at 12:00!"

Immediately, the boys sprang into action. John rushed through the doorway and taking two steps at a time soon confronted the villain. Shots were heard from the upstairs room and the wood-be assassin fell face first out of the window landing on a surrey.

We raced to the body and after rolling it over, it was Julie Randall.

Looking out the window from above, John spoke first saying, "She got what she deserved."

Tourists gathered around the body and soon City Marshal Ramsey was on the scene.

I said, "We were bringing Peggy Holmes to your office, but I guess the wife had different ideas."

City Marshal Ramsey said, "I can take it from here. Thanks guys. I'll make sure she's protected until federal marshals arrive."

"I have to ask, Ramsey, what are you using as an office?"

The City Marshal responded, "We've taken over the Chamber of Commerce building."

"Do you think she'll be safe there?" I asked.

"I won't let her out of my sight until the feds relieve me," the City Marshal responded.

I gave Peggy a hug and said, "Let me know if you need anything."

She smiled and nodded as she and the City Marshal disappeared into the crowd.

I turned to John and said, "I don't trust that City Marshal. I think he's in bed with Richard Randall."

"What makes you think that?" John asked.

"First of all, the City Marshal had explosive training while he was in the army and secondly, I noticed the flash drive in his office after the explosion. After I stole it, I plugged it into my computer and I saw Richard Randall's illegal shenanigans. I think the good City Marshal was black-mailing the MichCan Corp. Vice President and blew up his own jail to help Randall escape. Finally, Carolyn texted me and informed me that the deputy found in the explosion was already dead. He was stabbed in the back probably by his own boss."

"You mean he killed one of his own deputies?" asked John.

"That's right. The City Marshal saw a chance to make a fortune and he took it. I doubt if Randall knows that the flash drive made it through the explosion."

John replied, "If that's true, why isn't Randall miles away by now"

I replied, "Because he wants to rescue his real love."

"Who's that?" asked John.

"Let's follow the good City Marshal and solve this mystery once and for all." Together, we made our way to the Chamber of Commerce building and slowly slid the door open. We could hear people talking as we passed through the doorway. Peeking around the corner, I had my proof. Drawing my Glock, I entered the room and shouted, "Well, isn't this a nice scene. There sat City Marshal Ramsey, Richard Randall, joined by Peggy Holmes sitting on Randall's lap.

I said, "Nobody move." Peggy jumped up and shouted, "Thank God you're here. They were just about to shoot me. They were partners and were going to murder me."

I responded, "Save your theatrics, Peggy."

"What are you talking about? My life was in jeopardy. I was almost blown up at the environmentalists' headquarters. They were going to shoot me the other day when you had Jenni disguise herself as me, remember" retorted Peggy.

"Julie Randall wanted you killed because you had moved in on her man and she didn't want you to get any money. In addition, I checked your work record. You were never late the two years you worked there. David Wells had a soft spot for you and didn't want you hurt. I assume he had ideas of how you'd show your appreciation. I had the flash drive tested for finger prints and besides Randall's, yours were all over it. Now how do you suppose your fingerprints got on his flash drive? I think you were Randall's little birdie inside the eco-terrorist's organization that kept him apprised of what was happening."

Peggy panicked and reached across the table and grabbed Ramsey's pistol from its holster. Before she could even point the weapon, several shots were fired from the pseudo-detectives. It was safe to say that she probably was dead before she hit the floor.

Both City Marshal Ramsey and Richard Randall raised their hands and Ramsey muttered, "You know you'll have a tough time proving everything in court."

Looking at Randall, I stated, "Not if your partner wants to save his life. I think he'll be only too happy to testify against you."

Both vanquished felons looked at the floor. That night the boys and I returned to our families at the hotel pool and enjoyed a cold one knowing we had solved the *Murder on Mackinac Island*.

Part II

The Governor's Assassination

Chapter One

The leaves were just beginning to bud and the flowers were not yet in bloom. The island was just starting to transpose its metamorphic transformation into a beautiful island brimming with beautiful flowers and gorgeous trees.

At this time, many of the island visitors had not yet arrived. The locals were waiting until Memorial Day when the heavy tourist trade commenced. College students were returning to their tasks of helping fleece the tourists.

Store owners had re-opened their establishments with re-stocked inventory. Windows were being cleaned and sidewalks swept.

The horse wranglers had just unloaded the mounts and were walking them to the stables. The steeds' job of mundanely pulling carriages was soon to commence. The first major public event to jump start the season was the governors' convention.

Annually the Great Lakes chief executives held a summit to discuss common problems. Their unofficial goals were simple; attract industries to the area and seek out political allies if they had higher aspirations.

The Conference of Great Lakes and St. Lawrence Governors and Premiers is an organization of the chief executives from Illinois, Indiana, Michigan, Minnesota, New York, Ohio, Ontario, Pennsylvania, Québec and Wisconsin. Through the organization, the governors and premiers wanted to expand the regional economy and protect the world's largest system of surface fresh water.

The conference originally began in 1983 and over years of work by the US's Council of Great Lakes Governors encouraged environmentally responsible economic development.

The original goal was to create a non-partisan forum to promote regional agreements on issues of concern for the Great Lakes region. Later, the Governors of New York and Pennsylvania accompanied by the Premiers of Ontario and Quebec joined as associate members. In 2015, the organization launched the Conference of Great Lakes and St. Lawrence Governors and Premiers, to signify the increasing bi-national cooperation. Since its inception, the Conference has led regional efforts to protect the environment and accelerate the region's economy.

In the following years, the Governors and Premiers entered into a number of agreements developed through the organization. In 1985, the Governors and Premiers signed the Great Lakes Charter, a regional water management agreement. The Governors later signed the Toxic Substances Control Agreement, resulting in the establishment of the Great Lakes Protection Fund. It also helped provide impetus for the Great Lakes Water Quality Initiative in the 1990s.

Three years later, the governors signed the Economic Development Agreement, and along with the two Canadian Premiers, created Great Lakes of North America, a tourist promotional arm of the organization.

In 2003, the organization identified priorities to restore and protect the Great Lakes. These priorities served as the basis for the Great Lakes Regional Collaboration. That year, the federal government launched through the Great Lakes Restoration Initiative over $2 billion in federal funding to help achieve their priorities.

In 2005, the organization completed the creation of a binding, regional framework to manage and protect the water supply of the Great Lakes through the St. Lawrence River Basin.

The organization's goals are to enhance economic competitiveness, grow the regional economy and create jobs. Additional initiatives include promoting exports, increasing maritime transportation, and promoting tourism through better marketing.

Naturally, the organization's main goal is to protect the region's waters, but also fight aquatic invasive species like the Asian Carp.

It was also a perfect time for up and coming politicians to make avenues for political support. During national election years, it was common for aspiring presidential candidates to attend the conference and "kiss the ring." It was a win-win for both the aspiring politicians that had higher expectations and the governors to give themselves a sense of king-makers.

The main hotel on the island stood to gain in advertisement and recognition. They had hosted the get-together as long as anyone could remember. The famous saying "what happens in Vegas stays in Vegas" also applied to this shindig.

Many stories were told "off the record" that some executives saw this as an unofficial vacation. The term "boys will be boys" definitely described the week-long affair. Even when female governors had the audacity to break the male-only rule, they were candidly ignored when the boys got together after hours.

The media reported that the governors were protecting the quality of the Great Lakes water, and preventing the infiltration of Asian Carp, the dangers of the oil pipeline through the Straights, and other topics that gave the appearance the governors were hard at work.

Truth be told, the governors were great at giving wonderful lip-service to these important topics, but they usually blamed the federal government for lack of funding and recommended a committee to examine the problem further. In other words, nothing happened.

Security was paramount and the state police were assigned to provide for the safety of the governors and their staff. Two of the troopers were our old friends, Jenni Durant and Kelly Sanderson. When push came to shove, it was more like babysitting a group of frat boys on a week-end. It was normal for certain staff members to arrange a clandestine rendezvous and later have the young women and sometimes young men to be covertly escorted to the mainland by state troopers.

That spring, things were not going to be the same. The daily seminars were scheduled with each governor giving his/her speech expressing their concern for the welfare of the Great

Lakes and how that topic impacted their respective state.

The media was thrilled to cover each governor giving an emotional oration that usually finished with the governors pounding their fists and beads of sweat forming on their brows. Back home, the state electors were so impressed that they felt their governor should be re-elected to protect the Great Lakes.

After the speeches were finished and the cameras turned off, it was party time. The hotel had all it could do to keep the ruckus down and the damage to a minimum as the state chief executives raised holy hell.

Luggage carts could be seen being pushed down the hall with young ladies shouting encouragement to their benefactors as they participated in mock races. It was up to the staff employees to guarantee discretion so as to prevent the debauchery that predicated the drunken orgies.

Chapter Two

It was protocol for the host, Michigan Governor Jim Hutchinson, who had presidential aspirations, to greet each governor or premier as they arrived. The first to step off the horse carriage was Ohio governor Olivia Moore. She was followed by Wisconsin's Ethan Wilson, Illinois governor Michael Davis, Indiana's George Thompson, and the other female governor at the conference; Minnesota's Charlotte White, Pennsylvania's Theodore Harris, and New York's Asher Clarke. The two Canadian premiers usually arrived together; Ontario's Evelyn Harrison and Quebec's Lee Trembly.

Smiles and warm embraces were the order of the day. Once behind closed doors the hackles appeared. They all had their own itinerary and they weren't going to be overshadowed by the others.

According to Illinois Governor Davis, the Asian Carp problem was important and he wanted the Great Lakes Committee to free up more money to maintain the electric fences. But Ohio Governor Moore had a diabolical scheme to circumvent the Committee, so all the money ended up in her state's coffers. Minnesota's governor Charlotte White was more concerned about opening up more foreign ports for Duluth and Superior. Wisconsin's governor had a deep distain for Ohio Governor Olivia Moore that will be discussed later.

Pennsylvania's Theodore Harris had presidential aspirations and he needed the Great Lakes' governors to support him in that endeavor. He wanted the support of both Ohio Governor Moore and Minnesota's Governor White, but he wasn't sure how to accomplish that. How could he walk a fine line and not risk antagonizing both of them?

Chapter Three

Behind closed doors, petty jealousies and hatreds overflowed as each state executive saw their agendas as the most important. It was complete obstinance on the other executives' part that they couldn't see solutions their way.

Each executive wanted to emerge as the spokesperson for the convention and there lied the rub. Nobody would concede that another governor or premiere had a better idea and therefore be accused of being a lackey for someone else.

Needless to say, the staffers and interns were busy trying to placate the animosity that was displayed those days and partook in damage control to soothe bruised egos. By the end of the week, the governors could hardly tolerate one another.

Surviving the photo op after their arrival, the governors and premiers had retired to their rooms to relax and prepare to do battle after dinner.

Olivia Moore had just finished her shower when a knock occurred at the door. Forgetting the customary check before opening the door, she was pleasantly surprised to see her number one fan, Ed McCallister. Closing the door, Ed and Olivia embraced and held each other close.

"Ed, we mustn't be seen together," started Olivia.

"What's a little suspense?" replied Ed McCallister.

"If your boss, Governor Hutchinson, found out, you'd be fired," Olivia retaliated.

"He's taking a nap and he won't move until I wake him," answered the Michigan governor's assistant.

"Is that right? Well then we'd better hurry," she replied.

In another hotel room Governor Hutchinson was reviewing his speech he would give later that evening. Posturing in front of the mirror, he slowed his pace and raised his voice for affect. His wife exited from their bedroom and waited for him to finish.

The governor looked down at his speech and scribbled a comment on its side. His wife, Dorothy, clapped exuberantly, and shouted, "You'll have them eating out of your hand." He never heard the end of her sentence. A shot rang out and the governor clutched his chest. His wife rushed to his side and said, "Jim, stay with me. I'll call for help."

She pressed 911 on her phone, but before she could make contact, the door was flung open and state troopers burst in with weapons drawn.

"He's been shot. It must have come from the window," his wife Dorothy shouted.

One trooper rushed to the governor's side and started CPR. Others rushed to the window after viewing the small circular hole; scanning the perimeter. By now, the assassin had disappeared into the shrubbery. Dozens of troopers secured the building and more scoured the gardens. There was no shooter to be found. Word spread throughout the hotel that the governor had been shot. The politicians as a whole raced to the site of the assassination, but they were denied access to the crime scene.

EMT's arrived and before long, a helicopter landed on the front lawn and later lifted the critically wounded governor to the hospital in St. Ignace, with his grieving wife at his side. Every employee was interviewed with hopes of someone seeing something suspicious. Nothing turned up, except two staffers having romance in the hotel garden.

Lieutenant Governor Ben Conrad was summoned from Lansing. He arrived within hours via a state police helicopter. Immediately, he was apprised of the situation and ordered the hotel locked down. FBI agents arrived and assumed control of the case citing national security. Homeland Security was being kept apprised.

The next morning the governors and premieres were full of remorse regarding the assassination. Hutchinson had gone from a scoundrel to a Polly Anna. Nobody wanted to be quoted saying anything negative in case the Michigan chief executive didn't survive.

The Lieutenant Governor was transported to the St. Ignace hospital where the governor's status was listed as critical. Hutchinson had been shot, but the bullet miraculously missed any vital organs. After consoling the governor's wife in the hospital room, Lieutenant Governor Conrad escorted Mrs. Hutchinson to a private room where they could converse in private.

The Lieutenant Governor tried to console the governor's wife. Conrad began, "You know if there's anything I can do just ask."

Dorothy Hutchinson responded, "It's times like this, I appreciate good friends like you."

"You and I go back to college. If Jim hadn't outmaneuvered me, I'd like to think you and I would be a couple. But you got a great guy. Jim has been a great mentor to me. He helped me work my way through the state house and the senate. I'll always appreciate he picked me to be his running mate. Everything I have, I owe to him." murmured Ben Conrad.

Dorothy replied, "It's a two-way street. You helped get a lot of bills through the state legislature. He's indebted to you just as much as you are to him."

They held hands and prayed for Jim's recovery.

Chapter Four

Meanwhile, at the newly rebuilt Mackinac Island Sheriff's Office, the FBI had gathered all the local law enforcement from the county, including state troopers, Durant and Sanderson. Homeland Security informed them there was no increase in chatter by IS or any other terrorist organization.

Special Agent Sam Davidson warned, "Everyone use caution and that this is only a preliminary investigation. We have a lot of suspects including the Wildlife Assistance and the Bridge Painters' Guild and Artists Union. Even a few of the small decentralized eco-terrorists groups have to be interviewed."

Dividing assignments, each of the law enforcement agencies were assigned possible suspects. Jenni volunteered that Kelly and she would check on the Bridge Painters Union and the Wildlife Association.

Jenni replied, "I like the Wildlife Association myself."

Kelly Sanderson responded, "I think the Bridge Painters' are the likeliest candidate. They're a pretty gritty bunch. They have an incredibly dangerous job and to be told by the governor they had to take a pay cut is pretty nasty."

"Let's talk to them first. Maybe, your hunch is right," agreed Jenni.

FBI special agent Josh Wallenstein added his input saying, "We have a lot of suspects. We have to be careful that we'll spread a wide net, but not one too wide that we can't do a thorough job."

One sheriff's deputy asked, "Could it be an eco-terrorist organization. Hutchinson has come out in favor of protecting the oil pipeline."

Wallenstein replied, "It's certainly a possibility. We're running checks on the main ones now, but as you know most eco-terrorist groups are decentralized and don't have an organization we can track."

"Maybe, it's a wildlife organization. The governor has put some stiff limitations on the deer hunters and there's talk of banning baiting in the Upper Peninsula."

Wallenstein replied, "We can't rule one of them out either. They take their hunting very seriously up there."

"We're going to do the obvious, canvass the entire city, island, and every place north of Gaylord. We're also trying to find out who had a personal grudge against the governor. We're examing the threatening letters the governor received over the years. Maybe, something will show there."

Meanwhile, at the Wildlife Association office, their president was speaking into his cell phone. "Did you hear?" asked Russ Higgins.

"Yes, someone shot the governor," replied Tom Conway.

"We'll have to see if he makes it. I don't think it was one of us. If it was, he'd be dead," retorted Higgins.

"I suppose you're right. I assume we'll get blamed for it."

The two men had helped found the Wildlife Assistance organization twenty years ago. During lean winters, they had lobbied the Department of Natural Resources to provide feed for the deer. If the DNR refused, some of them provided feed anyway, running afoul of the DNR.

Higgins and Conway fought the deer feed ban in five Lower Peninsula counties. The problem started in 2015 when chronic wasting disease, or CWD, a contagious, neurological disorder related to "mad cow disease," was discovered in white-tailed deer. The DNR wanted to keep the disease from spreading, but the Wildlife Association tried to limit the DNR restrictions. If the disease spread to other parts of the LP as well as the Upper Peninsula, baiting would certainly be banned throughout the state.

"We better email our members and give them a heads-up that we're probably going to be investigated as a possible suspect," added Higgins.

"I suppose you're right," conjectured Conway.

Another concerned group wondering if they were going to

come under scrutiny was the union given the task of maintaining the Mackinac Bridge. The governor had recently denied them a pay increase as well as reducing their health benefits. Dozens of angry union emails and texts were sent to the governor. Would some of those threats come back to haunt them? Fred Gainer was the president of the state painters' union and his right-hand person was union steward, Mitsy Webster.

They had debated the governor's negotiator for over a year, but they were unable to obtain a raise and had to accept an additional 10% increase on their insurance. The membership was less than thrilled when given the offer. They could either take the deal or risk going the summer without a job. They voted for the former.

After learning of the assassination, Gainer told Webster, "We're in for it now. The state police are going to tear us apart. We threatened a work stoppage and even picketed the governor's residence. I have to think the cops are going to make a leap of faith and confiscate all of our union computers."

Mitsy Webster concurred, "I suppose we'd better walk a fine line. You don't suppose one of our union members sought justice themselves and shot the governor?"

Gainer replied, "I doubt it, but some of them were angry that they didn't get a pay raise and have to pay more for our insurance."

"Maybe, we'd better call a meeting and clear the air. Some of the boys will be pretty worked up over this. We don't want any bad publicity."

"Okay, how about if we call a meeting for the day after tomorrow for 1:00?"

"That would be good. We have to keep our brothers calm. We don't need anybody going off half-cocked claiming responsibility or shouting negative comments regarding the governor," stated Gainer.

The next morning, the two state troopers drove to the Mackinac Bridge and approached their query. After asking several laborers whom could they speak to regarding the shooting, one of them pointed skyward toward the main arches.

"That's our local president on the catwalk," stated one of the general laborers.

Kelly and Jenni decided to wait for Gainer to return to the ground before trying to interrogate him.

Soon, Gainer exited the bridge elevator and Jenni shouted over the generator's noise, "Are you the local union president?"

Fred Gainer nodded his head in affirmation. Kelly asked, "Could we talk somewhere quieter?"

Gainer pointed to the tarp hanging over the edge of the bridge. Trying not to act nervous, they followed him under the tarp and down a flight of scaffolding to a bird cage. Finally, Gainer turned and asked, "How's this?"

Gainer began, "I'm Fred Gainer, President of Local 587. How can I help you?"

Trying to hide her fear of heights, Jenni started, "As you know, someone shot the governor a few days ago, and your union personnel sent some terrible threats to him. In your union, you have a few men with criminal records of violence. We'd like to talk to them at the sheriff's office tomorrow morning."

Gainer reared back and let them have both barrels, "Just because we stand up for ourselves doesn't make us killers. Sure, we sent some nasty notes to the governor, but so would you if you risked your life every day and got nothing for it."

Kelly Sanderson handed Gainer a list of suspects and said, "We'd like to see them tomorrow morning."

Gainer asked, "Do they need an attorney?"

Jenni replied, "Only if they're guilty."

Gainer quipped, "The prisons are full of innocent men. They just can't afford expensive attorneys."

Kelly answered, "Have those men at the sheriff's office in the morning."

Gainer reluctantly nodded his head as the troopers returned to the bridge.

Exiting the bridge, Jenni stated, "We might as well interrogate the Wildlife Association leaders as well."

Kelli concurred, saying, "They're an unusual bunch. They love the outdoors and the wildlife, but would they go to that extreme to protect their hunting rights?"

Following the Wildlife Association's address on their GPS, they arrived at their destination.

Entering the front office, they were met by the two leaders, Tom Conway and Russ Higgins, who appeared to be expecting them.

Kelly started, "I suppose you know why we're here. The governor's been shot and we're checking out anybody that might have a grudge against him. You're on record opposing some of his attempts to restrict your hunting and fishing rights. Maybe, you decided to remove Governor Hutchinson yourself."

Higgins began, "Nothing could be farther from the truth. We didn't vote for him, but we'd never do anything like that. We had a meeting right here the time the governor was shot."

Kelly asked, "Were all of your members here?"

Conway retorted, "Of course not, but we can vouch for all of them!"

Jenni asked, "We'd like a list of your members."

Higgins scoffed and said, "In your dreams."

Kelly responded, "If you have nothing to hide, I'd think you'd be happy to cooperate."

Conway replied, "We have constitutional rights, and not giving you our membership list is one of them."

Jenni asked, "Can anyone besides your membership corroborate that you had a meeting?"

Collins retorted, "As a matter of fact, yes. The local newspaper sent a reporter here to cover our meeting. It seems some media support us."

Kelly responded, "We'll naturally have to verify that. Who was the reporter?"

Collins added, "Her name is Sue Wenton. After we adjourned, she even asked us some questions about our immediate problems."

"Okay, we'll keep in touch," Jenni Durant spoke as she and

her partner, Kelly Sanderson, left the Wildlife Assistance office. Entering their cruiser, Jenni said, "If they know something, they're sure being coy about it."

Kelly Sanderson responded, "I agree, but I don't see them as a possible assassin group."

Chapter Five

At the hospital, the governor had regained consciousness. Looking around the room, he saw his wife, Dorothy, his aid Ed McCallister, Lieutenant Governor Conrad and several strangers that were probably law enforcement agents.

His wife spoke first, "Dear, the doctor said you're going to make it, but you need to rest. Don't try to talk."

The Lieutenant Governor spoke next, saying, "Jim, everything is under control. All you need to do is what Dorothy says; rest. The state is in good hands."

The Governor closed his eyes and appeared to be relieved.

The two suits stepped forward and one of them spoke, saying, "Governor, we know you're in a lot of pain and have been through a lot. My name is Special Agent Sam Davidson and this is my partner, Josh Wallenstein. We're with the FBI. We don't expect you to tell us anything yet, but we just want you to think back to just before the shooting. Try to remember anything you can. We'll stop by tomorrow and see if you're up to talking. Now, you do what your wife and friend said, get some rest." The FBI agents nodded their respects to the governor's wife and departed.

After they left, Lieutenant Governor Conrad said, "Don't worry Jim, they'll catch whoever is responsible. Even as we speak, all of the law enforcement in the county is interviewing every possible suspect. Something will shake loose. You have to rest."

Looking at Dorothy, the Lieutenant Governor continued, "Dorothy, you need to rest also. I bet you haven't slept in days. Jim is okay. You need to find a bed and close your eyes. You're no good to anybody if you're exhausted."

Dorothy leaned into her husband and whispered, "I've phoned the children and they'll be here as soon as they can catch a flight."

The Governor motioned for her to leave, but Dorothy resisted, saying, "I'm not leaving your side."

The Governor moaned and again motioned for her to leave. She stood saying, "Okay, but I'll be here first thing in the morning. I love you."

She gave her husband a peck on the forehead and slowly exited with Conrad taking her arm.

Once in the hallway, Lieutenant Governor Conrad said, "I've taken the liberty of renting a house not far from here. You're welcome to stay with me. It'll be a lot more private than a hotel. The media will hound you mercilessly."

Dorothy thought for a while and agreed.

Returning to Mackinaw City, the FBI agents compared notes orally. Wallenstein said, "The governor has so many enemies it's hard to start."

Davidson agreed, saying, "You got that right. It's going to take time not having any eye witnesses or forensic evidence. We're going to have to pour through the hate mail and see if someone looks capable of the shooting."

The next morning Kelly and Jenni were driving their cruiser across the "Mighty Mac".

Jenni reminded Kelly, "We told Gainer to have his bridge painters at the sheriff's office this morning."

Kelly responded, "It'll take some time for them to catch a ferry to the island. We still have plenty of time to catch a ride ourselves."

As Kelly was driving, the accelerator suddenly froze. Trying to slow the vehicle down, she jammed the gear shift into neutral. The vehicle's speed continued to increase. Crossing the grids made it that much more difficult to control. She careened the cruiser against the median hoping to slow down.

Kelly remaining calm, spoke, "Something's wrong with the accelerator."

Jenni retorted, "I can see that. I know you'll get it under control."

The vehicle continued to accelerate smashing into the

guardrail and hurling over the edge. The vehicle crashed into Lake Michigan and took only seconds to submerge. Traffic had stopped and onlookers could only gaze at the horrific sight.

One driver emerged from his vehicle and raced to the sight of the air born cruiser. Some people gasped at the thought of the occupants dying so horribly.

Emergency vehicles arrived and along with the state and local police, but there was nothing anybody could do.

All of the drivers that witnessed the awful sight were interviewed and the Coast Guard was summoned to see if the occupants somehow miraculously survived. State Police divers were directed to the sight where the cruiser was last seen submerging. Mercifully, the two female bodies were removed from the wreckage and carefully transported to the hospital. A salvage tug arrived and pulled the pulverized cruiser to the surface and towed it to the dock.

Special Agents Davidson and Wallenstein were present as the cruiser was off-loaded onto a trailer and brought to a storage unit that was commandeered.

Later that day, State Police mechanics examined the fatal vehicle. They scoured the smashed frame for hours until one of the mechanics motioned for the two FBI agents to join them.

The mechanic started, "It looks like it was a vapor problem. On modern cars, the idle is controlled by the Electronic Control Module. An increase in RPM without pressing the gas pedal is called surging. That looks like what happened with this vehicle."

Davidson asked, "Was the vehicle tampered with?"

The mechanic responded, "It's hard to tell. They probably noticed it was rough handling. The idle was almost certainly high. I can't say for sure if someone deliberately tampered with the accelerator."

Davidson looked at Wallenstein and said, "Under the circumstances I have to believe the two troopers were murdered."

Wallenstein agreed, saying, "They must have rattled somebody."

Chapter Six

Meanwhile, in my home town, Victorious, centrally located in the beautiful Superior Peninsula, the pseudo-detectives and I were enjoying a cup of java at our favorite diner, Millie's. The main topic was the new baseball season that had just begun. All of our favorite teams looked great so far, but as we know, hope springs eternal.

My team, the Tigers, had recently unloaded most of their star players and were fielding a lot of youngsters in hopes of resurrecting their play-off hopes.

My friends included a number of esteemed retired police officers. Only the youngster, Tyler Baldwin was still active in law enforcement. My coffee brothers included my childhood friend, John Baldwin, and two other two crime-fighting partners, Ben Meyers and Mark Kestila.

Together, we had solved many atrocious crimes in Mesabi County over the last few years.

We were on our second cup when Tyler entered the restaurant with a somber look. Sitting down, he didn't say a word until his father, John, asked, "Is everything okay?"

Tyler still didn't respond. Now, we knew something was bothering him. After a lengthy uncomfortable period of silence, Tyler muttered, "They're both dead."

John asked, "Who's dead? What are you talking about?"

Another long period of deafening silence transpired before Tyler spoke, saying, "Jenni Durant and Kelly Sanderson. They're both dead."

All of us immediately peppered Tyler with questions that went unanswered.

"How did it happen?"

"Where did it happen?"

"When?"

"Were they on duty?"

Tyler ignored the questions as tears rolled down his cheeks. He tried to speak, but was unable.

I motioned for one of the waitresses to bring him a cup of coffee. Tyler stared straight ahead as if in a trance. We decided the best thing to do was leave him alone and he would tell us when he was ready.

Minutes later, Tyler had composed himself and blurted out the horrible news. He started, "This morning, Jenni and Kelly were driving across the Mackinac Bridge when their cruiser went spiraling out of control and careened over the side. They were both killed instantly on impact."

Nobody said a word. We were thunderstruck that our good friends, Jenni and Kelly, could be killed in such a way.

John started, "Does anybody think it's still an accident?"

Tyler shook his head saying, "Nobody knows yet!"

I nodded and said, "We'll leave as soon as we can."

We left the diner in total silence knowing we had to find out what happened to Jenni and Kelly.

After returning home and bringing my wife up to speed, she was supportive that my friends and I had to uncover the cause of the young troopers' demise.

Rendezvousing at the diner, we left for the city that usually represents fun and frivolity, but not this time.

After our arrival, we immediately sought the people responsible for the investigation. Entering the sheriff's office, I spotted two suits that I assumed were feds. I approached them and I asked, "Are you fellows in charge of the investigation of the deaths of the two troopers?"

One looked up and stated, "I'm FBI Special Agent Davidson. Can I help you?"

I continued, "The two troopers were good friends of ours and we want to know what happened."

The agent stated, "I'm sorry. It's an ongoing investigation and we don't share information with the general public."

John took a step toward the suit and growled, "We're not just anybody. We're retired detectives and don't try to blow smoke up our ass."

Both agents stood and glared at us. The other agent snarled, "I'm Special Agent Wallenstein. We don't care who you are. We don't jeopardize our cases by telling every Tom, Dick, and Harry that comes through the door what we're doing."

Ben replied, "Along with the two troopers, we have solved a lot of cases in the Superior Peninsula. Check us out and I think you'll change your minds."

Agent Davidson bellowed, "There's the door. Don't let it hit you on the way out. Good-bye."

I realized making threats wasn't going to get us anywhere. I retorted, "We're going to investigate their deaths; with or without your help."

We left grumbling among ourselves and promising each other we would not be deterred.

Reconvening at a coffee shop on Main Street, we started to reconstruct the events.

Mark began, "I wonder if their deaths had anything to do with the governor's attempted assassination?"

I replied, "Good point. Let's assume the two are tied together. I'll try and talk to the governor." John spoke, saying, "Tyler and I can stop at the local newspaper to see what we can discover."

Ben interjected, "Mark and I will track down some of the local police and see if they can provide an insight to what happened."

Learning that the governor's recovery was taking place in the St. Ignace Hospital; I decided that was my first destination.

Driving into the hospital parking lot, there were several state and local police vehicles present. It was clear to me, they would not allow me to simply waltz into the governor's room and start asking questions. I needed a ruse and one popped into my head. Most hospital laundries are located in the basement so I entered the front door and acted like I knew my destination. Descending the stairs, I heard a large tumbling noise. As I approached the laundry room, workers appeared to be preoccupied sorting and folding linen. Seeing a cart containing soiled hospital garb, I borrowed one of the scrubs and returned to the main lobby with the cart.

As I examined the directory on the wall, the doctors' offices were on the second floor. Now it became more challenging. Pushing the cart down the hall in hospital garb, I tried to act nonchalant.

I entered the office and nodded at the receptionist. It was an everyday affair and nobody raised an eyebrow. Opening the closet door marked soiled linen; I grabbed the gowns and closed the door. Passing one of the doctor's offices, I saw my treasure, a name tag resting on a desk. Leaving the cart and absconding with the treasure, I now started to ascend the stairway peeking through each floor as I continued in my quest for the state executive. Finally, opening a door, I saw several law enforcement officers huddled together. Assuming I had hit pay dirt, I meandered down the hall acting as if I owned it.

Passing the officers, they didn't challenge my credentials. Entering the governor's room, he was fast asleep. Knowing the officers were watching me, I picked up the chart and perused it. Slowly walking toward the patient, I gazed at the IV's pretending I was examing them.

The governor opened his eyes and said, "Hi, Doc. How am I doing?"

I whispered, "Good as far as I can tell."

He seemed to relax upon hearing those words. I continued, "Guess what? I'm not a real doctor, but I'm not here to hurt you either. My two friends, the state troopers, were killed yesterday, and I'm assuming their deaths are related to the attack on you. What can you tell me about your shooting?"

The governor immediately developed a feeling of apprehension. He replied, "I don't know anything. I was preparing my speech and suddenly I felt a deep pain in my chest."

I continued, "Let's cut to the chase. Who would be so desperate that they would try to shoot you?"

The governor responded, "As God is my witness, I have no idea who shot me."

I asked, "Do you think it was one of the eco-terrorist or wildlife groups?"

The governor shook his head and said, "No, I doubt t it."

"Could it be someone that doesn't want you to run for President?"

"That's always a possibility," he replied.

"Do you owe money to anybody?" I pursued.

"Naturally, I have a large campaign debt from the previous election, but that's normal. Besides, if they killed me, they'd never get their money, would they?"

I agreed with his rational. I slipped him my phone number and said, "If you think of anything call me." I departed the room and was relieved when I finally exited the hospital.

In the interim, John and Tyler entered the local newspaper office. There were only a handful of employees that appeared to be multi-tasking. They were so busy; John and Tyler had a hard time getting anyone's attention. After standing like two potted plants, finally one person noticed them and motioned for them to enter.

John started, "My name is John Baldwin and this is my son Tyler. We're looking into the strange accident that took the lives of the two state troopers and we're wondering if their deaths could be tied to the attempted assassination of the governor?"

The employee looked at them and asked, "You're kidding, right?"

"What'd ya mean?" asked Tyler.

"That's the million-dollar question around here. We're getting emails from all the major networks and news carriers. We're in the center of a shark-feeding frenzy. By the way, my name is Sue Wenton. Nice to meet you. Are you with the police?"

"No, not exactly. The two female troopers that died in the bridge tragedy were very good friends of ours. We're a group of retired police excluding my son, who is still active. We're from Mesabi County. Together, we've solved a lot of crimes in the Superior Peninsula."

"As you can see, we're pretty busy right now. What do you

want to know?" asked the female employee.

"The most important question is who would want to kill both the governor and the troopers?" asked John.

Sue Wenton replied, "It's anybody's guess. I was at the Wildlife Association the other night when the governor was shot and I don't think they're responsible."

"Why do you say that?" asked Tyler.

"They're a little ornery when it comes to their hunting and fishing rights, but I don't think they'd be that drastic," replied Wenton.

"Did anybody else have an axe to grind?" asked John.

"Sure, the bridge painters' union had to take a pay cut and they were pretty upset. In fact, their union president told me over the phone this morning, the two troopers were on their way to interview a couple of their union members when the troopers went over the bridge."

"Really, that's interesting," answered Tyler. He looked at his dad and said, "Maybe, we should follow up on that."

"John asked, "Is there any chance you know who they were going to meet?"

Sue Wenton answered, "No, but it shouldn't be hard to find out who their suspects were. Give me a minute and I'll call their union president, Gainer."

John and Tyler sat down and were impressed by the excitement that was transpiring in front of them. Phones were ringing with nobody answering them. The few employees were typing furiously on their computers ignoring everything around them.

In a few minutes, Susan Wenton returned and handed them a list with two names on it. She said, "According to Gainer, these are the only two men the troopers were going to interview."

John took the slip of paper and said, "Thanks."

After they exited the building, John and Tyler examined the list and said, "Well, we'll start with these two jokers."

The two investigators drove to the bridge and asked one of the general laborers where they could find the two men.

The laborer shrugged his shoulders and pointed at the foreman.

John and Tyler approached the man examining a blueprint.

John asked, "Excuse me, my son and I would like to ask a few questions to two of your men, Mike Hawkins and Red Boulder. Are they here?"

The foreman looked at them and replied, "No, they never showed up today."

"Can you tell us where they're staying?" asked Tyler.

"Most of the guys stay at the Northwood's Motel just outside of town. It's the cheapest place," answered the foreman.

John and Tyler thanked the foreman and departed for the aforementioned motel.

Driving into the parking lot, they could see why it was the cheapest. They walked into the office that was missing several lights in the sign. Ringing the bell, an elderly woman appeared and said, "No vacancy, can't you read?"

Tyler replied, "Actually, we're not looking for a room. We'd like to talk to two of your renters, Mike Hawkins, and Red Boulder."

After taking a puff of her cigarette, she mumbled, "Try number six."

John and Tyler left without fanfare and strolled down the dilapidated cabins until they reached their target.

Knocking on the door, there was no response. Tyler sniffed the air and asked, "Do you smell that?" Together, John and Tyler broke the door down and quickly covered their noses. The pungent odor was easily identified; LP gas. John and Tyler opened the windows and saw both beds occupied. The two detectives each grabbed one of the victims and dragged them outside. Performing CPR proved unsuccessful. After failing to revive them, John tapped 911 into his cell phone. He informed the dispatcher of the disaster and they continued to attempt to revive the victims while waiting for the emergency vehicles.

The EMTs and police arrived within minutes, but they also were unsuccessful trying to revive the two victims.

The deputy looked at John and Tyler and asked, "How did you two happen upon these guys?" John explained the whole scenario as to how they wanted to interview them regarding the deaths of their friends.

The deputy said, "It's too bad. They're not going to say anything anymore."

John and Tyler waited for the EMTs and police to depart. They walked around the building and noticed the bottled gas had been turned off by the police. After waiting for the gas to eviscerate, they entered the small domain bypassing the yellow police tape. They saw the slice in the stove LP gas hose and concluded that was the culprit. They scrutinized the small cabin and were about to leave when John, using his old police instincts, unscrewed the cover from the air vent. He gazed inside and shouted, "Hey, son, look at this!"

He removed a plastic bag and opened it. Inside were dozens of hundred-dollar bills. "How do you think a couple of painters saved up this much money?" asked John.

Tyler nodded and replied, "I guess they were involved in something illegal and got paid a tidy sum."

John replied, "I have to think someone wanted to cover their tracks and murdered those two sorry characters."

"Let's take the money, but we can't turn it over to the FBI, after all, we're not supposed to have it. If we can find out who gave these guys this money, it might lead to Jenni's and Kelly's murderer. It would confirm there's a conspiracy and not just some accidental deaths," stated Tyler.

John replaced the air vent and wiped it clean of finger prints.

Across town, Ben and Mark arrived at the state police headquarters. As they entered, they were overtaken by two large pictures of the deceased troopers hanging in the entrance.

Ben and Mark stopped to gaze at their young friends they would never see again.

After they had composed themselves, they approached the bullet-proof window. The trooper spoke into the mic and said, "I assume you knew the troopers."

Ben nodded and said, "Yes, we're retired police officers and the girls and us worked on a lot of cases in Mesabi County."

Mark asked, "Do you know if the families have set a day for the funerals?"

The trooper shook his head and said, "No, they're still trying to contact one of the family members. Can I help you?"

Ben stated, "We believe there's a connection between their deaths and the shooting of the governor."

The sergeant replied, "That's what some of us were just discussing."

Mark asked, "I don't suppose you could tell us anything?"

The sergeant shook his head and said, "No, I can't."

Ben asked, "What about the cruiser? Were they able to recover it?"

The sergeant replied, "Yes, but I can't tell you where it is. The state crime lab boys are on their way and they're going to go through it. One of our mechanics examined it but I can't tell you what he found."

Ben and Mark thanked the sergeant and gently brushed Jenni's and Kelly's pictures as they exited.

Once outside, Mark looked at Ben and said, "We have to check that vehicle. Maybe, the brakes were tampered with or something else. I've taken a few vehicles apart in my day and I want to go over that cruiser with a fine-tooth comb."

Ben replied, "I have an idea. This town isn't that big. Let's see what we can uncover. They drove around the city until they came to a small industrial park. As Ben walked alongside the units, he saw burn residue on the ground in front of one of the units. Bingo. Removing his cell phone, Ben dialed the number on the advertising sign on the front of the building. "Hello," as the voice on the other end answered.

"Yes, I'm Lieutenant Hanson with the state crime lab. We've just arrived to examine a state police vehicle. I understand you have it in your storage units."

"Yes, but I thought you weren't coming until tomorrow."

Ben continued, "There's been a change in plans. We're getting heat from higher-ups to get this thing done. Could you send someone to unlock the unit?"

The voice replied, "I can do better than that. I'll meet you there, myself." The voice proceeded to give Ben the directions to the storage unit.

After disconnecting, Ben looked at Mark and stated, "With his directions, I assured him we could find the storage unit."

Mark said, "While we're waiting, I want to check the trunk to make sure I have the necessary tools."

Shortly, an elderly man arrived and approached the two senior sleuths. Ben introduced himself and Mark using phony names. Fortunately, the man didn't ask for identification. He did say, "I'm surprised you're not in an official vehicle."

To reassure the owner, Ben and Mark flashed their old detective badges knowing the man wouldn't know the difference.

Ben quickly answered, "We travel in unmarked vehicles."

"Glad to help the state police," the man stated as he unlocked the storage unit and was about to enter when Ben said, "That's fine. We'll take it from here. We don't want to compromise any evidence we might find. We appreciate your help. We'll lock the door when we leave."

The man uttered something under his breath as he entered his vehicle and left.

Mark disassembled the brakes and after examining them closely, replaced them. He continued to disassemble the transmission, exhaust system, and even part of the engine. Ben watched with amazement as Mark finally stopped and pointed, saying, "Just as I thought, it was a vapor lock. The engine probably acted rough and stalled while idling, but once it was accelerated it couldn't be slowed."

Ben asked, "Could it happen by itself?"

Mark replied, "It's always possible, but the engine would have been a pain to operate. They'd have known about it and I doubt if they would have driven it. No, my guess, someone tampered with it."

Ben said, "Put everything back together and we'll bring the others up to speed tonight." After sanitizing the area, they locked the storage unit and left.

Chapter Seven

Back at the hotel, there was a knock on the door, but this time taking no chances, Governor Moore asked, "Who is it?"

The answer was, "Your Prince Charming."

Olivia Moore swung the door open and dragged Ed McCallister inside. She started, "Are you crazy? We definitely can't be seen together since your boss was shot."

The young Michigan staffer replied, "Relax, my job is to update every governor and premier on his status. We have lots of time. I saved you for last, so we can enjoy the night together."

The Ohio governor retorted, "It's just too dangerous. We'll have plenty of time later this week. Besides, shouldn't you be at the hospital?"

McCallister replied, Lieutenant Governor Conrad explicitly ordered me to stay here and keep an eye on everything. Right now, I like what I'm seeing. I have some champagne just outside the door. What say we wile away the hours like we did last year in Columbus?"

Down the hallway, they didn't know a certain staffer, Al Johnson, had taken their photos. Certain his boss, the governor of Illinois, Michael Davis, would be thrilled to use the sexual rendezvous between a lowly staffer and the governor's arch-rival, Ohio Governor Olivia Moore.

Every year the federal money spigot was being reduced to the states. It had now come down to each governor to grovel on their knees to Washington.

Lately, the Ohio Governor had outmaneuvered Davis due to her political affiliation. Governor Moore was able to get millions for infrastructure improvements. Meanwhile, Davis' state had languished.

There were grants destined to be shared by the nine Great Lakes governors and the two premiers. Moore, using her political clout was in line to snare the lion's share of the funds. Only a miracle could prevent that from happening and Davis had made up his mind he was going to use every ploy he could to make sure his state didn't get short-changed this year.

Davis had resorted to skullduggery employing one of his aids to employ clandestine methods to find anything disconcerting regarding Governor Moore's personal life. Davis was hoping a campaign check from a wealthy donor or a free trip out of the country courtesy of a lobbyist would be a welcome discovery. However, He didn't believe he would uncover a sexual rendezvous with a Michigan staffer. When told of this illicit tryst by his aid, Johnson, Davis was exuberant. Surely, Moore would be shamed into conceding.

It was bad enough Moore was pilfering the federal funds for infrastructure repairs, but he would be damned if that female pariah was going to sidetrack the money earmarked to fight the Asian Carp problem. He had approached the Wisconsin Governor, Ethan Wilson, with a plan to circumvent Moore's perennial pilfering of the Great Lakes funds.

Wilson was at first apprehensive. But he wanted to remind them Moore had outmaneuvered all of the mid-west governors and premiers last year in gaining grants that were ear-marked for all of the Great Lakes states.

In collusion with her two cohorts, the two Ohio U.S. senators, the wording was changed to refer to the funding as endowments and not grants coming out of the Great Lakes Committee. She was able to contrive the entire allotment for her state. Due to a technicality, only her state qualified under the rigorous stipulations set by the federal government.

With the bequest, Moore was able to maneuver the money into the tourist industry   refurbishing dozens of state parks and other tourist friendly investments. Whereas, the money was supposed to be spent fighting the Asian Carp problem that Illinois and Wisconsin were forced to continue using antiquated electric fences.

With Hutchinson shot, the Great Lakes Committee meetings

were in jeopardy. Most likely, they would not meet again this week, but maybe, Davis thought he could arrange one last meeting in an attempt to persuade the Great Lakes Committee to insist the funds be tagged as an endowment and not as a grant.

Davis was counting on his assistant, Johnson, to have the evidence on Ohio Governor Moore in her relationship with her young lover, McCallister.

Davis was too impatient to wait and decided to find his assistant and force the Ohio Governor's hand before he called a meeting. If Davis could humiliate her, she would be forced to acquiesce and be content with sharing the money.

Knocking on young Johnson's door, there was no answer. Not having a key card to his room, he tracked down a maid and asked, "I've knocked on my assistant's door and there's no answer. He has some important papers I must have. Would you be so kind as to open the door?"

Recognizing him as one of the governors, she smiled and replied, "Certainly, sir. Which room is it?"

Davis informed her of the room number and followed her. Arriving at the door, the maid swiped her card and the door popped open. The governor shouted, "Johnson, are you here?" as he entered. Once in the room, he was mortified to see his young aid hanging from the ceiling fan. "Help," he shouted hoping the maid was still within earshot. Fortunately, she came as quickly as possible and joined him, both looking aghast at the young man hanging. Thinking quickly, she tapped her cell phone and called the front desk. After explaining the appalling sight, she joined the governor on the couch.

Security personnel raced into the room followed by the hotel manager. One of the guards felt the young man's wrist for a pulse, but found none.

The hotel manager now in a complete state of shock, blurted, "This is horrible. We've never had a suicide in our hotel."

Knowing enough not to touch the body, the security personnel stood at the front door to keep curiosity seekers away as word spread.

Deputy Wilkerson and the EMTs arrived and tried to restore calmness to the scene. Having no detectives available to investigate, Wilkerson said, "We might as well get him down." The youth's body was laid on the floor as they awaited the M.E.

Old Doc Dunstan made his way into the room and kneeled over the body. Performing cursory procedures, he looked at the young deputy and stated, "He died about an hour ago. I'll have more to say after I have him on my table." The EMT's helped place the body in a bag and after zipping it shut, they left.

By now, the maid had given her brief statement to one of the deputies, and the Illinois Governor was trying to calm down so he could be coherent. Assuming he would be interviewed by the media, he wanted to appear presidential.

Davis had to be careful not to mention his young aid was last seen with Ohio Governor Moore. He could use that as a ploy to persuade her to forget her funds for the state parks.

Once he had relayed his story to the local deputies and appeared deeply distressed over the loss of his close protégé, he thought it would be a good time to visit his nemesis, Governor Moore.

As he approached her hotel door, he could see her door was ajar. Was this the time to inquire about her illicit tryst? He knocked, and called loudly, "Governor Morris, are you here?"

The room was darkened and he could see movement on the bed. "What do you want? I don't want to be disturbed?" she retorted.

Davis replied, "Your door was open and I thought you might like some company."

She hurled back, "Who are you kidding? You have no idea of my problems. Leave me alone."

Davis suddenly had a streak of compassion and couldn't bring himself to kick her when she was down.

Davis could hear her sobbing into her pillow and he felt it was better to leave her alone.

Chapter Eight

The Michigan Governor was resting comfortably and was awaiting a visit from his wife. The door opened and before he could identify the visitor, a pillow was placed over his face. Grabbing frantically to no avail, the governor eventually succumbed to the lack of oxygen. After removing the pillow and placing it next to the body, the assassin said, "Now the job is done right."

Time passed before Dorothy exited the elevator on her way to visit her husband. She spoke politely to the state troopers sitting at the end of the hall way.

"How are you today?" one trooper asked.

"I'm doing better today since Jim is recovering," the governor's wife replied.

"Since the governor is doing okay, we took a coffee break in the cafeteria. I hope you don't mind," stated one of the troopers.

"No problem, as long as Jim's getting stronger, everything's great," Dorothy answered and continued, "Have a nice day," she stated as she departed.

Upon entering her husband's hospital room, it appeared Jim was fast asleep. So as not to wake him, she gently strode over to his bedside expecting to see him in a deep sleep. Glancing at the monitors, there was no heartbeat.

Sounds of hysterics were heard from the governor's room; in seconds the troopers were in the room. Feeling his pulse and almost simultaneously starting CPR, the other trooper shouted down the hall for medical assistance. Within seconds, nurses and a doctor appeared with the crash cart and attempted to revive him. They hooked up the defibrillator attaching electrode patches to the governor's back and chest. The doctor shouted, "Clear" and a shock was sent to the heart. Nothing. The doctor shouted, "Clear" and again a second shock was sent but the result was the same. The doctor shook his head and said, "I'm calling it." After stating the time, he looked at the governor's wife and said, "I'm sorry. He must have died in his sleep."

Dorothy sobbed incessantly as the Lieutenant Governor Conrad burst into the room shouting, "Oh, my God! What happened?" Hearing the doctor's answer, he turned to Dorothy and said, "It's okay! Jim's in a better place." Dorothy continued to cry incessantly as the Lieutenant Governor guided her to a chair.

Coincidentally, we were enjoying our coffee at the hotel when the bulletin came over the radio. The announcer stated, *"Governor James Hutchinson is dead. The governor succumbed to his wound during the night. The entire state is now in mourning. Lieutenant Governor Conrad has ordered all state flags to fly at half-mast."*

"I could barely believe it," I started, "I just talked to him yesterday. He seemed to be recovering."

John said, "I wonder if something happened."

Tyler interjected, "There's just too many weird things occurring. If I could get permission, I wonder if I could get my wife to come here and perform an independent autopsy. Maybe, it would show something."

Tyler immediately called his wife, Carolyn, who was the M.E. in Mesabi County. Tyler stated, "I know you just returned home, but I have a question for you. Carolyn, as you've probably heard, the governor is dead. We think he might have been murdered. Would you be interested in returning and performing a separate autopsy if I can get permission?"

Carolyn replied, "Unless it's a real unusual murder, the coroner will determine if he was murdered. For example, if he was suffocated, he would have batikia, little blood spots, in the eyes from not being able to breathe. Let me know if you need me, but I really don't think it will be hard to determine the cause of death."

Tyler answered, "Okay, thanks."

After Tyler disconnected, he explained the answer Carolyn

gave that reassured us if the governor died from questionable circumstances the coroner would uncover them.

I said, "I think it's imperative we find out who gave the money to the bridge painters, but first let's pay a visit to the FBI agents." We finished our coffee and the five pseudo-detectives drove to the dock and took a ferry to the City Marshal's office to find the FBI agents.

Disembarking from the ferry, we wanted to convince the FBI a conspiracy was afoot. Entering the office, we saw an officer seated behind the City Marshal's desk. We approached him and identified ourselves. The officer spoke, "I've been appointed temporary City Marshal until a new one is selected. I'm Deputy Wilkinson. Can I help you?"

I began, "We were looking for the two FBI Agents, Davidson and Wallenstein. Do you know where they are?"

The deputy responded, "They're in St. Ignace tending to the governor's death. It's sure something he died after seeming to be recovering."

"That's for sure. We have our own theories about that, but we have to keep investigating. It was nice to meet you." We left the City Marshal's office and decided we needed a new plan.

Arriving in the LP, we were surprised to hear the news the governor was going to be buried tomorrow. He was Jewish and the custom, of course, was to bury him within 24 hours according to the Torah.

John started, "If they do that, there certainly won't be an autopsy."

Mark added, "That means whatever evidence his body contains will be buried with him."

I agreed, saying, "We'll have to solve these murders without the governor's forensic help."

Chapter Nine

That night Sue Wenton was staying late at the newspaper's office reviewing her notes. The door opened and a familiar face stepped through.

"Hey, how are you doing?" asked the reporter.

"Fine, but we have a lot of problems going on in the city," replied the visitor

Wenton responded, "I can't keep up with all the happenings. And now with the governor dying, it's surreal."

"By the way, how's the job going?" asked Wenton.

"Okay, but with the governor's and the two state troopers' deaths, everything's murky. Some old detectives stopped by yesterday and asked a lot of questions," replied the visitor.

"Yeah, I know. They were here also," answered Wenton.

"Two of those detectives found the two bridge painters dead this morning," stated the visitor.

"I heard that. It seems like those old guys are everywhere. That young guy is kind of cute, but I heard he's married," responded the reporter.

"Never mind him. Just take care of me. By the way, you don't think they'll find out about our special relationship, do you?" asked the visitor.

"I hope not. I love you, but if it came out, we're lovers, I'd lose my credibility when it came to covering stories affecting you," replied Wenton.

"That's what I wanted to talk to you about. Maybe, we should cool it for a while. At least until everything blows over. What do you think?" asked the visitor.

"I suppose that's a good idea, but I'll miss you. We can still text and talk on our phones, but it's probably better if we're not seen together," Wenton responded. They gave each other a peck as the visitor departed.

Minutes later, the door opened again, and Sue Wenton without looking, sarcastically cried, "I thought you'd stay away longer than that." Upon gazing at the new visitor her eyes widened and asked, "What do you want?" The new visitor retorted, "I want you to stay away from her."

Sue Wenton replied, "Well, guess what? You're going to get your wish. We just agreed not to see each other for a while until all the excitement's done. There are you happy now?"

The new visitor responded, "You don't understand. I want you to stay away permanently. We have a lot to think about when we're working. If you care for her, you'll let her go for good."

The reporter responded, "I can't do that. We care very much for each other and not you or anybody else is going to stop us from being a couple."

The second visitor brandished a pipe and with a thundering blow smashed it into Sue's head. Blood poured everywhere. Her desk and the floor became saturated with the crimson liquid. The second visitor was so stunned; the murderer dropped the pipe onto the floor and rushed into the evening gloom.

The next morning, we were awakened by sirens blaring as emergency vehicles raced past our hotel room. We hardly gave it a second thought until we met for coffee later in the restaurant. It was the talk of the eatery. Apparently, someone had murdered the newspaper's main reporter last night. Hearing that news, we rushed to the scene only to be met by a cordoned yellow tape and some of the city's finest. We tried to gaze through the window, but the emergency personnel prevented us from seeing what was transpiring. We were resigned to wait until some of the police exited and try to glean some facts from them.

Finally, the interim City Marshal came out to have a smoke and I decided it was worth a try. Walking up to Deputy Wilkinson, I asked, "Can you tell us anything?"

The deputy shook his head no, but continued walking into the alley alongside the building. "How about now?" I asked.

Deputy Wilkinson said, "She was my step-sister, Sue Wenton. It was a vicious attack. The murderer hit her on the head with a heavy pipe. She didn't have a chance."

My first words were, "I'm sorry for your loss. We can do this another time." He said, "No, I want to talk about her. She was my hero."

I stated, "I wonder if someone murdered her in retaliation for a story she was doing?"

The deputy responded, "That's always a possibility, but she was very involved with the local LGBT organization. She was proud when she came out and helped others in this community to do the same. She really helped the young people that had doubts about their sexuality. Sue told me, some LGBT youths don't experience a supportive school environment. Occasionally, they are physically and emotionally harassed and sometimes even encouraged to commit suicide. She taught people their LGBT identify should be respected, or even embraced. She went to the local schools and talked openly about acceptance of each other."

The deputy continued, "I remember one young person that experienced unsupportive conditions in a local school. Sue told that person to be proud of being gay. She told me research has found that LGBT youth are more likely to experience stress and fear in school than are non-LGBT youths."

As he walked away, I could only say, "I'm sorry for your loss. She must have been a great young lady." I returned to my comrades with my head down. John asked, "What's the matter? You've been around grisly murder scenes before."

I responded, "Yes, but the victim was the deputy's step-sister. She was very involved in the local LGBT organization."

John shook his head and stated, "I can't imagine walking into a crime scene and seeing your step-sister's skull crushed."

Mark added, "I guess we have another angle on the case. Maybe, the murders were all related to gay-bashing."

I said, "I never thought about that. We'll have to consider that as a possible motive for the murders."

We reconvened at a local café and wondered if all of the murders could be caused by anti-gay sentiment.

John started, "I have to admit, so far that's the only thread the four deaths have in common."

Ben retorted, "I don't know if our two friends, Jenni and Kelly, were gay and if Governor Hutchinson was."

I added, "I guess we're going to have to find out one way or another. Ben and Mark, why don't you check into Jenni's and Kelly's personal lives?"

"John and Tyler, could you snoop around Sue Wenton's life. Try to find out who she was seeing. I'll try to tackle the governor's personal life."

With a challenge ahead of us, we departed to investigate an area we knew little.

Chapter Ten

Governor Hutchinson's funeral had just finished and we were contemplating our next move when we saw a distinguished looking woman enter the restaurant.

As she came nearer, I recognized her as one of the Great Lakes governors. She strode up to us and asked, "Are you fellows the retired detectives that help people?"

We stood and identified ourselves individually. She replied, "My name is Charlotte White. I'm the Governor of Minnesota."

I responded, "Of course. I saw you on television, but I wasn't sure what state you represented."

After sitting among us, she began, "I'm in dire straits. As you know, we have had a lot of problems. Young Johnson's death really bothers me. I suspect the young man was murdered because he knew something. I think the key to his death might be on his cell phone. Do you think you could find it? Can you help me? I will pay whatever fee you ask?"

I replied, "We're already pretty busy, but we'll try to find time to work on it."

She continued to provide more information on the circumstances of young Johnson's death.

Could it have been a suicide or did someone tie him to the fan and hang him? To do so would involve a strong person or persons and possibly drugs.

We couldn't spare a lot of our time, but since the Minnesota Governor suspected foul play, we decided to look into it.

"John, how about if you and your son try to discover the actual cause of death? Ben could you and Mark check to see if he was suicidal? I'll see if he had any enemies? Let's meet here tomorrow to see if any of us turned up anything."

We finished our Joe and departed.

John and his son drove to the local hospital where the autopsy was being performed. Entering the laboratory, they tried to be subtle as they drew near the elder pathologist, Dr. Dunstan. They were used to the young and spry Carolyn who could perform the autopsy and still carry on a conversation.

John started by asking, "Dr. Dunstan, could we talk to you after you finished the young man's autopsy?"

The senior pathologist looked up and asked, "Who are you?"

Trying to win his confidence, John retorted, "We've been asked to find out if the young man committed suicide or was, he murdered?"

"Are you with the police? I know most of them," replied the senior pathologist.

"Not exactly, we've been asked by a very important person to see how he actually died."

"It's pretty irregular, you know. The public isn't supposed to know anything. I usually only turn everything over to the police. I'm afraid I can't help you. Good day to you gentlemen."

John and Tyler left as if returning to a classroom after a visit to the principal's office.

Tyler said under his breath, "You know we're going to have to get those records."

John answered, "I know. We'll come back later when he's gone."

Later in the evening, John and Tyler visited the hotel bar frequented by the various governors' staffers. Striking up a conversation was easy since all of the young interns were eager to network with anybody, they thought was important. The two pseudo-detectives approached a table of gregarious millennials and asked, "Did anybody know Al Johnson very well?" There was a moment of silence until a young woman raised her hand and said, "We both work for Governor Davis. We were assigned different responsibilities, but we caravanned together on occasion."

John replied, "Great, can we have a moment of your time?"

After corralling her into a nearby booth, John and Tyler identified themselves and related they were trying to discover if young Johnson was capable of taking his life.

The young staffer answered, "My name is Cindy Gould. I can't say for sure, but he didn't appear to be depressed. He was Governor Davis' go-to guy. He had a lot of responsibilities, always working on something secret."

Tyler asked, "Is it possible, he saw or heard something that bothered him?"

Cindy answered, "No, nothing really bothered him. He wanted to climb up the ladder and by doing the governor's dirty work, he was sure to become important, especially if the governor became president."

"Do you know what he was doing recently?" asked John.

"I think he was involved with surveillance on someone important. You might want to check his cell phone. It's probably loaded with photos."

Tyler replied, "Thanks, you've been a big help." The two detectives left to try to find Johnson's cell phone.

Meanwhile, I wanted to ascertain if the young man was murdered. Entering a sleazy bar off the beaten path, I placed some money in front of the barkeep and ordered a drink. Gazing around the room, this was not the type of crowd you'd strike up a casual conversation with the patrons. As the drink was placed in front of me, I produced a photo of the departed Johnson and asked the bartender if he recognized him.

After gazing at the photo for an extended period, he motioned to a waitress. The barkeep handed the photo to the young server and asked, "Does he look familiar?"

She replied, "Yes, he comes in occasionally by himself, but he usually leaves with a female."

I asked, "Would you recognize the woman if you saw her again?"

"Are you kidding, he left with the Ohio Governor, Olivia Moore"

I replied, "Thanks, you've been a big help."

I left the liquor emporium looking for answers.

My next quarry was to seek out the Ohio Governor and find

out if she could've been involved with young Johnson's death.

The pseudo-detectives and I gathered that night to exchange information. According to Governor White, we suspected young Johnson was doing surveillance work so that wasn't a big surprise. John and Tyler reinforced the idea that the young staffer was riding Governor Davis' coattails. The guys were astonished to learn that young Johnson was seeing the Ohio Governor, but for reasons unknown. We disbanded and it was up to me to discover exactly what relationship Johnson and Governor Moore were conducting. John and Tyler raised the possibility of returning to the M.E.'s lab, but I overruled them pointing out it wouldn't serve a purpose.

Since there was no time like the present, I located Governor Moore's hotel room and after she opened her door, I was surprised to see Governor Davis seated. I introduced myself to her and after social amenities were exchanged, I shook both governors' hands. Governor Davis looked like he was caught with his hand in the cookie jar. Along with the two governors were Ed McCallister and Howard Pearce. McCallister introduced himself as Governor Hutchinson's aid and Pearce stated he served Governor Davis.

Governor Davis made an excuse he was visiting Governor White on topics relating to the Great Lakes Committee.

I replied, "Isn't it a little late to be discussing business?"

He realized I wasn't buying his song and dance so he changed tactics. He started, "Okay, Bennett, you caught us. I was trying to persuade Olivia to share the grant money with the rest of the states. We need that money for our states to fight the Asian Carp menace."

He continued, "Bennett, did you know, recently, a Michigan congressman and one of its senators separately introduced a bill that would direct the Army Corps of Engineers to prevent Asian carp from entering the Great Lakes. The act would guarantee the locks and sluice gates remain closed until a better strategy is developed. The act would also allow the Army Corps of Engineers to purchase real estate necessary for the construction and maintenance of the barrier. The corps also has the authority to eliminate and prevent the spread of the carp using fish toxicants, commercial fishing and netting, and harvesting."

Davis continued, "My state, Illinois, has counter sued Michigan in their attempt to close our waterways. Our Attorney General is arguing that closing the Chicago Sanitary and Ship Canal would upset the movement of millions of tons of vital shipment like iron ore, and grain as well as other cargo."

The Illinois Governor paused to catch his breath and then continued, "Our state would lose $1.5 billion a year, and contribute to the loss of hundreds, perhaps thousands of jobs. In response, Michigan has argued the value of the sport fishing and recreation industry, has already been adversely affected in other states. Large carp populations, has caused a drop by more than $3 billion in the recreational industry resulting in the loss of thousands of jobs. Thankfully, President Obama's administration supported our efforts to keep the canal open; with the support of government agencies, reports have consistently denied the Asian carp poses a threat. Now with a new administration, we're pessimistic regarding a favorable ruling. You can see why it's such a hot-button item."

I replied, "Yes, you're right, but not when it comes to taking a life. I think somebody killed young Johnson over the photos he had." Gazing at Governor Morris, I asked, "I understand you've been seen with young Johnson at a pub downtown. I don't suppose you have his cellphone in your purse?" She balked at the request and started to leave. I strong armed her and shoved her back into her chair. She exploded in a fury, screaming, "I'll have you arrested for assault and battery. How dare you attack a governor?"

I responded, "I don't care if you're the Queen of England." I grabbed her purse and dumped the contents onto the coffee table.

To my surprise, nothing but a wallet, a key ring, her cell phone and facial make-up items dropped onto the coffee table.

Governor Morris screamed, "I demand an immediate apology. Not if you leave, I won't press charges."

The smart thing to do was to leave, but that didn't describe me. Jeopardizing my future, I grabbed Pearce and frisked him. His pockets were empty. I now ordered McCallister to stand. He refused. Pulling him from his chair, I frisked his pockets. There was something in his coat pocket that I prayed was a cell phone. Holding it in the air, McCallister retorted, "That's mine. Now if you don't mind, leave." I felt I might as well roll the dice and reached into his other pocket. Bingo. Another phone emerged and I said, "Interesting that you have two cell phones."

McCallister responded, "Of course I do. One is my personal phone and the other is for state business."

Thinking he was probably right, I nevertheless, tapped both phones. One of them showed an itinerary of Michigan state phone numbers. Feeling like the captain of the Titanic, I tapped the other phone and it came to life. To my amazement, it showed a young man standing with his arm around Governor Davis. I shouted, "I doubt if you'd have a cell phone with Governor Davis as your screen saver." I tapped the camera app and I saw a young man being accosted by McCallister and Governor Moore.

The pictures continued to roll and Governor Moore appeared to be demanding the cellphone. The slideshow continued until a scuffle began. The picture became blurry, but the audio still gave a blow-by-blow account. A woman's voice was heard that I assumed was Governor Moore's. A struggle could be heard as the video only showed feet moving about the room. Al Johnson could be heard shouting, "No, you can't have the camera!" He continued to cry for help until a thud was heard. Governor Davis interjected, "My God, you murdered him."

Dialing 911 I requested the police to come to Governor Moore's hotel room.

There was dead silence until some deputies arrived. I handed the cellphone to one of them and I stated, "Be very careful with that. There's some crucial evidence on it regarding Al Johnson's murder. After you watch it, you can take Governor Moore and McCallister into custody."

The deputies watched a cursory portion of the video and placed the governor and the Michigan aid under arrest. After the police removed Moore and McCallister, Governor Davis stated, "I never meant for it to go this far."

I replied, "What did you think might happen when you push people to the brink?"

I had to ask, "How did McCallister come into possession of Johnson's cell phone?"

Both Davis and Pearce stared at each other, before Davis stated, "Alright, we had worked out a deal. My aid, Pearce, was able to bribe someone in the police to give us the phone. In exchange Moore would share her grant with the rest of us. I was starting to realize the power some people could wield."

Dumbfounded, I stated, "You mean a police officer stole the cell phone from the evidence?"

Davis chuckled and said, "Wake up, Bennett. It happens all the time. Don't be naive."

Disgruntled, I returned to my cohorts where they were rehashing the day's events. I replayed the evening's happenings as they developed. I knew the cellphone by itself would not be enough to convict the Ohio governor, but I had a feeling her lover would confess to prevent him from taking the fall for his overlord. Because of the late hour I thought we could say we solved *The Murder of Carp Noctem.*

Chapter Eleven

That evening, Ben and Mark wandered the streets trying to get a glimpse into a world they knew little, but now had to explore. It wasn't like bars advertised who they catered to as patrons. Most of them were college kids blowing off steam from working in their menial jobs on the island. As they meandered from one bar to another, Mark said, "You ever feel like a fish out of water? I have hemorrhoids older than most of these kids."

Ben retorted, "Try to blend in. Act like you're going through a middle-age crisis."

Mark replied, "I did that ten years ago."

Ben answered, "Just see if you see anybody that's different."

Mark retorted, "Have you looked in the mirror lately?"

The bantering continued as they moved from one bar to another. Being desperate, Ben asked a youth, "Is there an alternative bar near-by?"

The youth smiled and replied, "Yes, but I think there's an age limit to enter."

Ben stared hard at the youth and said, "I don't want to repeat myself. Comprende!"

The youth responded, "Okay, gramps, don't get your Depends in a knot!"

Ben was about to grab the youth by the throat when he blurted, "There's the Pink Flamingo up the street. You might try there. But I don't think you're going to find anyone your age."

As they walked away, Mark gave the smart-ass youth a knee-drop for good measure and added, "It's past your bedtime."

Walking through the dark streets, they came upon a bar that looked like it might entertain people that preferred an alternative lifestyle. Madonna's *Vogue* was heard as the senior sleuths approached the entrance to the Pink Flamingo.

Mark looked at Ben and said, "This should be fun. Do you

want to lead or do you want me to show you how it's done?"

Ben muttered, "Shut up and get in there and don't drink from anything you don't open yourself."

The two older detectives walked through the doors and entered into a Brave New World. Everyone was dancing to *Walking on the Wild Side* and it was hard to tell which side of the plate a batter preferred. Mark mumbled, "I think there are a lot of switch hitters in here."

Ben rolled his eyes and didn't respond. "We're supposed to be investigating. Let's get to it." After ordering a beer, they tried to blend in, but that just wasn't going to happen. Ben tried to strike up a conversation with a youth wearing a hair net and dark leggings. The person only moved away without responding. A short staunch person with a butch haircut approached them and asked, "What's the fuzz doing in a place like this?"

Ben produced pictures of Jenni and Kelly and asked, "Have you seen these women in here?"

The short staunch person responded, "I doubt it. They look like a couple of cops with those haircuts." Ben and Mark continued to ask around, but with little success. After a lengthy time hearing the same frustrating answers, they decided to leave. As they were walking through the door way, they heard, "Keep walking and don't look back." Naturally, they assumed they were being mugged. Both had their Glocks ready as they turned around on the sidewalk. Facing them was an attractive young woman with a shaved head. Her body was covered with tats with earrings adorning her appendages.

Ben started, "If you're going to try to rob us, you're making a big mistake. We have two 9mms aimed at your heart."

The young woman replied, "Don't be stupid. You two old farts were made the second you entered the bar."

"What do you want?" asked Mark.

"I heard you asking about Jenni and Kelly."

"Did you know them?"

"You could say that," she replied smiling.

Ben replied, "It's late and I'm tired. What information do you have?"

She answered, "They'd accompany your chief executive when he was in town."

Mark asked, "You mean the governor would go in there?"

She smiled again and said, "Not only would he go in, but he usually had his boy toy with him. They'd all be in drag, but most of us recognized him. He'd go in the back room and your girls would enjoy themselves."

Mark struggled to get the words out, "You mean, the governor and his boyfriend would come in here and Jenni and Kelly would accompany them?"

The young woman smiled and replied; "Now you're catching on. I'd see the gov's limo in the alley. It was kind of a dead give-away if you know what I mean."

Mark asked, "Can you describe the man that was with the governor?"

She replied," You'll find him in the state with the most famous dog of all."

Ben asked, "Can I ask your name?"

She stepped back into the shadows and replied, "I was never here."

Ben and Mark commiserated as they strode to their hotel.

Ben asked, "I wonder what she meant by finding Hutchinson's lover in the state with the dog that's the most famous of all."

Meanwhile in the LP, John and Tyler entered the city's newspaper office. The room had been sanitized since the horrible murder. In its place was mass confusion. The few employees were busy trying to print information while simultaneously edit stories on their computers. An older man walked out of the back room and shouted, "Get out of here. This isn't a tourist stop."

John replied, "Actually, we're trying to discover who may have killed your reporter and the two state troopers along with the governor."

The older man bellowed, "The FBI removed everything from Sue Wenton's desk. Help yourself."

With that, John and Tyler slowly sauntered over to the late

reporter's desk and examined it. Relying on his old police instincts, John slid the top drawer out and reached inside. He pulled out a small notebook. Casually, replacing the drawer, they were careful to leave without drawing attention to themselves. Coincidentally, Tyler noticed some stained paper on the floor. He reached down and placed it in his pocket.

Once outside, they flipped through the notebook that appeared to be a calendar. Every date was marked from morning through evening. Most of them were routine interviews and meetings. However, the letters MW kept appearing in the late evenings. Having something to contemplate, the two detectives strode toward their hotel.

Before returning to the island, the pseudo-detectives and I had a good review of the facts. The hatred against the LGBT community must be at the heart of the murders. Sue Wenton's murder was connected to a person with "MW" initials and we had to figure out what state had the most famous dog.

We brainstormed for hours, when I had an idea. Twelve states have state dogs. Thumbing through the states with state canines, I came across the answer. Armed with that information, I returned to the main hotel on the island and felt confident the governor's lover would be revealed.

I realized interviewing the Hutchinson family was not an option. They had returned to Detroit to conduct a reverent funeral for their beloved governor. Contemplating my options, I decided to pay a visit to one of his nemeses. Touring the hallway of the hotel, I knocked on doors until I discovered one that I felt would prove most beneficial.

Because both Harris and his aid, Pearce, had already encountered me, I knew a disguise was in order. I donned a wig, beard and thick glasses hoping they wouldn't recognize me.

Making my way to Governor Harris' door, I knocked loudly. Opening the door, a young staffer asked, "Yes, may I help you?"

I replied, "Yes, I'm looking for Governor Ted Harris. Is he available?"

The young staffer had protected his mentor well over the years and was about to implement one of many excuses he had used prior. "I'm sorry, the governor is indisposed."

Pretending to be a reporter, I persevered, "I'm from the *Detroit Globe* and I was just wondering if the governor had a comment regarding the Michigan Governor's demise?"

Before the young staffer could respond, a voice was heard from behind the door. "Howard, let the man in. We don't want him to catch his death of cold in the hallway, do we?"

The young staffer opened the door and I was allowed to enter into the presence of perhaps the next President of the United States. I reached into my coat pocket pretending to retrieve my credentials. The governor smiled and stated, "Don't bother. I'm sure everything's in order. We're all friends here. This is my aid, Howard Pearce. He's my right-hand man."

I waited for the staffer to depart before I began. After I was sure we were alone, I asked, "Governor, how well did you know Governor Hutchinson?"

The Pennsylvania Governor had grown up in the political arena and could eat amateur reporters like me alive.

He paused for effect and began a long extrapolation of facts dating back decades. I pretended to pay attention and type his pearls of wisdom into my notebook.

After a long dissertation, I interrupted him and asked, "Did you and the governor ever have any disagreements?"

Naturally, the Pennsylvania chief executive played down any differences. The Governor continued to sing the deceased governor's praises and extol his virtues. I allowed him to continue until I felt the moment was right. I interrupted and asked, "Have you any knowledge of the governor's personal life?" Governor Harris was caught slightly off guard with the question and replied, "We've shared many dinners together in each other's official residences, but no, I've never socialized with him. Why do you ask?"

I now decided to step on thin ice by asking, "I've heard he was bisexual. Care to comment?" the governor also knew he was being led into a box canyon. He replied, "No, I've never heard that."

Jeopardizing my interview, I continued, "I understand, sometimes when the governor is on the island, he likes to visit some bars after hours. Have you ever accompanied him?"

The governor was now on full alert. He responded, "No, I never have. I prefer to have a few toddies among a few friends where it's nice and quiet."

Removing my disguise, I stated, "I guess I'm confused, some patrons of the Pink Flamingo remember the two of you attending together. Let's quit pussyfooting around. I have witnesses that can put you in that bar with the governor in full drag. I don't care what your personal life is, but I want to find out who murdered those two-state troopers and probably is responsible for the other two deaths."

The governor's face had now lost its color. For one of the few times, he was speechless. He answered, "Okay, but this stays between us?"

I replied, "I only want the truth. Tell me everything you know about all of the murders or the local paper will have a nice headline tomorrow."

The governor stammered and finally spoke, saying, "Jim and I were lovers. Jenni and Kelly would accompany us to the bar and we all needed to keep it quiet. That stupid Lieutenant Governor Ben Conrad followed us one night and spilled the beans to Jim's wife. She was heartbroken that Jim opted for our lifestyle."

I asked, "Do you think she could be responsible for her husband's death?"

Governor Harris answered, "Definitely, she would rather die than have her husband outed. The embarrassment would devastate her. She comes from old money. When Jim met her, he didn't have two nickels to rub together. Jim was a smooth talker and he was able to steal Dorothy away from Conrad. I doubt if Conrad ever forgave Jim for doing that."

"What about the other murders?" I asked.

The governor replied, "I don't know anything about them. You'll have to solve them yourself."

"Your secret is safe with me, but if Conrad knows about you and Hutchinson, you can bet he will use it as a political ploy against you," I stated.

The governor answered, "I suppose you're right. If I'm elected President, I can always give him a nice job in the government. After all, look what's there now?"

I couldn't argue with that. Without shaking hands, I left the governor to consider his options. I had my own problems.

Chapter Twelve

The pseudo-detectives and I rendezvoused in the morning for coffee and exchanged information.

Ben started, "Bill, how did you know to go to the Pennsylvania Governor with your suspicions?"

I replied, "Easy, the state dog of Pennsylvania's the Great Dane."

After explaining the Pennsylvania Governor's dilemma, we now had to zero in on who shot and probably later murdered Hutchinson as well as who was responsible for the other murders.

Tyler added, "By the way, I had that slip of paper analyzed at the county lab and they were able to learn that there were traces of phenolic on the paper."

Mark asked, "What's that?'

Tyler responded, "Phenolic is a resin formed by the condensation of phenol, when added with an aldehyde, is used in the manufacture of paints."

Upon hearing that, all of our eyes light up. I said, "It's time to pay the bridge painters' union a visit."

Together, we drove to the bridge and upon arriving; we dispersed in search of our prey, the painters' union president, Fred Gainer. We were hoping he could help us identify who might have wanted Sue Wenton dead.

Gainer was near the top of the bridge and could see us maneuvering. He believed the game was over and did a Peter Pan from the top. There was a thud and we all looked away upon seeing the sight of what was once a human being. The laborers gathered around him and one of them laid a drop cloth over the pulverized body.

I stepped forward and said in a low voice. "I'm sorry he did such a drastic thing. We suspected one of the painters' union members murdered Sue Wenton, but we didn't know who it was." Just then, the union steward knelt down near the draped body. She started, "Oh, Jim, he was so protective of me. He always worried about me when I was on one of the catwalks. He was like a big brother to me."

I asked, "May I ask your name?"

She replied, "I'm Mitsy Webster. Fred was our union president. We worked closely together."

I thought to myself, "Mitsy Webster. Could we speak privately?" I asked.

Once we were away from the crowd and hearing the sounds of the emergency vehicles in the distance. I asked, "We've had time to review Sue Wenton's calendar. It seems she spent a lot of evenings with an "MW". Care to comment?"

The union steward thought for a moment and said, "I guess it's out of the bag. Sue and I were lovers. Fred disapproved of us being together. He couldn't understand homosexuality."

I said, "Do you believe he was capable of murdering your girlfriend?"

She nodded and started to weep. She said, "After Sue's murder, I had my suspicions. I confronted him and he admitted to bludgeoning her with a pipe. I was debating what to do when he must have thought I told the police. He assumed you were the authorities and were coming to arrest him."

I led her over to the interim City Marshal, Deputy Wilkerson and I said, "I think Ms. Webster has something to tell you."

The pseudo-detectives and I returned to the hotel to plan our next action.

Chapter Thirteen

Later, that evening we watched on television in the hotel lobby the governor's funeral and agreed it was a fitting send-off for a man that served his state faithfully.

John stated, "I wonder if the family will return to the island or just send for their things."

I responded, "I bet they come back. Something tells me there's some unfinished business."

"What makes you say that?" asked Mark.

"I have a hunch the governor's murderer wants to tie up a loose end. Mainly eliminate the Pennsylvania Governor.

Sure enough, the next morning, the hotel was abuzz with the arrival of the governor's widow and her entourage.

It was now time for me to once again seek out the now humble Pennsylvania Governor and make him a proposition he couldn't refuse.

Knocking on his door, his young aid opened it and asked, "What do I owe the pleasure?"

I replied, "Is the governor available?"

This time, staffer, Howard Pearce, didn't bat an eye and replied, "He's indisposed, but you're welcome to enter and have a seat."

Following his recommendation, I found a nice overstuffed chair that was to my liking and promptly put my feet on the coffee table which I knew would drive Pearce nuts.

After an expeditious interval, the governor entered and shook my hand with trepidation. He started, "I thought I'd seen the last of you. I understand your crew solved the murder of the newspaper reporter. Congratulations."

I responded, "I wish that was the last of it, but as you know, we still have three unsolved murders. I believe whoever killed them will be coming after you."

The governor now showed great concern. "Why do you think they'll come after me?" he asked."

"You're the last person that could destroy Jim's Hutchinson's legacy," I answered.

"I have an army of police around me when I travel. There's no way anyone could get a shot at me."

I rebutted, "The murderer is going to be very close to you."

"What are you talking about? You're loony."

"Maybe, but I think you better take precautions," I argued.

The governor thought for a moment and stated, "How about a compromise. I'll hire you and your boys until the perp is caught or until I return to Harrisburg. Deal?"

Under the circumstances, I felt I couldn't refuse since I opened the door.

The boys and I set up around the clock protection and only his closest aides were allowed to get near him. Along with the state police, we felt we had the Pennsylvania Governor pretty well protected. We were wrong.

As I expected, the Hutchinson family returned to the island. Staffers were seen removing the governor's personal belongings while the Lieutenant Governor stood silently by the Governor's widow. Friends and politicians came to pay their respects as the state's first family prepared to leave the island.

I took it upon myself to accompany Governor Harris as he paid a formal call on the state's former first lady.

The Pennsylvania Governor was the model of sensitivity as he said, "Dorothy, I'm so sorry for your loss. Please feel free to call on me if there's anything I can do. Don't hesitate, your husband and I had our differences, but we always put our state's interests first."

Dorothy said, "Thanks, Ted. That means a lot. Even though you had political differences, I know the two of you were close. I think it would be wise if we just forget some transgressions between you and Jim."

The Governor replied, "I couldn't agree more."

As Governor Harris approached the Lieutenant Governor, he

said, "I think we should talk later. I'll need a good person like you to run my presidential campaign. Between the two of us, I think we'd make a pretty good team. Don't you agree?"

Hearing this, Conrad lit up and smiled. He replied, "You can count on me when the time comes. Whatever has happened prior is water under the bridge. I think the country needs a good person like you."

As they were finishing their conversation, a skirmish broke out in the hallway. We could see the state troopers were trying to contain a distraught woman. She managed to wiggle herself free and thrust herself through the doorway. Glocks were drawn from every direction as my comrades and I were prepared to defend both Governor Harris and the Michigan now former first family from a deranged maniac. Upon closer inspection, I realized it was Mitsy Webster. She was shouting threats against the Hutchinson's. She wrangled herself free of the troopers and produced a pistol. She shouted, "You Son of a Bitch. You ordered my Suzy to be killed. She was going to break a story about your queer husband and you couldn't stand it."

Glaring at the governor's widow, Mitsy continued shouting, "She was going to break the story about your husband and his lover-boy. She was in the next room and saw you shoot your husband. You had already poked a hole in the window and would rather be a widow than have to face the embarrassment of having a homosexual husband."

The troopers had regained control of Mitsy when Dorothy held up her hand. She shouted, "Stop. She's right. I did shoot my husband. When Jim wasn't here, I shot a hole in the window and swept up the glass shards."

The Lieutenant Governor interjected and shouted, "Dorothy, don't say another word. Nobody's going to believe this hysterical woman with an axe to grind."

Dorothy continued, "I can't take it. I shot my husband and I have to face the consequences."

I asked, "Why did Jenni and Kelly have to die?"

The governor's widow responded, "They knew too much.

They were involved with Jim's sexual trysts. Eventually, one of them would have talked. They knew I abhorred his life style and was disgusted by it."

I continued, "Why were the two bridge painters murdered?"

She said, "I asked Ben to find someone to solve the problem."

By now, the lieutenant governor was begging Dorothy to stop relaying the story, but she continued. She said, "I knew Ben worshipped me and would do anything I asked. He paid those two men to fix the troopers' cruiser. I didn't think the troopers would die in the crash; I only wanted to scare them into keeping quiet. Ben murdered the two painters on his own by slicing the LP gas valve in their cabin while the victims slept."

The pseudo-detectives led the governor's widow across the room and handed her and Ben Conrad over to the state police paving the way for them to face justice.

With a heavy heart, we had solved the *Governor's Assassination*.

Part III

The Odorous Murders

Chapter One

Most of the governors were despondent, with one deceased and several accused of crimes. New York Governor, Asher Clark, called a meeting of the remaining governors and premiers. As the participants entered the meeting room, there was an eerie silence among them. Pennsylvania's Governor Davis had left the island earlier in the day believing there was nothing more that could be accomplished.

Governor Clark decided he would pick up the gauntlet and lead the remaining participants and try to achieve some positive accomplishments. One of the major problems he wanted addressed was the dumping of sewage into the Great Lakes.

The culprits were easy to identify. Combined antiquated sewer systems including outdated storm water run offs into the streets, along with pesticides from lawns and plants contributed to the horrible mess adversely affecting the Great Lakes.

The New York Governor raised his voice and said, "We have to develop a plan that will once and for all alleviate this problem."

Clark continued, "Now that Congress has passed The Clean Water Act (CWA) which is the centerpiece of addressing pollution in U.S. waters. Under section 312 of the CWA, vessel sewage may be controlled through the establishment of areas in which discharges of sewage from vessels are not allowed. These areas are also known as "no-discharge zones" (NDZs).

Clark was only too happy to tell the other governors and premieres in attendance that his own states, New York, along with Michigan, and Minnesota have "No Dumping Zones" (NDZ) regarding the Great Lakes while Minnesota shares a zone with Wisconsin.

Governor Thompson of Indiana stated, "There is a bill in Congress that would give communities 20 years to make the necessary upgrades to their infrastructure before fines are increased from \$37,500 to \$100,000 a day per violation. The money collected from fines would flow into a Great Lakes Clean-Up Fund."

Wilson of Wisconsin, retorted, "There are 30 million people that depend on the Great Lakes for their drinking water. We have to protect them now. We can't wait twenty years."

Thompson added, "My state is in the forefront of trying to deal with sewage. One thing we're doing in my state is restoring wetlands. The bacteria found in wetlands will do the same thing in sewage plants."

Governor White from Minnesota quipped, "That's all well and good, but in my state we have over 10,000 lakes. If we designated some areas as wetlands and not others there would be a confrontation among our sportsmen."

Ontario Premier Harrison bristled and stated, "As you know, Toronto generates a lot of sewage. Over a hundred years ago, our sewer system, like many others in their time, allowed sewage to overflow into creeks, rivers, and Lake Ontario."

Harrison continued, "As the city's population grew and most rain-absorbing green space has been paved, rain and snow overwhelm the system more than once a week. When this happens, wastewater escapes into the natural environment or is intentionally released to the lake by treatment plant operators. Because the pipes and our waterways are connected, illegal and poorly-built plumbing also directs sewage into the lake instead of to a treatment plant. A few years ago, massive amounts of rain fell on Toronto, overwhelmed our facilities and knocked out power to at least one wastewater treatment plant. The city was forced to release more than 1-billion liters of raw sewage into Lake Ontario in a single day."

Contemplating her next argument, she continued, "Our personnel responded to the flood by sampling recreational water spots around the city and working with local media to alert the public about water quality problems. It took a week for Toronto's waterways to return to normal conditions." In conclusion she stated, "The City of Toronto will spend close to $1.5-billion in the coming decades to improve the network of pipes underneath city streets. We are only human and my country is doing everything possible to combat this ecological disaster. I resent your insinuation that Canada doesn't care about the disaster. After all, don't forget, it was your country that turned Lake Erie into a dead lake forty years ago."

Governor Clark conceded and stated, "It won't do us any good to point fingers. Let's talk about solutions."

In a conciliatory tone, Ontario Premier Harrison stated, "The city of Toronto dumps more than nine billion gallons of raw sewage into Lake Ontario every year. A few years ago, Canada passed a law that any ship longer than 5 1/2 meters in length had to have a sewage disposal tank."

Premier Trembly offered Governor Clark an olive branch by stating, "Upgrading existing sewage treatment and infrastructure is the most important priority, but we don't have a lot of money. We need both our federal governments to realize we have an ecological disaster that has to be addressed immediately. Don't you agree Governor Clark?"

The New York Governor nodded his head in affirmation and volunteered, "Let's have a drink and call it a night. In fact, let's take a day off tomorrow and tour the island. I'll arrange everything. Agreed?"

The others smiled and toasted the idea.

Chapter Two

Later that night, Mackinac Island Chamber of Commerce Director, Mary Archer, received a phone call from the Governor of New York, Asher Clark. Upon his request, the Chamber Director had quickly choreographed a collage of sites for the executives to visit the next day. The New York Governor explained he wanted to relieve the stress the remaining governors and premiers were enduring. With all of the carnage that transpired over the last few days, the others were under a lot of pressure.

It wasn't bad enough that each had their own agenda at the conference, but with the assassination and accusations flying, the remaining executives still wanted to accomplish something.

Archer tentatively arranged a visit to the three most famous caves; Skull, Arch, and the Devil's Den. Naturally, the trip would include a visit to Main Street with a stop at some of the famous fudge shops. Knowing a few of them were Catholic, St. Anne's Church would be included, with a final stop at the state park. If the executives were inclined, the tour would also include a visit to Fort Holmes. It was here that the post doctor kept a soldier's digestive tract open so he could observe the digestive procedure.

The Chamber of Commerce Director explained the itinerary to Governor Clark in the morning and he was satisfied hoping to divert the other executives from their animosities.

Gathering at the hotel veranda the next morning included along with the Chamber Director and Governor Clark, were Governors Thompson of Indiana, Wilson of Wisconsin, White of Minnesota as well as the two Canadian Premiers Trembly of Quebec and Harrison of Ontario.

The state police were represented by none other than the captain herself, Menendez and several troopers. After procuring the necessary bicycles, the entourage pedaled their designated route with Chamber Director Archer providing colorful information as they arrived at each site.

The trip was proceeding famously, as there were amble jocularity and breath-taking views of the Straits. Archer failed to mention the horrible murder that occurred on the route and concentrated on showcasing the island's beauty.

Governor Clark pedaled alongside Mary Archer and said, "This is going better than I could have hoped. Everyone is very relaxed and it's obvious they are enjoying the day."

Mary Archer replied, "Thanks, Governor. It's pretty easy to act as a tour guide with all of the island's beauty."

Overcome by the heat, Ontario Premier Harrison stopped at one sandy beach and dived into the beautiful unspoiled water. She encouraged the others to follow, but the rest refused. Emerging from the pristine aqua shoals, she splashed them until they harangued her with threats.

It continued until Governor Clark waded into the shallows and retaliated with playful retribution. Fortunately, it was hot so the execs dried quickly as they continued on their way.

Traversing the island, they felt exhilarated as they approached St. Anne's Church. The two Canadian premieres quickly attached their bicycles to a rack and entered. The others, realizing it was part of the tour, stepped inside. After touching the baptismal font water, the two premiers proceeded to the front to genuflect in front of the tabernacle. Out of respect, the others sat and prayed.

Enjoying the humbling surroundings, the execs left feeling closer to God. Upon stepping into the bright daylight, the serenity was broken by loud retorts of gunfire. A bicyclist had pedaled by the dignitaries, shooting Quebec Premier Trembly.

He collapsed immediately while the state troopers returned fire. Tourists dived to the pavement and horses reared their heads.

After being wounded, the attacker fell to the ground settling in his own blood. The troopers rushed to the attacker and after kicking the weapon aside, removed the bicycle helmet. The assassin appeared to be a youth. After hand-cuffing the young attacker they checked his wound. An ambulance was summoned as the youth shouted nationalist slogans in French.

The execs still sat stunned, as the Ontario Premier explained, "In 2011 there was a national election. The Coalition Avenir Quebec won and neither favored seccession nor acquiescing. In fact, the CAQ presented itself as neither favoring the current arrangement with Canada, which is the position of the Quebec Liberal Party, nor breaking away from Canada." She continued, "They describes the party's approach as *nationalism*, which means putting Quebec's interests first while remaining within Canada."

The City Marshall arrived and along with the State Police secured the area. The youth was treated by the EMTs and removed under heavy police guard as vacationing doctors could only watch as the life of Premier Lee Trembly ebbed away.

The remaining chief executives decided enough was enough. After making sure Premier Trembly's body was transported to the mainland, they returned to their hotel. Even Governor Clark had to admit the conference was a complete failure. The remaining executives booked passage on the next ferry to the mainland hoping to forget this abysmal nightmare.

Chapter Three

Returning to her hotel room, Ontario Premier Evelyn Harrison removed her earrings and placed them on the dresser. *What a week*, she thought to herself. *First Hutchinson, now Trembly*. If they only knew the power of *Bondye*. She walked over to her night stand and stared at the dolls. She removed the pins from both dolls symbolizing Hutchinson and Trembly. Clark thinks he's going to be the driving force on the Great Lakes. *Wait until he sees what I have in store for him,* she thought.   P r e m i e r Harrison was actually born in Haiti and moved to Ontario as a little girl. Her grandmother embraced her in the magic of Voodoo. As a little girl, the Premier came to embellish her grandmother's magic. There were many potions and rituals that would help her deal with life's problems. She loved the concept of reincarnation and many gods that she could worship. Once she got into politics, she had to keep her beliefs to herself. Non-believers wouldn't understand.

"With my allegiance to *Bondye*, nobody can stop me. I will take over this conference, then return home and become Prime Minister of all of Canada" she told herself.

She knelt before her altar and prayed to *Mawu*. She called upon the spirit, *Lau*, to come to her and give her the power to continue her carnage eliminating each executive one by one.

Harrison set the mood by turning the lights low and accompanied by taped Haitian drum music, she called to *Lau* to help her in her next ritual; eliminate her arch rival Asher Clark. For hours she summoned her god finally sticking a nail through the heart of the Clark doll.

Meanwhile, Clark was sipping a glass of wine and suddenly felt a sharp pain in his chest. His aid, Preston Cooper asked, "Are you alright?"

The governor replied, "I just felt something. It must have been the spicy dinner I ate."

Cooper replied, "Let me get you some antacids."

After the governor consumed them, he sat down, but he continued to feel the chest pain. Clark looked at his aid and said, "I think I'll go to bed."

Hours later, Governor Clark sat up in bed still feeling a severe chest pain. His wife, Diane, sat up next to him and felt his forehead. "Are you okay?" she asked.

He replied, "I don't know. I've had this sharp chest pain all night. It won't go away."

"Let's go to the hospital." She queried.

"I suppose I should, but I don't want this to get back home," he answered.

"Nonsense, everyone goes to the ER. Nobody will think any less of you. Besides, it might be something serious," she relayed.

Dressing and slipping out the back door, the governor and his wife hoped to check in at the local ER without fanfare. A horse-carriage was secretly arranged to transport the couple to the hospital. Once there, personnel recognized him and ushered him into a secluded room. A doctor was summoned immediately, and the usual tests were performed. After examing them, the doctor smiled as she approached the Clark's. The doctor began, "Good news. Nothing showed on the EKG or any other tests."

"Hopefully, it was something you ate that didn't agree with you. I want to keep you overnight as a precaution." The Governor shook his head and stated emphatically, "No way. I'm going back to my hotel."

The physician knowing it was fruitless stated, "Call me in the morning if you still have the chest pains."

The Clarks exited the hospital and were met by a plethora of media that had been tipped by a hospital employee.

The governor gave a forced smile and a thumb's up as he entered his vehicle and returned to their hotel.

The next morning Governor Clark was preparing to board his plane when he suddenly lurched forward. His wife tried to break his fall but could only slow his momentum. Looking into his eyes, the Governor's wife could see he was unconscious. She cried for help and immediately, staff and airport personnel tried to perform CPR until the medics arrived.

Unfortunately, the governor was gone. His wife was inconsolable as she followed her husband's body to the ambulance. Sitting next to him during the ride, she cried unconsolably until they reached the hospital.

The Ottawa Premier enjoyed watching the evening news with the lead story being the sudden death of the New York Governor. Harrison said to herself, *Clark must have realized she sent an evil spirt named "anvwa mo" to take him to the next world.*

Now there was nothing to stop her on the road to political glory.

An autopsy was performed and natural causes were listed as the culprit. Our interest was piqued so we had to pay a visit to the grieving widow and the governor's assistant. We waited a few days out of respect. Knocking on the widow's hotel door, I could hear ample noise inside. The door opened and the Governor's aid, Cooper, stated, "This isn't a good time?"

I answered, "I know it, but we would like to speak with Mrs. Clark if it's alright."

Cooper closed the door, and in a few minutes, it was reopened and a red-eyed attractive middle-aged woman appeared. She asked, "Yes, may I help. you?"

I started, "Mrs. Clark, My name is Bill Bennett and my friends and I have been helping solve some of the crimes on the island. I know this is a horrible time for you, but I would like to ask a few questions."

She opened the door and invited me inside. Gazing at the room, it was apparent she was packing to leave.

I began, "I know the governor's death was caused by natural causes, but I have to ask did he have any enemies at the conference?"

She paused for a minute and answered, "Everything has been so surreal this week with Jim being murdered and Olivia accused of it. I just don't know what to think."

I continued, "Please, it's very important. It's just too much of a coincidence with your husband passing at the culmination of everything else."

Mrs. Clark wiped her eyes and responded, "The only person I know, earlier in the week, he had harsh words with was the Ontario Premier, Evelyn Harrison. But I don't think she even saw him in days."

Preston Cooper stepped forward and spoke, "I have to insist you leave Mrs. Clark alone. She has been through a lot and she has to rest."

I nodded my head and said, "Thank you Mrs. Clark for your time. You have been most helpful. I'm sorry for your loss." Cooper saw me to the door closing it emphatically. I got the message.

Outside the hotel, my compatriots were waiting and I was anxious to relay the widow's thoughts. I said, "The only person her husband had a disagreement with recently was the Ontario Premier."

Mark asked, "I wonder what the disagreement was!"

I answered, "I don't know, but I'm going to look into it."

I couldn't wait to get to the internet and see what disagreements Ottawa and New York could have. I returned to my room and tapped in Ontario/New York problems. For starters, they share a 445mile-long border including four bridges and countless rivers. There were so many opportunities for disagreements I was overwhelmed. Both sides were still pointing fingers going back to the 2003 power black-out. Countless accusations of poorly maintained roads added to the animosity. Deciphering this menagerie would take a genius and I certainly wasn't in that discussion.

Rejoining my fellow sleuths, we enjoyed a cold beverage while pondering if the New York Governor could have been murdered. The circumstances certainly didn't warrant it and we couldn't very well make any accusations.

The only thing I could suggest was a good old-fashioned break-in. The others gave a look of consternation and after debating that possibility, they concurred. We had to consider we would be breaking into an international leader's hotel room. We knew she had even tighter security with two governors now deceased and another accused of murder.

The next problem was to develop a plan that would allow us ample time to enter and see if the governor could be a suspect or were, we wasting our time.

After considering several possibilities, we decided we needed a ruse to get everybody out of the hotel. A fire alarm would suffice for that. The real problem was getting a key for Harrison's room.

Tyler proposed, "I could try to sweat talk one of the cleaning ladies and remove her key." But with everything electronic that was going to be a challenge.

We had performed many card reader thefts in the past. It just took a little coordination. Most general access cards use a magstripe, but sometimes they use a radio transmitter in the pass card. We decided to use the latter since it would be a lot quicker.

Tyler was charged with waiting in the hallway near the Premier's room. When one of the cleaning employees was near the Premier's door, he would alert one of us to pull the fire alarm. With all the commotion, he would pass near the employee and activate the radio receiver. The Premier's door would receive the command and automatically unlock it.

With so much commotion, nobody would notice the door ajar. We just had to make sure this ruse was performed when the Premier was not in her room. We were in position for the scam to commence. Ben was casually sitting in the lobby reading the morning paper. Once the Premier and her entourage left the premises, he would contact Tyler. Tyler would have to lure a cleaning lady to stop in front the Premiere's hotel door, Tyler would text Mark to pull the alarm. Trying to avoid detection, Mark would don a Halloween mask and proceed to the nearest fire alarm.

John would follow the Ontario Premier throughout the island making sure she wasn't a problem. I would be waiting in the stairway to assist Tyler in his break-in.

Everything went great. Premier Harrison left early in the morning accompanied by her aids and security. Tyler next texted Mark to start the show. The alarm sounded and organized chaos ensued. Everybody exited their rooms; some fully dressed, some in bathrobes. Tyler detained a maid asking for directions to the closest exit. While she was providing him with the information, he activated the radio receiver opening the Premier's door.

I remained out of sight until the hallway was clear. After making sure the coast was safe, I joined Tyler and we entered the room. We checked the obvious places where something incriminating could be hidden. Just then, I heard, "Oh, my God, Bill come here!" I walked briskly into the adjourning suite and together we stood in awe of a Voodoo altar.

There were two dolls in various stages of disarray. The third one was still intact with a large needle in its stomach.

Tyler asked, "What do we do now?"

I thought for a minute and said, "Let's take a seat and wait."

He replied, "Are you crazy? We have to get out of here. We saw what we wanted. She's a lunnybird."

I know, "But in this case I want to confront this lunnybird."

The alarm was discontinued and slowly the guests returned. Hotel security showed, via closed circuit monitors, someone wearing a Donald Trump mask pulling the alarm.

John texted me that the entourage was returning and it wasn't long before I heard voices. The Premier and her aids entered the room and upon seeing us, the aids immediately called for security. I shouted, "Go ahead, Premier, let everyone see your photos in the other room. I'm sure it would make great press in the Ontario newspapers."

Premier Harrison held up her hand and motioned for everyone to leave. The aids put up a mild protest, but she was determined to see us without them.

I started, "That's a nice altar you have. Can I assume, the dolls represent the Governors?"

She shouted, "There nothing illegal in that room. Get out!"

I countered, "If it doesn't bother you, why did you dismiss

your aids and security?" I continued, "I'll make you a deal. You pack up and leave this island and you take your religion with you."

There was a moment of silence before she replied, "I guess I can leave. I've done what I came to do!"

"If you and your cronies aren't gone in two hours, I'll come back with the media and they'll have a circus with that altar. Do you understand?"

She nodded and Tyler and I left hoping we had prevented any more deaths. Premier Harrison walked over to another doll on the table and stuck a needle in its stomach and whispered, "*Enlevement Bennett.*" (Kidnap Bennett)

Chapter Four

With the governors' conference being classified, on all accounts, a failure that included two executive's dead, one disgraced, and one governor in custody, we thought it might be a good time to escape by enjoying our favorite summer pastime, fishing.

I was entrusted to secure a fishing vessel and equipment. All of us had years of experience on inland lakes, but our knowledge of sailing the Great Lakes was minimal.

Meeting at the dock the next morning, we were armed with refreshments and sustenance. After purchasing our licenses and bait, we decided we were ready. After weighing anchor, we teased one another of how we would individually be the one to reel in the biggest fish.

A few miles from shore, we dropped anchor and the challenge began. We knew Lake Michigan was abundant with many game fish including Chinook and Coho salmon, yellow perch, lake, rainbow and brown trout, smallmouth bass and steelhead. Giant sturgeon were known to inhabit the abyss but few anglers tried to catch the Sasquatches of the deep.

Some of the fellows wanted to catch Chinook salmon so they used appropriate bait. I wanted to reel in a sturgeon. I replaced my smaller line with 40 lb. test and attached a short shank hook. My bait as usual, was night crawlers. The only problem was I had to get my bait on the bottom. The sturgeon uses their four barbells to feel the bottom for crayfish or other small crustaceans. In order to land the big one, I had to allow the bait to lay on the bottom and jig the line in hopes of getting a strike.

Meanwhile, the others were having great fun reeling in Chinooks. Some of them landed steelheads while others settled for lake trout. Needless to say, there was sufficient questioning of my fishing skills as they filled the cooler and I was without a nibble.

Suddenly, my drag pulled and my line shot out. I knew something big was on the other end. I released the drag and let the line run. When the tension released, I slowly reeled the line, knowing the only way I was going to catch this monster was to wear it down. Minutes passed and my friends reeled their lines in an attempt to help. My arms were starting to ache, but I wasn't about to let this creature snap my line and escape. Slowly, the line was reeled in and we could see a dark shadow moving below the surface. It must have been over seven feet in length. Ben navigated the craft so the behemoth couldn't slip under us and snap the line. Back and forth, the battle raged as the beast fought for its life.

After an endless struggle, the giant specimen was finally pulled alongside and it had to weigh at least 150 pounds. John shouted, "Bring it closer and I can grab his gill with this hook." At this time my conscience got the better of me and I said, "Take some pictures and we'll let it go."

There was a moan from my buddies, but I just couldn't bring myself to bring this beautiful living thing aboard. Reluctantly John held my pole as I reached over the side and yanked the hook from its mouth. In seconds, it disappeared back to the depths of Lake Michigan. I savored the thrill of bringing the creature alongside the boat and that was enough for me.

On the way back, the others bragged about their exploits to each other, but I had a wonderful memory to savor.

John stood next to me and stated softly, "For what it's worth, I would have done the same thing."

I guess that's what friends do.

Chapter Five

We were nearing shore when we saw a large vessel portside. It appeared the men had a large hose extending into the water. Being curious, we steered a course toward the vessel. A shot rang out, and we ducked for cover. We knew it was a warning shot, and for one of the few times, we were unarmed.

Mark shouted, "Who are those sons-of-bitches?"

We continued to muse among ourselves why someone would shoot at another ship in broad daylight.

I said, "They must be doing something illegal to call attention to themselves."

Mark suggested, "Maybe they're handling drugs."

Ben interjected, "They might be doing some illegal fishing."

Keeping our distance, we followed the boat to shore, staying out of sight. The boat tied up at a public dock and after we were certain that they had gone ashore, we moored next to it. We had to have a look at what activity this crew could be involved with to risk one of them shooting at us.

To our modest surprise, we saw the name of a septic transport company on its side. We realized what these lowlifes were doing.

After securing our vessel and removing our catch, we decided to pursue this mystery. The wastewater treatment plant was located nearby, so I felt it would be a good time to check the validity of our concerns.

After entering the building, I approached the administrative assistant and asked to see the manager. She left and returned with a middle-aged clean-cut man. I introduced myself and he likewise replied, "I'm Gabe MacLeod. How can I help you?"

I had to be clever in case this man was involved as well, so I explained I was doing a piece for a tourist magazine. I asked, "We know the island is world famous, but how does this facility handle over 17,000 visitors daily."

He smiled and replied, "When sewage enters the plant, we have a system that pumps it through a series of screens to remove debris and grit. As a matter of fact, we have two head works, a smaller one for the winter and a larger one for the summer.

Sewage next continues through primary clarifiers where heavy sludge and debris settle to the bottom, and then it continues to the oxidation towers. From there, the wastewater continues to the next tank, where bacteria digest and break down organic matter. The treated water is next sent to a second clarifier, where particles are allowed to settle. The water at the top of the tank is skimmed off and sent to the chlorine contact tank for disinfection and the final water is returned to Lake Huron.

Throughout the wastewater treatment process, solid material is diverted for disinfecting by pressing the water out of it, and the resulting sludge is pumped into a wagon and transported to the holding facility, where it is shipped to a landfill."

I thanked him for his time and pretended to write his information down in my notebook. Returning to my comrades, they were eager to hear my report. After listening to my spiel, John reflected and said, "It's obvious, the septic transport boat isn't bringing it to any landfill. They're cutting corners by dumping it into Lake Michigan."

Ben concurred saying, "We have to stop this before it gets any worse."

Mark asked, "What's our plan?"

I looked at Mark and smiled.

He replied, "Don't even think about putting me undercover on that sewage boat."

"As a matter of fact," I said, "That's exactly what I was thinking."

"Get out of here," retorted Mark.

Ben added, "I think you'd be perfect for the job. You'd fit right in with that clientele."

"In your dreams," answered Mark.

"Listen, we have to find out what they're up to. If you nose around, maybe, they'll hire you," I replied.

Ignoring the chuckles from the others, Mark relented and said, "What do I have to do?"

"Let's find out where they drown their sorrows and you try to buddy up to them," I answered.

We walked the streets until we saw a bar that fit the bill.

I peeked in the door and saw a host of red-neck ruffians displaying wife-beater shirts and faded Trump hats. I looked at Mark and said, "It's show time. We'll enter a few minutes later and we'll back you up if you need us."

Mark mumbled under his breath as he entered, "Tell my wife I love her."

Bellying up to the bar, Mark ordered a drink. The bartender slid the suds over to him and grabbed the money. Looking around the room, Mark tried to gauge who might be employees of the sewage transport boat. He motioned to the barkeep and said quietly, "I'm looking for a job. Do you know anybody who's hiring?"

The barkeep motioned to the scurvy crew in the back corner and stated, "You might try those lugs. They haul sewage to the mainland. It depends how desperate you are for a job?"

Mark replied, "I haven't eaten in three days. Right now, I'd do anything that puts bread on the table."

Sauntering over to the rough-looking outfit, Mark started by saying, "I hear you might be hiring."

One of the burly men looked up and asked, "Do you have an arrest record?"

Mark answered, "Depends on what state you're in."

The crew chuckled and the behemoth stood and said, "I'm Rock Winston. These are my boys. That's Axel Hale, Elliot Brown and the little one is Brick Griffin.

Mark introduced himself and nodded at the seated individuals. "What do I have to do to earn my keep?" asked Mark.

"Tomorrow morning be at the pier at 5 o'clock sharp. It's your job to take care of the sludge."

Mark grimaced at the thought of dealing with the sewage. Winston continued, "Pick up a pair of rubber gloves and boots."

Mark sat down and commiserated with them for several hours. We observed the events from the other side of the room keeping vigilance on the new mate on the sewage scow. I stated, "It looks like Mark is blending in pretty well."

Ben agreed saying, "I always knew he had hidden talents."

John interjected saying, "It would be too dangerous to follow them on Lake Michigan. We'll have to hope Mark can keep them believing he's just a good ole boy."

Tyler stated, "It's too risky for Mark to wear a wire. If they found it on him, they'd feed him to the fishes."

The next morning, Mark was there promptly and was greeted by the other three mates. It wasn't long before they saw the sewage scow chugging toward the dock; without stopping the four mates jumped aboard. The skipper threw the boat in reverse and set sail to rendezvous with their odorous cargo.

Likewise, we were waiting out of sight near the wastewater treatment plant. Hearing the boat arrive, the crew quickly went about their business. Hooking up the treatment's hose to the boat, it took little time before the treatment's employee shut the slurry valve off and unhooked the hose. The scow's skipper turned the boat and proceeded to steer out to the lake presumably to unload on the mainland.

Once under way, one of the crew handed Mark a shovel and motioned for him to remove the cover of the vat and stir the sludge to prevent it from settling. Mark, gasping for air to the guffaws of the others, trying to catch gulps of fresh air as he stirred the sludge. The others had their own work and didn't attempt to provide him with any assistance.

Once in the middle of the lake, Winston turned his engine off and double-checked his radar searching for blips on the screen. Satisfied they were alone, the captain motioned for the men to hook up the hose to the vat and within minutes, brown slurry was pouring into the pristine lake.

The skipper kept a close eye on the horizon while the crew continued to release the ghastly mess. Once the outpouring slowed to a trickle, the crew climbed inside the vat. Mark had to oblige while fending off the dry heaves. Together, they swept the vat clean; shoveling and sweeping the residue into the lake. With the feat completed, the crew climbed out of the vat and continued sweeping the debris into the water.

The first mate, Axel Hale, handed Mark a hose and motioned for him to return inside the vat. With Mark again breathing painfully, he descended the ladder and sprayed the remnants of the sludge over the side. With that completed, Mark reemerged thinking he was done for the day.

Elliot Brown, smiled as he approached Mark, said, "Now you can wrap the hose." Mark wanted to say something defiant but realized this was neither the time nor the place. Obediently, he coiled the hose. He didn't think he'd survive the ordeal and it wasn't soon enough when he saw the island on the horizon.

Winston approached him and said, "Buddy, you did okay for your first day. You'll learn to do it faster as you get more experience."

The boat motored into a slip and Mark couldn't wait to escape. Winston shouted, "We'll see you here tomorrow same time."

Mark muttered to himself, "Over my dead body."

I knew it was going to be a confrontational homecoming when Mark laid eyes on us and I said to the others, "Go easy. He's had a gut-wrenching experience. Be glad it wasn't one of us."

I purposely planned to meet Mark in a public place hoping it would belay his anger. It didn't work. Upon seeing us he tied into us and no matter how much placating we did, he was not going to be deterred from giving us hell for allowing him to go on the voyage of the damned.

He ranted and raved indefinitely using every vile word he knew. There was absolutely no consoling him as we finally had to escort him outside and allowing him to cease his wrath. After he finished his tirade against us, Ben worked up the nerve and asked, "So, did they dump the sewage into the lake or not?"

That started another round of uncontrolled fury. I looked at Ben and said, "Nice going!"

Back inside the tavern, it took several pitchers of Mark's

favorite brew to quench his thirst. It didn't help that the rest of us sat on the other side of the table to avoid Mark's fumes.

Mark finally settled down and appeared to be able to participate in a coherent conversation, I began, "I assume they dumped the sewage overboard. Now that you can confirm that as an eyewitness, we'll have to come from another angle. Ben, could you and Mark visit the wastewater plant and John, could you and Tyler pay a visit to the site where the sludge is supposed to be dumped? I'm going to nose around City Hall. I have to think someone there must know what's been happening." We agreed to meet back in a few days.

Chapter Six

The next day, Ben and Mark arrived at the Mackinac Island Wastewater Treatment Plant. Entering, they saw a clean-cut middle-aged man staring at a wall of flashing lights. The man stepped forward and asked, "What can I do for you?"

Ben stated, "My name is Ben Meyers and this is Mark Kestila. Our wives are shopping and we're just killing time. We work in a wastewater treatment plant back home and wanted to see how you handle sewage." The man replied, "My name is Ralph Beloit and I'm one of the treatment specialists. I'd be glad to show you around; follow me." Ben and Mark fell in behind the specialist as he gave them a tour of the facility. As they proceeded, Ben and Mark pretended they knew what he was saying.

Along the tour, Ben asked, "How much sewage do you handle daily?" The wastewater specialist replied, "During the height of the season, June, July, and August, 15,000 to 20,000 gallons of the bio-solids will be processed at the screw press each day. During the winter, the plant stockpiles the sludge in a 49,000-gallon tank until the screw press begins operating in the spring. The heavy sludge is moved by boat to the mainland and deposited into a landfill."

Mark asked, "How much is dumped into the landfill?"

Beloit replied, "I'd guess about 5,000 gallons daily."

Ben and Mark tried not to look disgruntled upon hearing how much volume was being dumped into Lake Michigan.

At the completion of the tour, Ben and Mark thanked Beloit and prepared to leave when the Systems Operator stated, "We're hiring right now if either of you fellows are interested."

Mark retorted, "I've seen enough sewage on this trip. Thank you."

The specialist gave them a puzzled look as the two senior sleuths left.

Upon exiting the plant, Ben texted John informing him where

the landfill was located.   John and Tyler arrived at the site and realized they'd better be on guard.   Knocking on the door marked "Office" they waited for a reply and entered after being acknowledged.

"Yeah, what'd you want?" asked the seated employee.

John began by saying, "My name is John Baldwin and this is my son, Tyler. We're trying to find out how much sludge does the boat from Mackinac Island dump at your landfill every day?"

The employee stood and said, "I run this place. I don't know exactly. Why do you want to know?"

Tyler replied, "We're just curious?"

The employee stood and said, "I don't think that's any of your business. Don't let the door hit you while you're leaving."

John and Tyler left mumbling to themselves.

Tyler started, "He's definitely hiding something. He would have looked it up if he wasn't concealing something."

His dad agreed saying, "You got that right. Maybe, we'll have to come back tonight and check the records. I noticed there were some file cabinets along the wall."

As they were leaving the landfill, they happened to see a shovel operator. Tyler said, "Maybe, he can tell us something."

John and his son approached the employee introducing themselves and made small talk. The shovel operator replied, "I'm Tony Davis. I've worked here nearly thirty years. What do you want to know?" Tyler asked, "Do you know how much the Mackinac Island scow brings here daily?"

The employee chuckled and replied, "You mean if it comes. We only see it a few times a month."

Having their answer, the senior sleuths left.

After Ben and Mark had left, the office manager tapped his cell phone and waiting for the other party to acknowledge him, the employee said, "I just had a visit from two guys asking about the amount of sludge the scow dumps here."

The voice on the other end asked, "What did you tell them?"

"I kicked them out of my office," answered the employee.

"You did the right thing. Thanks for the heads-up. I'll be ready if they come my way."

I entered the Mackinac Island City Hall and was met by a courteous administrative assistant.

I approached the young lady and asked, "I'm writing a story on the island and I'm curious how does the island handle such a large daily influx of tourists?"

The young employee replied, "We have a great wastewater treatment plant. Let me see if our mayor is available. She can tell you more than me." Returning shortly, the young gal said, "Mrs. Rodman will see you. I told her you were a journalist and you were doing a story about our island."

Upon entering the room, the woman stood and extended her hand and said, "I'm Abby Rodman, mayor of the island."

I replied, "I'm Bill Bennett and I'm doing a piece on tourism."

She asked, "How may I help you?"

I responded, "I'm doing a story on problems that tourist sites have to overcome. One thing I am curious about is how you handle so much volume of sludge considering the incredible number of tourists that visit daily."

Mrs. Rodman responded, "We have a contract with a consulting engineering firm. Our treatment facilities deteriorated and had to be updated a few years ago. The company took into account the larger differences between our summer and winter months. The consulting firm did an outstanding job designing and constructing a unique system to our needs. It cost over $6 million."

I pressed asking, "Yes, but what happens to the sludge that can't be processed?"

Rodman replied, "We transport it to a landfill on the mainland."

"Can you tell me how much is transported?" I asked.

"Why in the world would your readers want to know that? I don't see the point," she replied.

"I actually write for a technical magazine and that would be right up their alley," I retorted.

"I suppose I could look it up, but It'll take time. I'll have my administrative assistant, Sandy, get back to you," she replied frankly.

I could tell I'd worn out my welcome, but I wanted to find out the difference between what the island shipped to the landfill and how much actually arrived.

I thanked her for her time as I handed my phone number to her. I was eager to discover if the other senior sleuths had any luck.

Phoning my compatriot, Ben, I asked, "Any luck at the wastewater treatment plant?"

Ben responded, "Some. They supposedly ship 5,000 gallons daily to the mainland, but as we know, it gets dumped into Lake Michigan."

I stated, "Okay, thanks. I'll phone John and see if he had any luck."

Upon answering his cell phone, John replied, "No, nothing at all. After we introduced ourselves, he showed us the door. We're going back tonight and rifle through the file cabinets."

I replied, "Don't get caught."

John retorted, "Oh, yee of little faith."

That night John and Tyler waited for the last employee to vacate the premises and drove to the office. Parking behind the large equipment, they approached the office. Using his lock-key set, Tyler made quick work of the front door lock and they entered.

John said, "Why don't you start on the other end and we'll work toward each other."

Both detectives started removing folders and skimming through each one. Tyler examined one thick folder and whispered, "I think I found something. Here are the dates the landfill employees removed the sludge. It's current through last month." He started to photograph the entries while John now tapped on the office computer and accessed the files identified as **Mackinac Island Account.** John said, "Look at this, the records show the boat brought sludge here yesterday, but we know that didn't happen."

John tapped the Print icon and soon the recent entry was

printing. John looked at Tyler and said, "I think we have the evidence, now we just have to get out of here."

As they were leaving, they heard an automobile stop outside the office. John and Tyler dived behind the office furniture. The door opened and two individuals entered the room. They turned the lights on and proceeded to the file cabinet. One of them removed some files and removed a few of the accounts. "Be sure to delete all of the files," ordered the first burglar. The other person turned on the computer and started removing them. After they had finished, the two individuals exited the office. John and Tyler crept over to the front door to ensure they were leaving.

To their surprise, an argument ensued and one of them brandished a pistol, shooting the second individual. John grabbed Tyler's arm and prevented him from rushing to the victim's aid. They continued to watch the melee unfold. The individual who murdered the other stepped into a payloader and proceeded to drive toward the body. Scooping the body up into the bucket, the driver inched toward the landfill. Releasing the bucket and dropping the body into the hole. The individual returned the payloader to its original location.

John whispered, "Can you believe that?"

Tyler replied, "I sure didn't see that coming."

They continued to watch as the murderer descended the payloader and drove off into the night.

Once the murderer was out of sight. Tyler did the unthinkable; jumping into the hole. He rolled the victim over and shined a light into the victim's eyes. It was the employee they had talked to earlier.

Tyler searched the victim's pockets removing some papers, wallet, and keys. He climbed out of the hole and said, "Obviously, he was involved in the plot. I wonder who shot him?"

John said, "I think we better get the hell out of here before we become the suspects."

Checking to make sure the murderer had left; the two sleuths found their automobile and returned to Mackinaw City.

Chapter Seven

After John and Tyler shared their experience with us, we had to wonder who the murderer could be. Could it have been one of the men from the sewage scow, an employee of the land-fill, or perhaps somebody I met at city-hall? The list of suspects was formidable and we had to pare it down.

I asked John, "Could you tell if it was a woman or man that murdered the other?"

John responded, "No, not really."

Tyler spread the victim's items on the table and we proceeded to examine them. His wallet produced no evidence that would help. His cell phone had a list of phone numbers and the keys were a combination of vehicle and house keys.

"We have something to pursue," I said. "John, how about you and your son take the key ring and Ben, could you and Mark interview Mark's old cronies? The best place to find them will probably be the bar. I'll start phoning these numbers and see if I get a hit."

There were several cell numbers and after phoning various family members of the victim, one call surprised me. After dialing the number, the voice on the other end went through a litany of city hall phone numbers. I looked closer at the number on the cell phone and dialed the extension number. I tapped the number and the voice on the other end replied, "City Manager's Office. May I help you?"

I disconnected and now had one major suspect.

Meanwhile, across town, Mark was experiencing déjà vu. Along with Ben, they entered the musky hole in the wall that passed for a bar. As usual, it was full of rough necks that engaged in raucous arguments. Knowing Ben had his back, gave Mark a feeling of security, as they approached the sewage scow crew. Roy Winston stood and shouted, "Well, you came to ask for your job back and you brought along a friend."

Mark replied, "Not exactly, we're private detectives and we're here to stop your shenanigans. You and your crew have been dumping sewage into Lake Michigan and it stops now. Get it."

Winston immediately stood and prepared to throw a haymaker, but Ben beat him to it knocking Winston head over teacups across the table. One by one, the others stood, but before they could even swing Ben and Mark had them on the floor. Only Winston tried to get up again and he was quickly felled by Mark with a fist to the throat. The skipper immediately fell to his knees gasping for air.

Mark continued, "I'm going to ask some questions and you're going to give me some straight answers. Understand!"

The four downtrodden men pulled themselves into their seats and Mark proceeded, "Now, we want to know who was paying you to dump the sewage into the lake?"

There was a moment of silence until Ben pulled out his oversized hunting knife saying, "We can continue this discussion outside if you want."

Winston remained silent, but the other three crew members' spirits were broken.

One by one, each blurted out what little they knew. Putting the whole scheme together, Ben and Mark understood the lackeys on the sewage boat were to dump the mess into Lake Michigan and return. They had no contact with anybody else. They received an envelope weekly with their cash payment enclosed. Ben said, "If I were you, I'd turn myself in or get off the island. If we see you idiots again, we'll turn you in to the police. Get out of our sight." The four bumbling criminals stumbled out the door. Mark looked around and noticed nobody was even looking their way. Mark said, "I guess we picked the right place to question those fools."

Later, after enjoying a hearty meal, John stood and said, "Well there's no time like the present," as he led Tyler through the doorway. He continued, "I think the best thing we can do is wait until dark and try the wastewater plant, then city hall, but first let's start with the landfill, because it'll be a process of elimination. Naturally, we can forget about any keys that open anything there."

Overlooking the landfill, and catching some shut-eye, the two sleuths waited until sundown. Once the moon was glimmering and the employees had left, John and Tyler once again approached the front door of the office. After a few unsuccessful keys failed, one opened the front door and through a process of elimination, a few more could be discounted as they opened the various storage rooms along with the back door. John said, "Now we earn our keep. Let's go to the wastewater treatment plant and later city hall."

After they arrived at the plant, all of the remaining keys were tried on the front door but to no avail.

"Well," Tyler said, "That leaves just the city hall." The two sleuths strolled into the alley behind the city hall and after trying several keys, one opened the back door.

"Bingo," John said as he smiled.

They crept through the hallways trying keys to various doors unsuccessfully, until they came to the mayor's office. The last key available worked as John turned it. The door opened and the two amateur cat burglars stepped into the darkened lair.

Tyler whispered, "I guess we can narrow down our suspects tonight. Someone who works in this office must be tied to the sludge dumping; maybe, even the murderer."

They quietly closed the door and exited the building. They couldn't wait to share their newfound information with us. As they stepped into the alley, they heard a voice say, "Don't move or it'll be your last."

Both men reached for their Glocks, but before they could, a gun was pressed against John's head. The voice ordered, "Hands, I want to see your hands. If you reach for your guns, this one gets it." John and Tyler slowly raised their hands and now were at the villain's mercy.

Chapter Eight

After several failed attempts to reach John and Tyler, I knew something wasn't right. I said, "Something's wrong. It's not like them not to answer. We'd better look for them."

Meanwhile, John and Tyler had been trussed like lobsters complete with blindfolds and dumped into the back of a truck. As they were driving, they could hear the sounds of seagulls getting louder; realizing they were approaching water.

The truck stopped and John and Tyler were dragged from the truck and hauled onto a boat. They heard a voice say, "You know what to do." John and Tyler assumed the worst.

Meanwhile, we were scouring the island and were slowly driving along the docks when we noticed the sewage scow leaving. Mark immediately said, "They don't move sewage at this hour; something's wrong."

We procured a boat and pursued them. The scow had a head start, but we knew we had to find them. Mark said, "Head due east to the sight where they usually dump the sewage."

Ben steered in that direction and before long we could see the boat. We slowed down and wanted to see what their play was.

Using binoculars, I was able to identify two gunny sacks in the back of the boat that were squirming. I assumed they were our cohorts. I said, "I think they got John and Tyler tied up and I assume they plan to dump them overboard."

Ben shouted from the captain's chair, "We'll have to wait for them to stop. If we increase our speed, they might just dump the guys overboard."

I retorted, "I agree. All we can do is wait."

The tramp boat continued to chug along finally coming to a halt. We could see some men muscling the two large bags to the edge. Ben gunned our motor and we increased our speed, hoping to get there in time. That wasn't going to happen. We saw the two large bags dumped overboard and we had only one choice. As the scow disappeared in the distance, Mark and I readied ourselves to dive into the murky water. Ben maneuvered the boat to where the scow had dumped our comrades and together, Mark and I dived into the unknown.

We didn't know how deep our buddies had sunk, but we had to find them. Unfortunately, the two sleuths sunk like rocks, not being able to use their hands or legs to slow their demise. Faster and faster I swam downward hoping against hope I could feel one of them. At long last, I felt some material and strained to stop its falling. The weight was unbearable, but I slowly was able to stop the body's free fall. Somehow, I found the strength to pull the body toward me and begin the ascent. My lungs were bursting, but I had to make it to the surface. It wasn't long when they gave out and I felt water pouring inside my lungs. Just then, I felt something grab my collar and pulled the two of us upward. I don't know how, but we reached the surface and I was nearly unconscious. Ben helped me and our trussed-up comrade aboard. I laid on the deck and strained to get air into my lungs. I looked at Ben and said, "Thanks for pulling me to the surface."

Ben replied, "What are you talking about? I didn't leave the boat. I kept circling the area hopping I'd see either you or Mark surface."

Mark emerged from the deep and he dragged his friend to the side of the boat. We helped Mark along with our tied-up friends onboard. We cut the ropes free of our two comrades and expected the worst. As we untied them, it was clear both John and Tyler were unconscious. Appling CPR, both were resuscitated after minutes of chest pumps. It was truly a miracle. On our return to shore, Ben looked at me and asked, "What were you talking about when you thanked me for pulling you to the surface?"

I shrugged my shoulders and said, "I must have been hallucinating."

Recovering from near death, John was able to mutter, "Keys, the keys opened the City Manager's office." We now had our first lead.

On shore, the four sewage scow employees were reluctant to face the wrath of their employer. Upon tying up at the slip, they made their way toward their fuming overlord. The skipper had the audacity to call their chief and hint that a problem had developed.

As they approached the individual standing at the end of the dock, their boss asked, "Did you get rid of the two bodies?"

The scow's skipper whimpered in a low voice, "Yes, but we had company."

"What do you mean, you had company?" the individual barked.

Winston again answered in a low voice, "I think it was their friends who sped toward us as we dumped the two guys overboard."

The individual persisted, "What happened after that?"

"I don't know. We got away as fast as we could," retorted Winston.

One of the deckhands added, "We saw them dive into the water, but I doubt if they could save them."

"You idiots. All you had to do was dispose of those two men and we'd be home free. Now, we have to deal with those old men. Even if they couldn't save their buddies, they'll know it was you that dumped their buddies into the drink. You better catch the first ferry off the island. Keep going and don't come back," their boss insisted.

"What about traveling money. We're going to need some to get out of here," Winston replied sheepishly.

"I'll get some money together and pay you before you leave. Come to the wastewater plant tonight. Make sure you're not followed," their boss ordered.

The four men disappeared into the darkness and found solace at their water hole until it was time to get what they believed was rightfully theirs. Arriving at the treatment plant, they found the front door unlocked. As they entered, they saw a light in the back room. Following Winston, the crew ambled toward the light hoping for a pay-off. Instead, as they entered the room housing the chorine vat, they were met by their boss.

The double-crosser ordered, "Climb the stairs!"

Chaos followed as one of them shouted, "What do you mean? You promised us a pay-off for us to disappear."

I'm giving you a pay-off, now get up those stairs," the murderer bellowed.

The men climbed the stairs and looked down into the menacing vat. Winston shouted, "Boss, you don't want to do this. We've done everything you told us to do."

The back stabber retorted, "You idiots screwed up a good deal. You're going to disappear for good." One by one the fiend mowed them down and watched as each of them fell into the chlorine vat.

The villain shut the light off and left the plant.

The next morning, after the wastewater treatment crew arrived, the employees were surprised to see some of the gauges were incorrect. Performing a cursory sweep through the plant, they were aghast seeing four bodies badly decomposing in the chlorine vat.

Law enforcement and the EMT's arrived, but the bodies were badly decomposed in the heavily chlorinated water. Mayor Rodman entered the premises and said, "I just heard. Do we know who they are?"

One deputy replied, "We checked their wallets and it seems they're the crew that transports the sludge to the mainland."

Mayor Rodman asked, "How were they murdered?"

The deputy replied, "All of them were shot by a small caliber revolver. The M.E.'s on his way and he'll be able to tell us more."

The Mayor continued, "I just don't understand why all of them were murdered?"

The deputy replied, "This was a pretty rough bunch. They might have been transporting meth or other drugs back and forth to the island."

The Mayor nodded her head and said, "I bet that's what happened. With all the college students working here, I'm sure there's a ready market for the drug. I'll have to speak with the

City Marshal and see what he thinks."

Shortly, the new City Marshal arrived at the horrific scene. Upon entering the room, the mayor couldn't wait to quiz him regarding the cause of the four murders.

Rodman approached the new city marshal and stated, "Well, Jeff, you sure have an unusual challenge your first day on the job."

City Marshall Jeff Mitchell answered, "I worked for Homeland Security for ten years but I never saw anything like this. I couldn't believe it when one of my deputies updated me on this."

Rodman continued, "One of your deputies thinks it might be drug related. We have hundreds of young people on this island and some of them certainly use illegal narcotics. Do you think the four victims could have been transporting drugs to the island?"

The City Marshall replied, "I don't know. I'll have to look at everything. That's certainly a possibility. I'm going to keep my options open."

The mayor left the plant believing she had pointed the locals toward that answer.

John and Tyler rested most of the day allowing Ben, Mark and me to pursue other leads. By now, we had heard about the deaths of the four sewage scow crew members. Mark started, "I can't say as I'm sorry to hear about their deaths. What they did to John and Tyler was reprehensible. Now we have to find out who murdered them."

I answered, "John said one of the keys opened the City Manager's office. Let's go there."

It wasn't long before Ben, Mark and I were entering City Hall and gazed on the administrative assistant. Her nameplate read Sandy Evans. "Excuse me," I began, "Is it possible to see the Mayor?"

The young assistant looked into the main office and said, "I'll see if Mayor Rodman is available."

We took a seat and hoped the Mayor had some answers. Soon the Mayor's door opened and she gazed hard at me and stated, "I thought you were a journalist?"

I replied, "My name is really Bill Bennett and these are my friends. Yesterday, two of our comrades were almost drowned and overnight the four perps that tried to kill my friends were found dead at the wastewater treatment plant. We found a set of keys on the victim from the landfill, and one of them opened your door. Do you know why?"

Mayor Rodman reacted very strongly saying, "I don't like being deceived and if someone stole a key from my ring, I have no idea how they did it. Besides, many island employees have a key to our door."

"Could you tell me who?" I asked.

"I'm afraid I'm not at liberty to divulge that since you're not really police," she related.

"I just think it's interesting that someone from the landfill had a key to your office."

"You can think whatever you want, but don't insinuate anyone here is involved in anything illegal. Good day," the Mayor bellowed.

The three of us left bidding her adieu.

As we walked past the administrative assistant, the young lady smiled at us; dialing her cell phone after we left.

She said, "Those old guys are getting close. They took the key ring from the one you murdered at the landfill. What do we do?"

The voice on the other end replied, "Relax. If anything, they'll probably suspect the Mayor. Sit tight and act natural. Remember, let your boss take the heat."

Chapter Nine

(A Robbery Gone Awry)

"Wait for me," Benny shouted to his playmates as they raced to the bus. They had fundraised all year and now they were getting their reward. A whole weekend on Mackinac Island. They had sold candy bars for Halloween, pumpkin pies for Thanksgiving, and a host of other items to reach their goal. That was all forgotten as the youngsters raced to the bus anticipating a week-end of fun with their classmates. It had become a tradition for the students at Kaiser Elementary in Grand Blanc to make it an annual event. School was out officially so the Mackinac Island Middle School would be available.

The Grand Blanc teachers and parents had been planning the event since the beginning of the school year. Over the years, it had gone splendid. There were only a few scrapes and bruises to show, but considering they were responsible for over 100 youngsters, every year had been a success.

Because of the long bus ride north to Mackinaw City, the bus caravan left immediately after lunch. They had decided to use the island's school gymnasium as their home port. Unbeknownst to them there was danger afoot. A gang of desperate men had decided to rob the First National Bank of St. Ignace Mackinac Island.

After being pent up in the school buses for the entire afternoon, the students were thrilled to run from the ferry parking lot to their waiting boats. The adults whose task was to keep everyone safe had their work cut out for them. Before they boarded the ferries, a head count was in order. Once, that was completed, there was a mad scramble for seats. Every youngster wanted a top birth. Those who were unable to secure a seat topside had to settle for a seat below. Needless to say, there was ample complaining by the youngsters who were denied the top deck.

Meanwhile, the desperadoes had decided the island bank would be easy pickings for several reasons. First, it had never been robbed and the bank employees would not expect it. Second, the thieves only had to dock their boat at the public marina and it was a short hike down Main Street to the bank, easy in and easy out.

The gang was comprised of Eddie Sawyer, Gunner Slade and Mick Thorne. They had grown up in Hell's Kitchen, New York. All three had only known a life of crime. They had been passed from one foster home to another with the same result. They were incorrigible. After school, they bummed around doing odd jobs but the pay wasn't good. Feeling they deserved more, they took to a life of crime. Over the next fifteen years they each amassed a criminal rap sheet that was as thick as a New York Phone Directory. Their last robbery landed them incarcerated for stealing autos for a chop shop. They decided they should go big-time. It proved successful as they moved around the country hitting convenience stores.

They didn't get rich, but they made enough to survive as long as they kept moving. A few weeks in one place were usually enough before the local law got too close. They would disappear into the night and emerge days later on the opposite coast. As long as they didn't try to establish roots or become romantically involved everything was fine.

Eddie Sawyer saw himself as the unofficial leader since he was older. Gunner Slade was content to allow Eddie to call the shots. After all, things were going pretty well. Mick Thorne, at first, liked the gypsy life, but after several years of being on the run and a few near misses, he wanted out of the gang. *Would Eddie and Gunner allow him to walk away and leave? He was pretty sure Gunner wouldn't care, but Eddie was a different story.*

On Mackinac Island, the trio cased the bank weeks in advance and investigated the marina. They had practiced many times how they would tie up at a slip and walk the few blocks to the bank. They believed Friday afternoon would be the best time because there was a greater influx of tourists coming for the weekend and the bank would have extra money to accommodate them. They walked past the City Marshall's Office and weren't impressed.

They were positive Gunner and Mick could intimidate the tellers to hand over their cash in their drawers while Eddie drew down on the Bank Branch Manager and force her to open the main vault.

Timing was of the essence. They believed they could accomplish the heist if they could keep the tellers away from their alarm buttons.

Eddie added, "I think we'll make a haul with this robbery." Mick found the courage to say, "Eddie, this is going to be my last robbery. Nothing against you or Gunner, I just don't have the desire to continue this way. I want to settle in one place. I've been wandering for fifteen years and I want to put down roots."

Eddie thought for a moment and said, "Okay, Mick. This is your last gig with us. If you want out, you're out." As he walked away, Eddie said to himself *you're going to be out permanently.*

The youngsters offloaded from the ferries like the marines at Iwo Jima. The adults tried to catch up, but soon realized it was hopeless.

Mrs. Anderson, the principal, said to the stressed-out parents, "Don't worry. By tomorrow, they'll be too tired to run anymore. The ride home on Sunday will be like a day in heaven." The parents seemed to like hearing the good news.

The students separated into two groups, boys and girls. The first point of interest for the boys, of course, had to be the fort. The boys especially liked seeing the canons and the barracks where the soldiers were quartered. The girls chose to go to the butterfly house and were thrilled when the butterflies landed on them.

The first day was completed with a bike ride around the island. The chaperones envisioned a gentle ride enjoying the beautiful scenery. That wasn't going to happen. Instead, the term "Hell on Wheels" probably best described the ride. The entire group of children pedaled as fast as possible until they left the parents and teachers behind.

The adults envisioned casually stopping at the various

caves that dotted the route. Again, that was a pipedream. The chaperones didn't lay eyes on the youngsters until they rounded Mission Point.

The Kaiser Middle School students returned their bicycles and ran to check on their new digs, the Mackinac Island gymnasium. By the time the chaperones arrived at the school, the students had each laid claim to a place on the gym floor. It was with great delight the parents were glad to see the entire Kaiser student body safely enclosed for the first time since they left the ferry. It would also be the last time.

The trio of thieves had commandeered a boat docked in Mackinac City and motored to the island marina. Tying up at a vacant slip, they reviewed their plan once more. Just before closing time, they would enter the bank and through terror immobilize the tellers and depositors. They knew the bank employees had been trained not to be a hero so they didn't expect any trouble from them. The depositors were an intangible. Hopefully, they could be persuaded their deposits weren't worth their lives. The robbers inhaled ample amounts of meth and snorted cocaine to provide them with courage. Walking past Doud's Grocery Store, Eddie asked, "Does everybody have their mask?" Both Gunner and Mick answered affirmative. Eddie continued to pepper them with questions regarding their weapons and roles during the robbery. He didn't want any foul-ups. This time they were going for big money.

Ben, Mark and I decided to see what doors the keys on the ring would open. Walking on Main Street, I suddenly realized I was running short on cash. Seeing the local bank, I decided to pay a visit to the ATM. Ben and Mark joined me as we entered the bank to withdraw some money.

Meanwhile, the robbers arrived at the bank and donned their disguises. Checking to be sure it was five minutes to closing, Eddie shouted, "Okay, let's do this."

The three of them charged inside the bank and Eddie shouted, **"This is a robbery. If you don't want to die do what you're told!"**

Gunner motioned for the tellers to step away from their alarm buttons and Mick ordered the depositors to lie face down and put their hands behind their heads. Everyone did as they were told. With so many customers in the bank, we complied along with the rest of the bank clientele. The branch manager said in a calm voice, "Take what you want. We won't resist." Looking at her tellers, she said, "Give the robbers what they want!"

Eddie countered, "Listen, I give the orders. Open the vault or this teller gets it." The branch manager motioned toward the vault and said, "It's not locked. Take what you want and leave."

Eddie entered the vault while Gunner and Mick kept the rest subdued.

Eddie filled one bag quickly and shouted, "Throw me another one," Eddie shouted.

Gunner complied and kept his weapon trained on the tellers. Mick continued to keep us subdued when one of the elderly ladies started to go into convulsions. Her body started shaking as Eddie shouted, "What's going on out there?"

Gunner replied, "Just an old lady going spastic. Nothing to worry about."

The branch manager shouted, "Let me help her."

Gunner motioned for the manager to see if she could help.

After a cursory check, the manager looked at Gunner and said, "She needs a doctor."

Gunner replied, "That's not going to happen. Sit still and we'll be out of here shortly."

Eddie exited the vault with two bags of currency. Meanwhile, Gunner seizing his opportunity, pushed the tellers further back and emptied the drawers. Mick started to shake at the possibility the old lady was dying. He shouted, "Let's get out of here! We have enough!"

Eddie turned on Mick and said, "Not until we check below the tellers' stations and see what goodies they have."

With Gunner cleaning out the drawers and Mick mesmerized by the unconscious woman, I removed my cell phone and tapped 911. I laid the phone on the floor hoping the dispatcher would hear what was transpiring.

Eddie was finally satisfied he had taken all of the small denominations and change. He motioned for the tellers and the bank manager to lay down which they quickly complied. Walking backwards with their guns trained on us, they started to exit. Once outside, they started to run toward the marina. A police officer, on foot, approached them followed by several officers on bicycles.

In a flash, we were right behind them. The bank robbers were caught in a cross fire. Eddie stopped and started to shoot at the officer hiding behind a car door. Gunner turned and sprayed the two police officers on bicycles. Both officers went down.

The three of us fired. Now in full panic, Eddie saw a brick building and shouted, "Run to the school." As they ran across the school yard the deputy and we continued to fire with one of our bullets striking Gunner in the back. He grimaced and shouted, "I'm hit!"

The three robbers dived through the double doors and ran through the hallway with Mick supporting Gunner. They entered the gymnasium and sprayed the ceiling with gunfire. All of the children screamed and threw themselves on the floor. Eddie shouted, "**I want everybody against the wall.**" He motioned for some of the youths to stand in front of the doorway. "**Do what you're told and nobody gets hurt.**" One of the chaperones approached the trio only to have Eddie shoot him point blank. Eddie shouted, "**Who else wants to be a hero**?" Everyone laid down and shivered at the prospect that they were now hostages.

Trying to maintain control, Eddie retorted, "**If you cooperate everything will be okay. Listen to me and only me.**"

By now the deputy in the police vehicle had radioed for help, but the dispatcher replied there wasn't anybody immediately available. He would have to hold them in the school until the sheriff's deputies and the state police could arrive.

Keeping our heads down, we maneuvered around the building. We had to get in the school quickly before this went bad. Approaching the back door, I hoped it wasn't locked.

Fortunately, I heard the latch click as I pressed down. Now we could go to work. We entered and quietly crawled down the hallway. The classrooms were dark, so we felt they weren't a problem.

Before I turned the corner, I heard the cries of children. "My God", Ben said, "There must be a hundred kids in there."

I belly-crawled toward the door and slowly raised my head enough to glance inside. There were over a dozen youngsters being used as human shields. I could identify three adults wearing masks. I motioned to Ben and Mark there were three bogeys. They crept behind me and I whispered, "I'll take the one on the far left, Ben, you take the middle one and Mark, take the one on the right. On three we go."

I counted slowly to three and I slid the door open and we poured in and took sniper positions. In a split second all three robbers were eliminated. We continued to peruse the room to see if there were any more. The adults immediately raced to the downed adult lying motionless. They began chest pumps hoping to save him.

We heard sirens outside as the state police burst through the door. We laid our weapons on the gym floor and raised our hands. Lieutenant Menendez looked at us and said, "Nice work. It was awful stupid, but nice work."

Watching the adolescents hug one another was rewarding. Without fanfare we had saved them from *A Robbery Gone Awry.*

Chapter Ten

We didn't have time to celebrate liberating the children as we had to meet the next day over coffee. John and Tyler felt well enough to join us. It was now time to brainstorm and I hoped someone had an idea.

John had a suggestion and we listened carefully. He stated, "Tyler and I didn't have time to try all of the keys on the ring. Let's run a comb through the city and see if we find any lice."

That night, we waited for the shops to close. Checking the door locks on Main Street brought no success. As we approached the police station, I held my breath and hoped none of the keys worked. Fortunately, none turned the locks. We continued working our way up one street and down another. We arrived at the Chamber of Commerce Office and feeling that it was probably a waste of time, we decided to give it a try anyway. To our surprise, one key opened the front door. "Oh, oh," Ben murmured under his breath.

Since the entire building was dark, there was no point in pursuing what we already knew. Someone in the Chamber of Commerce building was involved with the dumping of sludge in Lake Michigan along with another individual in the City Manager's Office. We locked the door and retired to develop a plan.

Rendezvousing at a local pub, several ideas were discussed, but none I thought would work. After hours of debating, and consuming a few pitchers, we reached a scheme that we hoped would succeed.

John's plan called for the police finding some incriminating evidence in the pocket of one of the four deceased.

"That's a good start," I stated.

Mark asked, "What evidence could he find that would lure the criminals into the open?"

Tyler added, "It'd have to be pretty waterproof to withstand hours of exposure in chlorine."

Ben interjected, "It's pretty obvious none of them kept a diary or journal."

We racked our brains until I said, "Yes, but would there be proof on the sewage scow? Could we pass the story that Winston marked his route on his GPS and see who takes the bait?"

Mark said, "I'll take the new City Marshal."

John added, "Tyler and I'll catch up with the Administrative Assistant, Evans, and if she's in her office, we'll talk to the Mayor also."

Ben stated, "I guess I'll take the Chamber of Commerce gal."

I stated, "I'll set up shop watching the sewage scow just in case someone comes. We dispersed and agreed to meet at the dock later that day.

Mark saw the City Marshall entering his office and said, "Hey, how are you doing? My name is Mark Kestila. My buddies and I are on the island trying to find out who tried to drown our two friends the other day. Also, we heard those four men that were murdered in the vat were dumping sewage into Lake Michigan."

The City Marshal replied, "I heard they were up to no good, but didn't know they tried to drown your friends."

Mark continued, "Skippers always mark their weigh points to help navigate. If you find his GPS, it'll show you his routes."

"Yes, that's right. That's the first thing I did after I left the plant. I found his GPS on the boat," replied Mitchell.

"Did you find anything on it?" asked Mark.

"Yes, and his routes were marked including his sewage dump," answered the City Marshall.

Mark left believing the City Marshall was innocent.

Meanwhile, Ben found Mary Archer in her office. As he approached her, he said, "Hey, my name is Ben Meyers and I'm on the island vacationing, but I heard some guys were kidnapped and hauled out to the middle of Lake Michigan and dumped overboard. Is there any truth to that?"

Mary Archer shot back, "Certainly not. That's just a rumor

and there's no truth to it."

Ben responded, "That's what I thought. After all, it would be easy to track down where the boat's been because everybody knows boat captains keep track of their routes on their GPS. Thanks for setting the record straight." Ben turned and left knowing he had planted a seed of doubt if she was involved.

By the time John and Tyler were able to arrive at the City Hall, Sandy Evans was preparing to close for the day. The two detectives entered and Tyler said, "I guess we're too late to see the Mayor."

The young administrative assistant replied, "Yes she just left. I can take a message if you want." John spoke saying, "We just wanted to talk to the Mayor. We were wondering if the skipper left anything behind on the boat that might tell us who was involved in the dumping the sludge in Lake Michigan."

Sandy Evans answered, "I'll tell Mayor Rodman first thing in the morning. Maybe, you should tell the City Marshal."

Tyler replied, "We'll probably go there next. Thanks for your time." The two men left while the administrative assistant was already dialing her phone.

The sun was setting in the distance and the pseudo-detectives and I had gathered near the dock. We were prepared for action and we weren't disappointed. We took turns catching some sleep as one of us kept surveillance.

It was my turn to keep an eye on the boat when I saw two silhouettes walking toward the scow. I nudged the others and within minutes we were ready.

Mark stated, "This'll be as easy as shooting fish in a barrel."

We waited for them to board the scow and we jumped into action. We raced onto the dock with Glocks drawn.

I shouted, "Hold it right there. Don't move."

Suddenly a burst of automatic gunfire rained down on us. We dived into the water and hid under the dock. The firing was non-stop. As fast as the shooter emptied his weapon, he reloaded and fired again. Bullets zipped by us as we swam under the moored yachts. We could hear the yachts being cut to pieces as we continued to dive deeper. Just then the shooting stopped. Feeling it might be safe, one-by-one we broke the surface gasping for air. The pier looked like Pearl Harbor on December 7th.

We climbed aboard the scow and grabbed the two criminals before they could make their escape. Shining a light in their faces, the two were the administrative assistant, Sandy Evans, and the Director of the Chamber of Commerce, Mary Archer. We shoved them to the deck and applied wrist ties.

We now looked along the pier for signs of the third felon. Standing next to a bleeding body was our old friend man-mountain, John Crane. We approached wondering how he got here.

Crane had worked several cases with us over the years and had helped us innumerable times. He had fought in every major war zone over the last thirty years. There was no obstacle he couldn't overcome. He was as crusty as they come, but I'd trust him with my life.

I asked him, "What brings you to this neck of the woods?"

Crane replied, "I figured you could use my help. You fool know how to get into trouble, but you don't know how to get out."

Mark took exception to that and took a step toward him. Crane smiled and said, "Easy old timer. I didn't mean anything by that."

Looking at the dead man on the ground, I asked, "Who's this?"

Crane replied, "I assume he was a hired gun that these two women employed."

John rolled him over and we saw that he had his throat slit. John stated, "Nice work. I hate to say it, but you saved us again."

Crane replied, "Of course I did. It's become a habit."

I reflected for a minute and then said, "Hey, wait a minute. It was you that pulled me from the depths of Lake Michigan. Wasn't it?"

I looked into the shadows but Crane was already gone. That's his *modus operandi*. He never wants acknowledgement. The women later confessed to murdering the landfill employee and Mary Archer admitted murdering the three sewage scow deckhands and their skipper.

I asked, "Why did you murder them?"

She replied, "I didn't want any loose ends."

I replied, "You're going to have a long time to think about what you did." We were glad to have solved the *Odorous Murders*.

Post Script

The Lilac Kidnapping

The island was coming alive bursting not only with visitors but with flowers as well. Every imaginable vegetation was on full display. The weather was perfect accompanied by a beautiful warm summer breeze blowing gently.

The Lilac 10K Race was only one day away and our own Tyler and his wife, Carolyn, were entered. Our job, as I saw it, was to station ourselves along the route to keep them hydrated and provide moral support. Both of them were in great shape and I hoped it would be a nice respite from the terrible tragedies we had helped solve.

I asked Tyler, "Where should we position ourselves to provide the best assistance?"

He answered, "The race begins at Windemere Hotel, then runs through Main Street. The route next turns uphill over the rolling hills through the wooded center of the island. The last leg is on the Shore Road. The race is easily accessible so you can see us at the start and catch us later. I appreciate you helping us. It's nice to have friends cheer us along the route."

I replied, "We wouldn't miss it for the world. I admire that you and Carolyn are able to compete in such an event."

Meanwhile, on the island, there was a sinister plot underway. Unbeknownst to us, an angry person bent on revenge was planning a kidnapping and murder; mine.

The morning of the race was perfect. We gathered in front of the hotel and with a shot, the participants started.

We had pre-planned the route to maximize our assistance by placing each of us at specified locations. We knew the race ran west through the quaint Mackinac Island downtown, turning left to a challenging steep hill. Mark would be waiting once they reached the top. As the race proceeded the route traveled through the wooded area of the island where I would be waiting.

The last portion of the race was on the Lake Shore Road with the Mackinac Bridge providing a beautiful panoramic setting. There, Ben would be available if needed. John would be waiting at the finish line to congratulate his son and daughter-in-law. We had it all planned and were in place.

Tyler and Carolyn were strong runners and set a respectable pace up the steep hill. Upon reaching the top, Mark was waiting and rehydrated them. The pace now became faster as the better runners started to separate themselves from the pack.

Tyler and Carolyn knew they had to increase their pace or risk falling behind. They had always run together and Carolyn motioned for Tyler to keep up with the first group. He shook his head and said, "I'd rather stay with you." Carolyn muttered, "Get going. I want you to finish as best you can."

Tyler replied, "No, we run as a team. I'd rather finish with you than win."

She gave him a disgruntled look, but Tyler knew he had done the right thing.

As they made their way through the woods, I was nowhere to be seen. The duo continued running until they saw Ben. There was no time to discuss my absence; time was of the essence. Reaching the Lake Shore Road, they now kicked in for the final push. Both Tyler and Carolyn felt exhilarated as they passed many runners, but couldn't catch the leaders.

Crossing the finish line, John gave both Tyler and Carolyn an exuberant hug. The runners looked for shade and replenished their bodies with energy drinks. John looked for their times and smiled when he saw them. After informing the duo of how well they did, Tyler and Carolyn once again hugged each other.

Mark, and Ben arrived and after hearing of their wonderful finish gave each of them a high-five.

Everyone was so concentrated on enjoying the minute, no one thought about yours truly. Finally, Ben asked, "Where's Bill. He should be here by now. I hope he didn't get lost."

John replied, "You know him. He's probably talking to someone. You know how distractible he is." Assuming I was preoccupied, they retired to a local eatery.

Earlier in the race, I watched as the first set of runners passed me and I prepared to cheer on Tyler and Carolyn. Looking down the trail, a friendly vender sporting long hair and sun glasses happened by and I saw my favorite beverage. I approached him and asked, "How much for that one?" as I pointed to one in his cooler.

Upon hearing the price, I didn't like it as I felt it was exorbitant, but I felt it was better to buy than go without. I paid the vender and waited for him to hand me one from the cooler. Instead, he asked, "I already have one opened. One fellow ordered it, but didn't want it. Would you take this one?" Being a good sport, I replied, "Sure. That'll be fine."

The vender left to sell his liquid refreshments and I quenched my thirst. As I was watching the runners, I suddenly felt delirious. Falling to the ground unnoticed, the villain returned and dragged me into the woods. Once the last runner had passed, he emptied the cart of ice and drinks and dumped me inside. The vender pedaled nonchalantly so as not to draw attention.

Chapter Two

After they had finished their meal, John stared at the pedestrians passing in front of him. He said, "I wonder where Bill is. It's not like him not to hook up with us. I've phoned him several times but it goes to voicemail."

Mark responded, "Maybe, he took a ferry back to the mainland."

Tyler answered, "No, he wouldn't leave without congratulating Carolyn and me."

Ben said, "I suppose we're going to have to spread out and find him." Each senior sleuth along with Tyler and Carolyn selected a direction and agreed to meet back at the restaurant. Ben and Mark entered the main hotel and scoured the premises with no luck. Tyler and Carolyn, even though exhausted from their race, walked eastward, while John scoured the docks. Hours later, they returned and had the same story to tell. No sign of me.

Meanwhile, my nemesis was preparing to remove me from the island and have his revenge. Hours later, I awoke finding my hands bound. I felt my prison was gently swaying back and forth so it was obvious I was in the hull of a boat. Smelling the aroma, it made it painfully clear I was back on the sewage scow.

The narcotic used by my kidnapper was slowly wearing off and my head was clearing. My attacker stepped into my cell and I was thunderstruck as I recognized my kidnapper. It was Dan Martin, the Immigration agent I had humiliated in an attempt to help one illegal get a visa to our country. He started. "I can tell by your reaction, Bennett, you recognize me. I'm glad you do. I'd hate to think you ruined my life and you had forgotten me."

I retorted, "You've got to be kidding. You went through all this trouble just because I helped one illegal alien get a work visa."

His face turned red and he shouted, "That one illegal alien

cost me my job. When my superiors discovered I had falsified an application they fired me immediately. On top of that, you poured salt into my wound by tricking me into losing at the casino."

I answered, "I didn't trick you. It was you that had hidden cards under your tie."

Martin continued, "I was riding a winning streak until you brought it all to an end. Now I'm going to return the favor. I'm going to destroy your world."

"I supplied you with GHB and I plan on doing something special to your wife and grandchildren."

It was one thing to kill me, but when he talked about hurting my spouse and grandkids, that was a horse of different color.

I tried to engage him to find out what his plan was. I started, "My friends are tearing this island apart. They won't quit until they find me. Besides, I don't think you're a murderer. I have met hundreds of them and you don't fit the bill."

I had achieved my goal. He responded, "Bennett, I'm going to enjoy killing each and every one of your brats and then offing your bitch. I'm going to make sure you watch every second."

I pressed by asking, "How do you plan to do that hiding on a sewage scow?"

Martin responded, "I read about your little fray with the sewage boys and I felt the one place nobody would look was right here."

I had to admit he was right, but I wouldn't give him credence.

I continued, "You still haven't told me how you're going to carry out such an ambitious operation."

Martin replied, "It's all set. I'm going to send a text using your cellphone to your wife that you want her to bring the grandkids to the island. When they cross the Straits, I'll be waiting. I'll give them a charge they won't forget."

I now realized he was just crazy enough to do it. I had to stop his maniac, but how?

Martin left and returned to the top of the boat. I tried to find a weak spot in the walls but the boat was built like a tank.

Suddenly, I noticed my watch. Martin was smart enough to

remove my smartphone, but I still had my smartwatch. If I could send an email to someone without Martin seeing my phone light up, I could circumvent this idiot's plan.

I hoped he had placed my smartphone somewhere on the boat and wasn't paying attention to it. If that was the case, I'd be in business. The other concern I had was the battery life on my smartphone. It only had a life expectancy of a few hours. I had to assume, it was nearly dead. Time was of the essence if I was going to save my family.

With my hands still tied, I tapped a message to my cohorts and hoped it was delivered.

After we were underway for a while, the door opened and a smiling Martin entered. He said, "You just asked your wife and grandkids to meet you at the dock. They're going to take the next ferry. We'd better hurry if we're going to meet them."

He stepped back on deck and I heard the engine start. With a slight jerk, the boat started to chug toward open water. I panicked for one of the few times in my life. I had to save my family but I was powerless. I looked through the porthole and saw the ferry approaching.

Martin turned the sewage scow in their direction in an attempt to intercept it. Banging on the window until my hands were bleeding solved nothing. What could I do? I saw a fire extinguisher attached to the wall and I grabbed it and smashed at the window. The window cracked and I sprayed the fire extinguisher out of the hole. I felt the boat slow down and Martin probably felt he had to take care of the problem or risk missing the ferry.

The door swung open and a furious Martin jumped down the steps. Even though my hands were tied, I lunged at the maniac and knocked him to the deck. As we struggled, he stabbed me in the stomach. Freeing himself, he scampered up the steps and locked the door. I knew I had to kill that deranged would-be killer. On the wall was the most beautiful thing I had ever seen, an emergency axe. After I removed it, I ran my bindings over it until I was free. Using the axe, I slashed at the door making quick work of it.

Emerging topside, Martin was ready and he kicked me as hard as possible. The force sent me flying onto the deck with blood cascading down my face, I charged Martin knowing he was armed with a hunting knife. I swung wildly at him with my ax but missed. He counterattacked and sliced my arm. I stepped back to regroup and I could see he had now removed a package from underneath. I lunged for it, but he pushed me away and holding the package turned his attention to the approaching ferry. I was trying to pull myself together for one last attack, but I didn't think I had it in me. He had to be stopped. I staggered toward him with all the energy I had, and swung at the package knocking it onto the deck.

Martin, now enraged as the ferry came closer, and he wasn't going to miss his opportunity to destroy my family. Just then, a motorboat approached from behind with Ben and my comrades aboard. First things first. I had to stop Martin. After he retrieved the bomb, I tackled him from behind knocking the package to the deck again.

By now, my buddies were alongside motioning for me to jump. I pointed at the ferry and the ever-resourceful Mark realized what I meant. He removed his pistol and fired several rounds into the air. Immediately, the ferry swerved away. Now with my family safe, I threw myself over the side and landed in their boat. Accelerating at warp speed, we soon distanced ourselves from the sewage scow. Seconds later, a loud explosion occurred that enveloped the scow. It dissipated into a million pieces fouling the air as it did.

I ignored my wounds as I braced myself against the boat and could see my grandchildren on the ferry; I collapsed. Days later, I opened my eyes and peered into a beautiful pair of brown eyes, my wife's. She started, "Well, sleepy head, it's nice to see you awake."

I answered, "I'm just glad to be alive."

Barb held my hand as I took solace in solving the *Lilac Kidnapping.*

Made in the USA
Monee, IL
30 October 2021